DEBBIE MACOMBER

One of America's favorite storytellers!

Praise for Debbie and her previous novels:

"One of the few true originals in women's fiction."
—Anne Stuart

This Matter of Marriage is "so much fun
it may keep you up till 2 a.m."
—*The Atlanta Journal*

"I've never met a Macomber book I didn't love!"
—Linda Lael Miller

"Popular romance writer Macomber has a gift for evoking
the emotions that are at the heart of the genre's popularity."
—*Publishers Weekly*

"Debbie Macomber's name on a book is a guarantee
of delightful, warmhearted romance."
—Jayne Ann Krentz

"Well-developed emotions and appealing characters."
—*Publishers Weekly* on *Montana*

"Debbie Macomber is the queen of love and laughter."
—Elizabeth Lowell

AUTHOR NOTE

As I've matured as a writer, I've learned that every book has its own timing. The plot for *Moon Over Water* was conceived back in the early eighties when I was still new to the writing business. Like other projects—every writer has them—it got filed away in a drawer, almost forgotten.

Then one day, in an all-too-rare burst of energy, I started cleaning the drawers of an old desk and stumbled upon a file of rejected stories and discarded plots. *Moon Over Water* jumped up and insisted its time had come.

Each day of writing was an adventure. Jack infuriated me, but then so did Lorraine. A wonderful writing teacher once told me, "Tears in the writer mean tears in the reader." That being the case, I feel I need to warn you. I laughed and cried and cheered. I wrote and rewrote myself in and out of corners, spent endless hours talking over plot points with my editor, who—in addition to everything else—deserves an award for patience. So here it is, *Moon Over Water*, nearly twenty years in the making. I hope you enjoy this adventure as much as I did!

With almost every book, there are a number of people to thank, and that's certainly the case with *Moon Over Water*. As always, I'm forever grateful to my husband, Wayne, who continues to love me after thirty years. His encouragement and loving support are the glue that holds me together. Much appreciation to Dianne Moggy and Paula Eykelhof, who make writing for MIRA such a pleasant experience. Thank you for making all my dreams come true. Special recognition belongs to my agent, Irene Goodman, master negotiator and talented cheerleader. Also to Renate Roth and Jenny LaCombe, my two able-bodied assistants, who help keep my life relatively sane. And last, but certainly not least, I'm thankful for Dr. Stephen Fredrickson's medical advice. He was the one who insisted there was no possible reason in the world to remove that bullet.

I eagerly look forward to hearing what my readers think about each book. You can write me at P.O. Box 1458, Port Orchard, WA 98366.

DEBBIE MACOMBER

MOON OVER WATER

MIRA

ISBN 1-55166-533-6

MOON OVER WATER

Copyright © 1998 by Debbie Macomber.

All rights reserved. Except for use in any review, the reproduction or utilization of this work in whole or in part in any form by any electronic, mechanical or other means, now known or hereafter invented, including xerography, photocopying and recording, or in any information storage or retrieval system, is forbidden without the written permission of the publisher, MIRA Books, 225 Duncan Mill Road, Don Mills, Ontario, Canada M3B 3K9.

All characters in this book have no existence outside the imagination of the author and have no relation whatsoever to anyone bearing the same name or names. They are not even distantly inspired by any individual known or unknown to the author, and all incidents are pure invention.

MIRA and the Star Colophon are trademarks used under license and registered in Australia, New Zealand, Philippines, United States Patent and Trademark Office and in other countries.

Look us up on-line at: http://www.mirabooks.com

Printed in U.S.A.

To Liz Curtis Higgs
Speaker, Writer and Friend Extraordinaire

One

"Eternal rest grant upon her, oh, Lord...." Lorraine Dancy closed her eyes as the first shovelful of dirt hit her mother's casket. The sound seemed to reverberate around her, magnified a hundred times, drowning out the words intoned by Father Darien. This was her mother—her *mother*—and Virginia Dancy deserved so much more than a cold blanket of Kentucky mud.

Lorraine had received word the evening of April first that her mother had been involved in a horrible freeway accident. In the beginning she'd thought it was some kind of cruel hoax, a distasteful practical joke, but the mud-splattered casket was real enough to rip her heart wide open.

Her chest tightened with the effort to hold back tears. A low mewling sound escaped her lips and her trembling increased as she listened to the priest's words in the gray afternoon.

After a while, the friends who'd come to say their last farewells started to move away. Father Darien gently took hold of Lorraine's hands and in sincere compassionate tones offered a few final words of comfort. Reaching deep within herself, Lorraine managed to thank him.

Still, she remained.

"Sweetheart." Gary Franklin, her fiancé, stepped closer and placed his arm around her waist. "It's time to go home."

She resisted and held her ground when Gary tried to steer her toward the waiting limo. She wasn't ready to leave her mother. Not yet. Please, not yet. It made everything so final...to turn her back and walk away.

This shouldn't be happening. This couldn't be real. But the reality of the moment was undeniable—the open grave, the nearby headstones, the muddy ground. Her fears assailed her from all sides, sending a chill down her spine. Lorraine wasn't sure she could survive without her mother's love and support. Virginia had been her touchstone. Her example. Her *mother*.

"Sweetheart, I know this is difficult, but you can't stay here." Gary again tried to urge her away from the grave.

"No," she said, her voice stronger this time. What made it all the more difficult, all the more painful, was the complete lack of warning. Lorraine had talked to her mother that very weekend. They were so close; it had been the two of them against the world for as long as Lorraine could remember. Not a day passed that they didn't connect in some way—with a conversation, a visit, even an E-mail message. On Saturday they'd spent more than an hour on the phone discussing plans for the wedding.

Her mother had been delighted when Lorraine accepted Gary's proposal. Virginia had always liked Gary and encouraged the relationship from the beginning. Gary and her mother had gotten along famously.

Just last weekend—just a few days ago—her mother had been alive. During their phone call Virginia had chatted endlessly about the kind of wedding she wanted for her only child. They'd discussed the wedding dress, the bridesmaids, the flowers, the invitations. Lorraine had never heard her mother sound more excited. In her enthusiasm, Virginia had even mentioned her own wedding all those years ago and the only man she'd ever loved. She rarely spoke of Lorraine's father. That was the one thing she didn't share with her daughter—at least not since Lorraine's early teens. Those were private memories, and it was as though Virginia held them close to her heart. They'd sustained her through the long lonely years of widowhood.

Lorraine couldn't remember her father, who'd died when she was barely three. It seemed her mother had loved Thomas Dancy so completely she'd never entertained the thought of remarrying.

No man, she'd once told Lorraine, could live up to the memory of the one she'd lost.

Her parents' love story was possibly the most romantic Lorraine had ever heard. When she was small, her mother had often told her how wonderful Thomas had been. In later years, of course, she hardly ever talked about him, but Lorraine remembered those long-ago stories—of her father being a decorated war hero and how her parents had defied everyone by getting married. They were the adventure tales, the marvelous bedtime stories of her early childhood, and they'd made a deep and lasting impression on her. It was one of the reasons Lorraine had waited until she was twenty-eight before becoming engaged herself. For years she'd been searching for a man like her father, a man who was noble. Honest. Brave. A man of integrity and high ideals. No one seemed right until Gary Franklin came into her life.

"Lorraine, everyone's gone." Gary's arm tightened around her waist.

"Not yet. Please." She couldn't leave her mother, not like this. Not in a cold wet grave when Virginia Dancy hadn't even reached the age of fifty. The pain was more than Lorraine could bear. As the agony of the moment consumed her, tears began to roll down her cheeks.

"Come on, honey, let me get you away from here," Gary murmured in a voice gentle with sympathy.

Lorraine took a step in retreat. She didn't want Gary. She didn't want anyone except her mother. And her mother was in a grave. "Oh, Mom," she cried, then broke into sobs, unable to stop herself.

Gary turned her in his arms and held her protectively against him. "Let it out, sweetheart. It's okay. Go ahead and cry."

Lorraine hid her face in his shoulder and wept as she hadn't since that night the state patrolman had come to her with the tragic news. How long Gary let her weep, she didn't know. Until her eyes stung and her nose ran and there were no more tears to shed.

"The house is going to fill up and you'll need to be there," Gary reminded her.

"Yes, we should go," she agreed, and wiped her nose with the tissue he handed her, grateful that Virginia's neighbor, Mrs. Henshaw, would be there to let everyone in. Lorraine was calmer now, more self-possessed. People would want to talk about her mother, and since Lorraine was the only one left in the family, she'd have to be in control of her emotions.

Together she and Gary started toward the parking lot. Away from her mother. Away from the only parent she'd ever known.

Lorraine's one comfort, small as it was, was the knowledge that after twenty-five years apart, her parents were finally together again.

* * *

Lorraine couldn't sleep, but then she hadn't really expected to. She should be exhausted. She *was* exhausted; she'd barely slept in days. This past week had been the most emotionally draining of her life. But even now, after the funeral and the wake, she was too restless to collapse into sleep.

Gary seemed to think that spending the night at her mother's house wasn't the best idea. He was probably right. Her sense of judgment, along with everything else, had been thrown off-kilter by the news of her mother's death.

The wake had been here, at Virginia's place. It only made sense that everyone come to the house. Lorraine's apartment was much too small to host the event, and a restaurant seemed too impersonal. Parishioners from St. John's Church where Virginia had faithfully attended Mass all these years, plus a large group of neighbors, co-workers and friends, had lingered to tell Lorraine how sorry they were. They, too, appeared to have difficulty accepting the suddenness of her mother's death.

Virginia had been an active member of St. John's and a devout Catholic. For twenty years she sang in the choir and worked tirelessly for her church "family." As a stockbroker with a large national firm, she'd made a name for herself in the business world. Turnover at the firm was high, and Virginia had learned that office friendships were often fleeting. Nevertheless, the house had been crammed with people.

Contrary to what Lorraine had assumed, she wasn't needed as hostess. Friends and neighbors arrived bearing casseroles, breads and salads, which soon covered the dining-room table. The extras spilled into the kitchen and lined the countertops.

Lorraine was grateful to everyone, especially Gary who'd been both kind and helpful. Yet throughout the wake, all Lorraine had wanted was to be alone, to grieve by herself without people pressing in on her. But that wasn't possible. It took her a while to realize that the friends who'd come were in need of solace, too. So she'd accepted their condolences and done her best to assume the role of comforter. Before long, she'd found herself depleted of energy, and she'd sunk into her mother's favorite chair. Sitting there helped her feel closer to the mother she'd loved so deeply. It eased the ache of loneliness that threatened to consume her in a room full of people.

An endless stream of sympathy and advice had come at her.

"Of course you'll want to keep the house…"

Lorraine had nodded.

"Naturally you'll be selling the house…"

Lorraine had nodded.

"Your mother was a fine woman…"

"We're all going to miss her…"

"She's in a happier place now…"

"...such a senseless tragedy."

Lorraine had agreed with one and all.

By the time everyone had left, it was dark. Gary had helped her with the cleanup and urged her to return to her own apartment. Or to his. He didn't seem to understand her need to stay here, but how could he? He'd never lost a parent.

"You should go on home," she'd told him. "I'll be fine."

"Darling, you shouldn't be alone. Not tonight."

"It's what I want," she'd insisted, yearning for him to leave. It was an unfamiliar feeling, and one she didn't fully understand. She loved Gary, planned to spend the rest of her life with him, but at that moment she'd wanted him out the door. She had to deal with her grief and pain in her own way.

"You need me," Gary said with loving concern.

"I do," she agreed. "Just not right now."

Disappointment registered in his deep brown eyes and he nodded with obvious reluctance. "You'll phone if you change your mind?"

Lorraine had said she would.

He'd kissed her on the forehead in a sweet gesture of love and consolation. Shivering with the evening's cold, Lorraine had stood out on the porch and watched him drive away.

She'd finished the remaining dishes, then wandered aimlessly through the house, pausing in the entrance to each room. Tenderly she caressed the things that had once been her mother's most prized possessions. She closed her eyes and pictured her mother and father together at last and the wonderful reunion they must have enjoyed.

Lorraine was comforted by the knowledge that Virginia had been happy during the last weeks of her life. She'd been thrilled at the news of her daughter's engagement, thrilled at the prospect of planning a large formal wedding. No sooner had Lorraine accepted Gary's proposal than Virginia had started making elaborate plans for the October wedding. She'd valued tradition and frowned on Lorraine's having chosen a small emerald necklace in lieu of the usual engagement ring.

"You have your wish now, Mom," she said aloud. The wedding ring on her left hand had belonged to her mother. The inside of the band was engraved with the words "I'll love you always. Thomas." The funeral director had given it to her that very day, just before he'd closed the casket. Lorraine had slipped it on and wouldn't remove it until the time came for her own wedding. Her mother had worn this ring since the day Thomas Dancy placed it on her finger, and now Lorraine would wear it, too.

"What am I going to do without you, Mom?" Lorraine said into the stillness of the night, her eyes welling with tears. It surprised her that she had any left.

She mulled over everything she'd done that had been a disappointment to her mother. She'd dropped out of medical school after her second year and trained as a nurse/practitioner, instead. Virginia had said little, but Lorraine knew her mother regretted that decision. She liked to think she'd made up for it when she met Gary, who sold medical supplies to Group Wellness, where Lorraine worked.

The fact that she'd become a lapsed Catholic had distressed her mother, as well, but Lorraine had never identified with the church the way Virginia had. She attended a nondenominational Christian church, but her mother would have preferred she remain Catholic.

"I'm so sorry, Mom," she whispered, knowing she'd let her mother down in countless other ways.

When she'd finished her emotional journey through the house, Lorraine had taken a hot shower and changed into a nightgown, one she'd bought Virginia the previous Christmas. After giving the matter some thought, she'd chosen to sleep in her mother's room, rather than her own. When she was frightened as a child, she'd always climbed into her mother's bed. Lorraine was frightened now, afraid of the future, afraid to be without Virginia, without family.

As she lay there sleepless, she gathered her memories around her, finding consolation in the happiness they'd experienced. Day-to-day life had been full of shared pleasures, like cooking elaborate meals together, watching the classic movies they both loved, exchanging favorite books. Virginia also worked for several church-sponsored charities, and Lorraine sometimes spent an evening helping her pack up boxes of food for needy families, or stuffing envelopes. Her mother had been a wonderful woman, and Lorraine was proud of her. She'd been devout in her faith, hardworking, kindhearted. Smart, but generous, too.

After an hour or so, Lorraine gave up even trying to sleep. She sat up and reached for the framed photograph of her parents, which rested on the nightstand. The picture showed Virginia as young and beautiful, wearing a full, ankle-length dress with a wreath of wildflowers on her head. Her long straight hair fell nearly to her waist. She held a small bouquet of wildflowers in one hand; with the other hand she clasped her husband's. Her eyes had been bright with happiness as she smiled directly into the camera.

The Thomas Dancy in the picture was tall and bearded, and wore his hair tied in a ponytail. He gazed at his bride with an identical look of love and promise. Anyone who saw the photograph could tell that the two of them had been deeply in love.

As recently as last weekend, when they'd been discussing Lorraine's wedding plans, she'd teased her mother about the photo, calling her parents "flower children." Virginia had been good-natured about it and merely said, "That was a long time ago."

Sadly this photograph was the only one Lorraine had of her parents together. Everything else had been destroyed in a fire when she was in grade school. Lorraine remembered the fire, not realizing until years later all that she'd lost. Her parents' photographs and letters, her father's medals...

Lorraine knew that Virginia O'Malley had met Thomas Dancy her freshman year in college and they'd quickly fallen in love. The war in Vietnam had separated them when her father volunteered for the army in 1970. He'd survived the war and come home a hero. It was a year later, during a routine physical, that something unusual had shown up in his blood work. That something had turned out to be leukemia. Within six months, Thomas was dead and Virginia was a young widow with a child.

Virginia's parents had helped financially for many years, but both of Lorraine's maternal grandparents had died in the early eighties. Her father's relatives were unknown to her. Her mother had one younger brother, but he'd gotten involved with drugs and alcohol and communication between them had been infrequent at best. The last time Virginia had heard from her brother was five years ago, when he'd phoned her asking for money to make bail. Virginia had refused. Lorraine's only cousin lived someplace in California, and she hadn't seen or heard from her since the summer she was thirteen.

In other words, Lorraine was alone. Completely and utterly alone.

The phone startled her, and she whirled around and grabbed the receiver. "Hello," she said breathlessly, uncertain who to expect.

Gary. "Just checking to make sure you're all right."

"I'm okay," she told him.

"You want me to come over?"

"No." *Why can't you just accept that I need this time alone?* His attitude upset her. This wasn't like Gary.

"I don't think it's a good idea for you to be by yourself," he said. He'd mentioned this earlier, more than once. "I know it's all a terrible shock, but the last thing you should do now is isolate yourself."

"Gary, please. I buried my mother this afternoon. I...I don't have anyone else."

Her words were met with an awkward pause. "You have me," he said in a small hurt voice.

She regretted her thoughtlessness and at the same time resented his intrusion. "I know how that must have sounded and I'm sorry. It's just that everything is still so painful. I need a chance to adjust.''

''Have you decided to sell the house?'' Gary asked.

Lorraine didn't understand why everyone was so concerned about what she did with the house. ''I...don't know yet.''

''It makes sense to put it on the market, don't you think?''

She closed her eyes and sought answers. ''I can't make that kind of decision right now. Give me time.''

She must have sounded impatient because Gary was immediately contrite. ''You're right, darling, it's too soon. We'll worry about it later. Promise you'll phone if you need me?''

''I promise,'' she whispered.

After a few words of farewell, she ended the call. As she replaced the receiver, her gaze fell on the clock radio. She was shocked to discover it was barely nine o'clock. It felt more like midnight. She lay back down and stared up at the ceiling, letting her thoughts creep into the future. Her mother wouldn't be at her wedding, wouldn't be there for the births of her grandchildren. Virginia Dancy had looked forward to becoming a grandmother; now her grandchildren would never know her.

Rather than deal with yet another aspect of her

loss, Lorraine turned her mind to Gary's unexpected call. He'd brought up a number of questions she still had to face.

The house had to be dealt with soon. If it sat empty for long, it'd start to deteriorate, not to mention attract vandals. Gary was right; she had to figure out what to do about it. Finances and legal issues posed another problem. She'd never even seen her mother's will.

She'd deal with one thing at a time, she decided. That was advice Virginia had given her as a child and it had always stood her in good stead. One step and then another.

The call from Dennis Goodwin, her mother's attorney, came a week after the funeral, when Lorraine had returned to work. She'd been expecting to hear from him. Dennis had told her at the funeral that there were a few legal matters that needed to be resolved and then he'd get in touch. He wouldn't need more than fifteen or twenty minutes of her time. He'd promised to phone the following week and set up an appointment.

True to his word, Dennis had called her exactly a week after she'd buried her mother.

Lorraine arrived at the appointed time, prepared to hear the details of her mother's will. The receptionist greeted her pleasantly, then reached for the intercom button. ''Lorraine Dancy is here to see you,'' she announced.

A moment later Dennis Goodwin appeared in the reception area. "Lorraine," he said, his voice warm. "It's good to see you." He ushered her into his office.

Lorraine knew that Virginia had both liked and trusted Dennis. They'd worked in the same Louisville office building, and during that time, he'd acted as Virginia's attorney of record for her will and any other legal matters.

"Have a seat," he invited. "How are you holding up?"

"About as well as can be expected," Lorraine told him. She no longer felt the need to brush aside her own grief in an effort to comfort others. The week since the funeral had been difficult. She couldn't have borne it without Gary's constant support.

"As you're already aware," the attorney said, leaning toward Lorraine, "I knew your mother for a number of years. She was one of the most talented stockbrokers I ever met. Back in the eighties, she recommended I purchase shares in a little-known Seattle company called Microsoft. Because of her, I'll be able to retire in a couple of years. In fact, I could live off that investment alone."

"Mom loved her job."

"She made several smart investments of her own," he added. "You won't have to worry about finances for a long time to come."

The news should have cheered her, Lorraine supposed, but she'd much prefer to have her mother back. No amount of financial security could replace what she'd lost.

She folded her hands in her lap and waited for him to continue.

"Your mother came to me four years ago and asked me to draw up her will," Dennis said. He rolled away from his desk and reached for a file. "According to the terms, you're her sole benefi- ciary. Under normal circumstances, our meeting wouldn't be necessary."

Lorraine frowned.

"But in the event of an untimely death, Vir- ginia asked me to speak to you personally."

Lorraine slid forward in her chair. "Mom wanted you to talk to me? About what?"

"Medical school."

"Oh." She gave a deep sigh. "Mom never un- derstood about that."

The attorney raised his eyebrows. "What do you mean?"

"It was a big disappointment to Mom when I decided to drop out."

"Why did you?"

Lorraine looked out the window, although she scarcely noticed the view.

"A number of reasons," she finally murmured, glancing down at her hands. "I love medicine and Mom knew that, but while I have the heart of a physician, I don't have the competitive edge. I hated what medical school was like—the survival of the fittest. I couldn't do that. Maybe I'm lazy, I don't know, but I have everything I want now.''

"How's that?''

Her smile was brief. "I do almost as much as a doctor, but without the bucks or the glory.''

"I believe your mother did understand that,'' Dennis said, although Lorraine suspected it wasn't completely true. "But she wanted you to know that the funds are available if you should change your mind and decide to go back.''

Lorraine's eyes stung as she held back the tears. "Did she tell you I'd recently become engaged?''

"She hadn't mentioned it. Congratulations.''

"Thank you. Gary and I only recently told…'' Lorraine let the rest fade. The attorney waited patiently, but she didn't trust her voice.

"If you reconsider and decide you'd try medical school again, I'll do whatever I can to help you.''

His offer surprised her. "Thank you, but I'm not going to do that. Not when Gary and I are about to start our lives together.''

"Well, I promised I'd mention it to you if the occasion arose. It saddens me that it has.''

Within a few minutes, Dennis finished explaining the terms of the will and handed her the necessary paperwork. When she'd read everything, he passed her another sheet of paper.

"What's this?" she asked.

"An inventory of the safe-deposit box. I went down to the bank yesterday afternoon and retrieved everything. I have it all for you here." He stood and picked up the manila envelope on his credenza. "I wanted you to be sure that every document listed on the sheet is accounted for."

Because she knew it was expected of her, Lorraine dumped the contents of the envelope onto the desk surface and checked off the items on the list. She'd previously seen or known about everything here. Or so she assumed until she found the opened letter addressed to her mother. How odd, she mused, studying its colorful foreign stamps.

"Do you know anything about this letter?" she asked the attorney.

"Nothing. Actually, it seemed odd to me that Virginia would put something so obviously personal in with documents that were all business-related."

"It's from Mexico," Lorraine said unnecessarily.

"Yes, I noticed that."

"Postmarked seven years ago." She withdrew the single page inside. After scanning it, she turned it over and read the signature. Gasping, she lifted her head to stare at Dennis Goodwin.

"You're...you're sure you didn't know about this?" She was unable to conceal her shock.

"Lorraine, I don't know anything about that

letter. I was your mother's lawyer, not her confidant. What she chose to place in the safe-deposit box had nothing to do with my role as her attorney.''

Lorraine sagged against the back of the chair and raised her hand to her throat. ''Could...could I have a glass of water please?'' Her mouth felt incredibly dry and her voice had gone hoarse. This couldn't be true. Couldn't be real. This was *crazy*.

''I'll be right back.'' Dennis stepped out of his office and quickly returned with a large paper cup.

Lorraine drank the contents in several noisy gulps and briefly closed her eyes, trying to take in what she'd learned.

''I'm sorry if something's upset you,'' Dennis said.

''You really haven't read the letter?'' she asked shakily.

''No, of course not. It would've been highly unethical to do so.''

Lorraine waited until she'd regained her composure enough to sound unemotional. ''It appears, Dennis,'' she said calmly, ''that my father isn't dead, after all.''

Two

The nightmare woke Thomas Dancy out of a sound sleep. He opened his eyes and filled his lungs with air. A breeze wafted in through the open bedroom window and a full April moon cast fingers of cool light into the room. *It's just a dream*, he reminded himself. One that came to him periodically. It was always the same, and despite the passage of almost thirty years; it hadn't lessened in intensity. He relived every gut-wrenching detail—and always woke up at the same point, trembling with fear and terror. Again, as he did every time, Thomas felt unabashed relief that it had only been a dream. Again, he reminded himself that the worst was over. He'd walked through that hell once, and lived.

Thomas threw back the sheet and sat on the edge of the thin mattress as the darkness and the effects of the nightmare closed in around him. Even now that he was wide-awake, the fear refused to release him, had seeped into his bones.

He'd lost so much, back in the early seventies.

By far his greatest and most profound loss had been his wife and daughter, but the dream had nothing to do with them.

In an effort to combat the lingering traces of depression—the dream's legacy—he formed a mental picture of Ginny and tiny Raine the day he'd left for Vietnam. Ginny had been so young, so beautiful. Her face had been streaked with tears as she held their daughter in her arms. Despite everything that had gone wrong in the years since, that particular image never failed to lighten his heart.

She'd come to the airport to see him off to war. A war he didn't understand and had no desire to fight. It had nearly killed him to leave his family that day. But in the end he'd been the one to do the killing.

Guilt surged up in him and he shook his head, refusing to allow his thoughts to stumble down that path. He rubbed his face with both hands, as if he could erase the last residue of the dream and all the memories it brought back.

He couldn't.

The trembling started again, and he stood and walked over to the window and stared into the night. He gazed at the reflection of the moon over the smooth water of the bay, off in the distance. He needed a reminder that the war and its aftermath were far behind him.

As memories of the war faded, they were replaced by thoughts of Ginny. Despite the years, despite her abandonment, he still loved her. He'd made a new life for himself here in El Mirador, and he'd come to think of Mexico as his home. He was a simple man, living a simple life. He'd never be rich, but then, money wasn't important to him. Ginny had understood that.

Ginny...

Earlier that night, before his dreams had erupted into the sights and sounds of a brutal war, his wife had come to him. He'd seen her as she was at twenty, and their love had seemed as real as the windowsill beneath his fingers.

His heart sang at the sound of her name in his mind. He remembered the first time he saw her on the university campus and how he'd dismissed her as virginal and uptight. But the cliché about opposites attracting was certainly true in their case. He'd embraced the beliefs of the late sixties—like student power and "doing your own thing"—ideologies she'd regarded with contempt.

As it happened, they'd attended the same English class and sat across from each other. Thomas took it upon himself to break through that barrier of reserve she held between herself and the world. Ginny was the challenge he couldn't resist. He didn't mean it to happen, but before he knew it, he'd fallen in love.

So had she.

A slow smile relaxed the taut muscles of his face as he recalled the first time they'd slept together. She'd been innocent, and while he was far from a virgin, that afternoon with Ginny was the first time he'd truly *made love*. The honesty of their lovemaking had forever changed him. Instinctively he'd known that, despite his other lovers, she was the only woman he'd really loved.

He wanted to marry her. His feelings had nothing to do with religion and everything to do with his heart. They met every day after class and took crazy chances to be together in either his dorm or hers. Once they'd made love, it was impossible to stop, and their physical need for each other grew until it dominated all common sense.

He realized Ginny was pregnant long before she suspected it. Good Catholic girl that she was, she'd refused to let him practice birth control. God knows, he'd tried not to get her pregnant.... But Ginny would wrap her legs around him in a way that drove him to the brink of insanity, refusing to let him withdraw early. It was as if she was purposely trying to make it happen.

By that time he was renting a two-room apartment off campus. His sole piece of furniture had been a worn-out mattress tucked in a corner. What cooking he did was on a hot plate. The lack of material wealth was of little concern to either of them. They were too much in love to care.

Ginny's conservative family was shocked by

the changes in her when she arrived home for the holidays with him in tow. Her hair was waist-length and her attire consisted of long cotton dresses and sandals. Her parents hadn't liked him then and liked him even less when they discovered he'd gotten their honor-student daughter pregnant. It didn't surprise him that her family strongly disapproved of their marrying. One of the things that distressed Thomas most in the years that followed was the rift he'd caused between Ginny and her family.

They wrote their vows themselves and at Ginny's insistence found a sympathetic priest who agreed to perform the ceremony. Their lovemaking had been good before they were married, but afterward it was incredible.

With a wife to support and a baby on the way, Thomas had been forced to drop out of college and find full time employment. At one time he'd seriously considered medicine as a career, but that had been an unlikely dream from the beginning. He and Ginny both knew that. Besides, the only way he could've attended medical school would have been on a scholarship, and his marks had fallen since his involvement with Ginny. Still, he wouldn't have traded his marriage for even a full-ride scholarship to the best medical school in the country.

Although they lived below the poverty level, Thomas and Ginny were blissfully happy. At Lorraine's birth, he was with Ginny as much as the doctors would allow. It'd been hell not to go into the delivery room with her. When the nurse came out and told him he had a daughter, Thomas broke into tears of joy. His heart had never known that kind of happiness.

Two days after they brought Lorraine home from the hospital, Thomas walked into a U.S. Army recruiting office and handed over his life to Uncle Sam. It wasn't what he wanted, but he had no real choice. Little did he realize when he put on that uniform how much he was about to lose.

The nightmare was about Vietnam. Again and again he relived the day he'd held David Williams in a blood-filled rice paddy and watched him die. He'd been helpless to do anything but scream in anguish.

He wrote Ginny about David, but words were inadequate to describe his loss. More than a friend had died that day. Part of Thomas Dancy had died, too. The young man he was, the innocent twenty-one-year-old who believed in the power of love and goodness, also bled to death in that rice field. From then on, he was able to kill without conscience.

He'd gone to war a kid, trying to provide for his family, and returned a killer. It'd taken Ginny's love to wipe away the ugliness of those long months in Vietnam. Halfway through his tour he'd flown to Hawaii on leave and never returned to the war. He despised what he'd become.

The army referred to him as a deserter, but Thomas knew that walking away then had saved his life. He would have lost his mind if he'd gone back. He'd hidden in San Francisco for a while and Ginny had come to him there, loved him, given him back his sanity. The bitterness and hatred inside him had slowly melted away until he was almost whole again, almost able to put all the horrors he'd seen out of his mind. But he felt a moral obligation to save others from what he'd experienced. Instead of fleeing to Canada as so many before and after him had done, he made it his mission to work toward ending the war. He joined an extremist group and made friends with its leader, José Delgado, who had family in Mexico. Because Thomas had some fluency in Spanish after four years of study, José insisted they speak the language when talking about their plans. It had started out as a safety measure and then later become a necessity.

"Thomas?"

Reluctantly he turned at the sound of his name.

"The dream again?" Azucena asked in a low whisper.

He nodded, not wanting to explain that his thoughts had been of Ginny and the daughter he no longer knew.

She slipped out of bed and walked to his side,

her bare feet silent against the stone floor. "Come back to bed," she urged in Spanish as she wrapped her arms around his waist.

"Soon," he promised, unwilling just yet to let go of the memories.

"Come," she enticed once more, splaying her fingers across his chest. "I will help you forget the bad dreams you have."

"Azucena..."

Her response was wordless. She kissed his neck and pressed her heavy breasts against him.

He needed her then as he'd needed her so many times before. Despite the advanced state of her pregnancy, he kissed her with little gentleness and she responded with a hunger that quickly ignited his own. When he would have stopped, she pulled him to the bed and drew him close.

Azucena deserved a much better man than he would ever be. She deserved someone who would love her completely for herself. A man who could give his name to the child who grew inside her. It shamed him that she was only two years older than his daughter, but that didn't stop him from burying himself between her thighs. In the moment of his release he cried out Ginny's name. It wasn't the first time, and he suspected it wouldn't be the last.

Lorraine had read the letter so many times she'd memorized it. She'd given up sleeping at her own place and spent the nights at her mother's house instead. While she stayed there, she slept very little. Exhausted and angry, she sat in the dark living room night after night and tried to make sense of what she'd learned.

She was vaguely aware that two weeks or so had passed since that afternoon in Dennis Goodwin's office. Morning dawned and bright light spilled into the room and still Lorraine hadn't slept. She wasn't capable of dozing for more than an hour or two. The deep satisfying sleep of those at peace with life seemed forever lost to her.

The mother she'd known and loved was someone whose existence had virtually disappeared. Virginia—or the person she'd pretended to be—was completely out of reach now. Her actions were beyond Lorraine's understanding—or forgiveness. Lorraine felt as if the foundation of her entire world had crumbled beneath her.

Although she knew each word of the letter by heart, she removed it from the envelope and read it once again.

Dearest Ginny,
Today is our daughter's twenty-first birthday. Where did all those years go? It seems only yesterday that I bounced Raine on my knee and sang her to sleep. It hurts to realize how much of her life I've missed.

I know you don't want to hear this, but I

never stopped loving you or needing you. I wish things could have been different for us. All I ask of you now is that you tell Raine the truth about me.

The decision to tell her I was dead is one we made together. At the time it seemed the right thing to do, but I've regretted it every day since. You know that. You also know I'm a man of my word. I've done as you wanted and stayed out of your lives, but I'm pleading with you now to tell Raine the truth. All of it. She's legally an adult and old enough to make her own judgments.

I'm teaching at a small school in a coastal town called El Mirador on the Yucatán Peninsula. You can reach me by phone at the number on the bottom of the page. The school will make sure I get the message.

Are you well, Ginny? Do you lie awake at nights and think of me the way I do of you? Are you happy? This is my prayer for you, that you've found peace within yourself.

I'll always love you.

Thomas

Three truths hit Lorraine full force each and every time she went over the letter. First and foremost, despite what she'd been told, her father was alive and well. Second, he loved her. Last—and what had the most profound impact on her—her mother had *lied* to her all these years.

There was a loud knock sounded at the front door, yanking Lorraine from her thoughts.

She wasn't surprised to find Gary standing on the other side of the screen door. "I thought you'd be here." He glanced into the living room and eyed the disarray.

"What time is it?" she asked, although it was obviously morning.

"You were due at work an hour ago."

"Is it that late already?" she asked. She drifted around the room, picking up books and papers and videotapes, piling them neatly on a shelf. Anything to avoid looking at him. Anything to delay telling him what she'd done.

"I don't know what to do to help you anymore," he said, lifting his palms in a gesture of helplessness. When she didn't answer, he walked into the kitchen and opened the cupboard, then pulled out a tin of coffee.

Lorraine followed him.

"It might be a good idea if you dressed for work," he suggested pointedly.

Rather than argue with him, she did as he asked, taking a quick shower and putting on her uniform, although she had no intention of showing up at the clinic. The scent of freshly brewed coffee greeted her when she returned. Gary handed her a mug and poured himself one.

"Let's talk," he said, motioning for her to sit at the table.

Once more she complied, because fighting him demanded too much energy.

He took the chair across from her. "Sweetheart, I know this is difficult, but you've got to get on with your life."

She didn't pretend not to know what he was talking about. "I realize that and I will."

"That's a good start." He sipped his coffee, then sighed heavily, as if he'd dreaded this confrontation. "You haven't been yourself ever since that meeting with your mother's attorney."

"I know."

He hesitated, as if unsure how far to press her. "I realize the letter upset you. Hell, it would've upset anyone, but you've got to come to grips with reality. Sleeping here every night, watching the same videos over and over isn't going to help." He paused and changed tactics. "It's been a month now, and you haven't dealt with your mother's death any better than when it first happened."

"You're right, I haven't," she agreed, cradling the mug with both hands, letting its warmth seep into her palms. Somehow she managed to go in to work most days, but she'd been late a number of times. Again and again she sat in front of the television and escaped into her favorite movies. Movies her mother had loved, too—romance, adventure, suspense, anything that would take her mind off the lies Virginia had told her. Lies *both* her parents had conspired in.

"What do you do here every night?" he asked. "Besides watch Humphrey Bogart and Cary Grant movies."

"Do?" It seemed he had only to look around for an answer to that.

He glanced back into the living room and frowned.

Lorraine tried to look at the house through his eyes and had to admit its appearance must come as something of a shock. She was as neat and orderly as her mother had been. Both were meticulous housekeepers, yet Lorraine had gone about systematically tearing every room apart. The house was a shambles.

"What do you hope to prove?" he asked.

Lorraine was stunned by his lack of comprehension. "I'm not hoping to *prove* anything. I'm hoping to find what else my mother saw fit to hide from me."

He stared into the distance as if it took some effort to assimilate her words. "Don't take this the wrong way, but have you thought about talking to a counselor?" he asked gently. He risked glancing in her direction.

"You mean a mental-health professional?"

"Ah…yes."

Lorraine couldn't help it. She burst out laughing. "You think I've gone off the deep end? That I'm losing it?" As her laugh turned to a giggle, she wondered if he wasn't far from right. At times the sense of betrayal and pain threatened to strangle her. That her parents, particularly her mother, had chosen to lie to her was incomprehensible.

"I know how difficult this is for you," Gary added, rushing his words. "I'm trying to understand, and I know the people at Group Wellness are, too, but there's a limit to just how accommodating everyone can be while you deal with this."

"I agree with you."

Gary's eyes revealed his suspicion. "You do?"

"I'm booking the next month off work."

"A month?" She could tell he was taken aback by the news. "That long? I think a week or two should be sufficient, don't you?"

"Not for what I have in mind."

"I thought we'd decided to save most of our vacation time for our honeymoon and—" He stopped midsentence and his eyes narrowed. "Have in mind? You have something in mind?"

"I'm going to see my father."

It was a moment before he spoke. "When?"

"My flight's scheduled to leave at seven o'clock Tuesday morning."

Gary stared at her as if he didn't recognize her any longer. "When did you decide this?" His voice was calm, which Lorraine recognized as a sign of anger.

"Last week." She'd known when she bought the ticket that Gary would disapprove. It was one of the reasons she hadn't discussed her plans with him beforehand.

"I see," he said in a hurt-little-boy voice. He reached for his mug and took a long swallow.

"I phoned the school where he teaches and talked to the secretary." Communication had been difficult, but the woman's English was far superior to Lorraine's high-school Spanish.

Gary's silence was comment enough, but Lorraine hurried on with the details, hoping to settle this before she left for Mexico. She didn't want to slight Gary or offend him, but she had to see her father, talk to him face-to-face. She had to find out what had driven him and her mother apart. Why her parents had allowed her to believe he was dead. There had to be a logical explanation for the lie; she prayed there was. Of all the emotions he'd revealed in his letter, the strongest was love, for her and for Virginia. And all these years they'd deprived her of that love. *Why?*

"Have you talked to your father?" Gary asked, his voice devoid of emotion.

She hesitated before answering, knowing Gary would find fault with this aspect of her plan. "Not directly."

"I see."

"The phone number is for the school where he teaches."

"So I understand." He sounded downright bored now.

"And he was in class when I called," she continued. Surely that made perfect sense. "I left a message giving my flight information and asking him to meet my plane."

"Then he returned your phone call?"

Again she hesitated. "Not exactly."

Gary snorted. "It's a simple question, Lorraine. Either he returned your call or he didn't."

This conversation had been unsatisfactory almost from the first. "I resent your tone, Gary. I was hoping you'd support me."

He released his breath in a long-suffering sigh. "I just wish you'd talked to me about it first."

"I'm sorry," she told him, and she was. "I realize this is unfair to you, but I have to find out what happened between my parents. My father's alive, and I want a chance to know him—to talk to him, to learn why they felt they had to lie. You can understand that, can't you?"

He took his time answering. "Yes," he admitted with obvious reluctance. "But like I said, I wish you'd involved me in this. We're engaged. I would've thought you'd want to talk it over with me before you booked the trip."

"I'm going to see my father, not quit my job."

"Taking a month off has...ramifications," he said.

"What do you mean?"

"Our honeymoon time," he shot back. "Group Wellness isn't going to give you a month off now and then two more weeks a couple of months down the road."

"Five months."

"Whatever."

"Gary, please. Try to see it from my point of view."

"See it from mine."

"Darling, I'm sorry," Lorraine said. "I was hoping you'd understand. I have to do this before I can get on with my life—with *our* life."

Slowly he nodded, as if his agreeing to her trip was a gift. "I still wish you'd told me first so I could've changed my schedule and joined you."

Joined her? Not once had Lorraine thought of asking Gary to accompany her. He couldn't come anyway, she decided with a surge of relief. Not when he was so recently promoted and training his replacement.

But that wasn't the real reason, and she knew it. She loved Gary, but she didn't want him with her. This journey into her family's past was her adventure, and hers alone.

Letting Lorraine travel to Mexico by herself had never sat easy with Gary Franklin. He loved his fiancée and realized this was a difficult, unsettling time for her. A measure of his love was his willingness to stand by and let her fly off on her own. Not only that, he'd offered to drive her to the airport—which meant getting up at 4:00 a.m. He glanced at his watch in the dashboard light. Quarter to five now. They'd discussed this trip countless times since the morning she'd sprung it on him, and he was convinced she was making a mistake. But Lorraine didn't want to hear that and had stopped listening to him.

Although his only intent was to protect her, shield her from further hurt, she refused to consider any outcome other than a joyful reunion with the father she'd never known. He'd long admired Lorraine for her common sense, but she exhibited little of it in this unpleasant matter.

Gary had liked Virginia, and her death had shaken him, too. He'd respected Lorraine's mother for her business savvy and the way she worked in what was still largely a man's world. Furthermore he trusted her judgment. Since she'd chosen to tell Lorraine a lie regarding her father, he figured there had to be a good reason. Gary feared that whatever it was would mean bad news for Lorraine, maybe even heartbreak.

Besides her unwillingness to listen to his advice, he couldn't help resenting the fact that she didn't want him with her. She hadn't tried to hide it, either, and that hurt.

He parked the car and gathered his thoughts as he approached the house.

"Ready?" he asked Lorraine when she answered the doorbell.

She nodded. At least she'd packed sensibly, he noted—just one medium-size wheeled suitcase. She wasn't like some women, who found it necessary to bring along every outfit they owned. She looked smart, too, in an off-white linen pantsuit, her blond hair neatly pulled back. She seemed a little uncertain, but obviously determined to follow through, no matter what happened.

"Do you have your passport?"

"Yes."

"Travelers' checks?"

She nodded.

"Insect repellant?"

"Gary! Honestly, you make me sound like a child heading off to camp."

He hadn't thought of it like that, but she was probably right. "Sorry," he said with a grin.

Because there was so little traffic this early, the drive to the airport didn't take long. He insisted on going to the gate with her. Then they stood there waiting, not knowing what to say.

"I don't want you to worry," she murmured at last.

"I'll try not to. Will you phone?"

She hesitated and shrugged lightly. "I don't know about the phone situation in El Mirador. My guess is the schoolhouse is the only place in town with a working phone.''

He wished she hadn't reminded him how primitive this village was likely to be.

''I'll write,'' she promised, ''and phone if I can.''

''Great.'' He had to be happy with that.

Her seat assignment was called and he waited in line with her before she entered the jetway. They hugged and kissed and he clung to her for a moment, then stepped back as she disappeared into the long tunnel that led to the plane. She'd vanished from view, and still Gary stood there.

Despite Lorraine's optimism, he couldn't shake the feeling that everything—in his life and in hers—was about to change.

Three

Jack Keller had never thought of himself as a big-game fisherman. But owning a thirty-two-foot twin-diesel cabin cruiser made about as much sense as anything else in his life, which was damn little.

He'd "retired" as a mercenary, gotten out of the death-defying game while the getting was good. At the end of his five-year stint he was sick of it all. Sick of the low-profile and corporate rescues Deliverance Company had specialized in. Jack was tired of fighting hotheaded terrorist groups and corrupt governments that used innocents in a cruel game of greed and revenge.

He had, however, been paid well for his skills, and he'd managed to save most of it. The major part had been wisely invested, and with the proceeds of the sale of his condominium in Kansas City, he could live comfortably in Mexico until he was a very old man. Growing old in the tropics appealed to Jack. Footloose and fancy-free, that was him. The boat was a bonus he hadn't expected. An inheritance of sorts from Quinn McBride, a friend whose life he'd saved a decade earlier. Jack had lived aboard *Scotch on Water* for the past three years. He'd stayed in the Gulf of Mexico for most of that time, dropped anchor here and there, made a few friends. The strongest of these friendships was with Thomas Dancy, another American expatriate who lived in the tiny coastal town of El Mirador.

Although Thomas was about fifteen years his senior, the two shared a camaraderie and a deep love of their adopted country. Thomas was a man of secrets, but Jack had a few of his own. It was because of Thomas and Azucena that Jack had hung around the Yucatán; in the past few weeks, though, he'd decided to expand his horizons. Lately he'd been thinking about heading to the Florida Keys, stopping off at some of those small Caribbean paradises along the way. He'd heard the people were friendly, and it didn't hurt any that the women were gorgeous.

Then again, he might return to Belize. He'd pulled into port at Belize City any number of times and he was impressed with the beauty of the country. His American dollars were always welcome; Jack had no problem with that. The women were warm and friendly—and there was a pretty *señorita* he was certain would be glad to see him. Jack couldn't quite remember her name, but no doubt it'd come to him in time.

Either Florida or Belize—he had yet to decide. Before he set his course for either destination, he needed supplies and figured he might as well check his mail, too. Not that he was expecting anything. He hadn't heard from Cain, Murphy or Mallory in several weeks, but he wasn't much for keeping in touch with old friends himself. His life as a mercenary was far behind him. These days he had little in common with the men of what used to be Deliverance Company. His friends were married now, and the last Jack had heard they'd settled into domesticity. Not Jack, though.

Standing on the flybridge, the sun in his face and a breeze slapping his unbuttoned shirt against his tanned chest, Jack set *Scotch on Water* in a westerly direction. He checked the chart and saw he wasn't far from El Mirador. It'd been a couple of months since he'd shared a beer with Thomas. Azucena must be ready to pop that kid of hers any day now, if memory served him right. Perhaps he'd arrive in time for the blessed event, and he and the new father could celebrate.

This was their third kid in six years. Good grief, Thomas was as bad as Cain and Murphy, but at least Thomas had an excuse. Azucena was a traditional Catholic and didn't believe in birth control. Sex without marriage, sure; birth control, no. Interesting logic, Jack thought with a grin. During one visit, Thomas had confessed how upset he'd been when Azucena turned up pregnant the first time around. In the years since, he'd apparently grown accustomed to fatherhood. Then again, Jack might, too, if he had a hot-blooded woman like Azucena warming his bed. There was some reason Thomas couldn't marry her, some reason in his past; he'd alluded to it but never explained.

A few years back, fool that he was, Jack had given marriage serious consideration. He found it hard to believe now, but he'd actually been ready to buy into the whole scene—wife, family and house in the suburbs. Luckily he'd escaped *that* trap...but at the time he hadn't felt especially lucky. In fact, it'd hurt like a son of a bitch when Marcie turned down his proposal. What really got him was that she'd married a plumber named Clifford instead. It still boggled his mind that a woman as smart and sexy as Marcie would find happiness with a slow-witted moose of a man named Clifford.

But they did seem happy. He found it remarkable, but had to admit he felt relieved; he wouldn't want her to be anything else. He'd received picture Christmas cards from her and Clifford for the past two years. The first one showed her standing proudly beside her big oafish hus-

band with her stomach extending halfway across
the room. She looked a good ten months' pregnant. Next year's Christmas card explained why.
Twins. He'd forgotten their names now, but they
were rather unimaginative, as he recalled. Billy
and Bobby or something along those lines. What
he remembered most was how happy Marcie had
seemed. Her face had glowed with joy as she held
one squirming toddler and Clifford hoisted the
other. Jack had kept the photograph tucked away
on the boat as a reminder that she'd made the
right choice in not marrying him. Other than that
one all-too-brief episode, Jack had realized a long
time ago that he wasn't the marrying kind. Nope,
not even close. He wasn't interested in settling
down with a woman, putting up with all that do-
mestic crap. He enjoyed his carefree life and
didn't need anyone messing with his mind. Or his
heart...such as it was.

No question, things had worked out for the best
when Marcie married Clifford. Jack would have
made a rotten husband, but there were times, al-
beit few and far between, when he wondered what
would've happened if Marcie *had* married him.

He'd drink a beer in her honor, Jack decided,
frowning into the wind. To Marcie and their lucky
escape.

The Boeing 767 landed in Mérida on the Yucatán Peninsula early that afternoon. As Lorraine

exited the aircraft, she peered over the customs counter, hoping her father had received her message and follow-up letter and had been able to meet her plane. The only photograph she had of him was the wedding picture, which showed him with long hair and a beard. He'd be fifty now, and Lorraine had no idea whether or not she'd even recognize him.

The map securely tucked in her purse showed that El Mirador was about seventy-five miles north of Mérida. She glanced around anxiously. It took an unusually long time to clear customs, with lots of people complaining about the unnecessary hold-up. From what Lorraine could make out, the small customs office was short-staffed because of some museum theft. Apparently every available officer was checking the luggage of passengers leaving the country.

After what seemed like an eternity, she was waved through. She collected her suitcase and carefully searched the waiting area, but saw no one remotely resembling the man in the photograph.

"Time for Plan B," she muttered to herself, grateful that she'd thought this out beforehand. She made her way across the airport to the car-rental booth.

"Can I help you?" the clerk asked.

"Great," she said, digging through her purse for her driver's license. "You speak English."

"Yes." The young woman flashed her a toothy grin.

"I need to rent a car."

"Very good."

"I'm not sure how long I'm going to be needing it, possibly an entire month, unless there's a rental agency I can return it to near El Mirador."

The friendly smile faded when Lorraine mentioned the name of the town. The clerk looked over her shoulder and said something in Spanish that Lorraine didn't understand. Right away the first woman was joined by a second, who appeared to be the manager. They spoke in rapid Spanish, and while Lorraine recognized a few words, she couldn't catch the gist of the conversation.

When they finished, the girl with the toothpaste-ad smile turned serenely to face Lorraine once again. "I'm sorry, but my supervisor says we have no cars available at this time."

Lorraine didn't believe it. "But you were perfectly willing to rent me one a minute ago."

"Yes." She didn't deny that.

"Why won't you now?"

"El Mirador has no roads."

"No roads?"

The clerk pulled out a rental agreement, silently

read it over and underlined the appropriate section
before handing it to Lorraine. People in the line
behind her were becoming impatient, so Lorraine
moved away and sat down to read the section the
other woman had highlighted. With the aid of her
dictionary, it did make some sense. Apparently
rental cars were not allowed on anything but
paved roads. In other words, El Mirador was well
off the beaten path, and the roads leading in and
out of it were either dirt or gravel. Getting there,
it seemed, would be no easy trick.

"Okay, then. Plan C." Except she had yet to
figure out what that would be. There *had* to be
another way to reach El Mirador. A bus. If she
couldn't get a rental car, she'd take a bus. Which
meant she had to find the bus station first.

That decided, she picked up her suitcase and
walked outside the air-conditioned airport. The
blast of heat made her stagger. She felt as if someone had thrown a hot towel over her head. Almost
immediately her linen pantsuit became damp and
clung to her like a second skin. Summers in Louisville could be stifling, but she'd never experienced anything like this—and it was only May.
She looked down at her limp wrinkled trousers
and sweat-stained jacket; this was what she got
for wanting to make a good impression on her
father. Had she been meeting anyone else, she
would have dressed less formally.

Joining the long line for a *colectivo*—cab—she patiently waited her turn. Unfortunately the taxi driver spoke little English, but with her pocket dictionary and traveler's phrase book, she was able to get her message across. The driver nodded repeatedly at every question, then loaded her suitcase into his trunk, which he tied closed with a frayed rope.

Lorraine climbed into the backseat and searched for a seat belt. There wasn't one. The instant he got behind the wheel, her meek and mild-mannered driver turned into a road warrior. Lorraine was tossed about the backseat like a sack of oranges, flung from one side of the vehicle to the other as he wove in and out of traffic. He switched from lane to lane, sometimes racing toward oncoming traffic at a death-defying rate. It would have helped had she found something to hang on to, but all she had were her wits, and those had scattered long ago. The one compensation was that she was too terrified to notice how miserably hot it was.

By the time she arrived at the bus station, she was grateful to have survived the trip. Her shoulder ached from being slammed against the side of the car and her jaws hurt from being clenched. She paid the fare with no argument but without any tip, either, and lugged her suitcase into the depot.

One thing was for sure: her presence certainly attracted a lot of attention. Every eye in the dilapidated place was focused on her. With what she hoped was grace and style, she squared her shoulders and made her way up to the window as if she'd done this every day of her life.

"I'd like a ticket to El Mirador," she said in English, forgetting to use Spanish.

The man stared at her blankly.

Lorraine reached for her phrase book and flipped pages. She discovered that mentioning the name of the town wasn't enough to achieve the result she wanted. She attempted a number of times to ask for a ticket, and each time the agent merely shrugged and looked blank.

Then he tried speaking to her. First he spoke slowly, then louder as if that would make her understand. After five minutes of this, she was ready to scream with frustration.

"Perhaps I can help."

Lorraine turned to find a smiling clean-cut man standing next to her.

"Jason Applebee," he said.

"Lorraine Dancy." She held out her hand, noting that his was bandaged. "You're American?"

He nodded. "I guess that's fairly obvious, isn't it? Around here I stick out like rice in a bowl of beans."

"I take it you speak Spanish?"

"Fluently." Then, as if to prove his point, he spoke to the man behind the counter. The clerk grinned, nodded and said something in return. His eyes moved to Lorraine; she couldn't miss the relief in his expression.

Lorraine didn't understand what either of them had said. By this point she was beyond translating even the simplest verbs. Jason turned to her. "Now, what were you trying to ask?"

"I need a ticket to El Mirador."

"You're joking," Jason said, his face lighting up. "I'm heading that way myself."

"Really? I thought it was just a small town."

"Actually, I'm going to a place not far from there. I was planning to spend the night in El Mirador."

"You mean there's a hotel?" If things didn't work out with her father, it was reassuring to know she'd have someplace to sleep that night.

"I guess you could call it that," Jason said, and they both laughed.

Lorraine paid for her ticket, and Jason bought his, as well. When they'd finished, they sat in the shade outside and waited for the bus, which was due to arrive, Jason said, in thirty minutes.

"Will you be staying at the hotel, too?" her newfound friend asked as he arranged his backpack at his feet.

"I don't know yet," Lorraine muttered. It had

been a long day already, with a plane change in Atlanta and a two-hour delay. "How long will it take to reach El Mirador?"

"A couple of hours, possibly more—if the bus doesn't break down, that is."

"Oh, great." She sighed loudly, wondering if anything else could possibly go wrong.

"Hey, it isn't so bad," Jason said. "You should've been at the dig I was on last week." He explained that he was a part-time archaeology lecturer at a small college in Missouri; she didn't recognize the name. He was here doing research for his doctoral thesis. He'd been in Mexico a month now, he told her, although this wasn't his first trip. Lorraine guessed him to be in his mid-thirties. He had short dark hair and the ubiquitous sunglasses, and wore a short-sleeved cotton shirt tucked neatly into khaki pants. The freshness of his clothes made Lorraine feel even more despairing about the condition of her own.

"So you were working on this dig?"

"Yeah, and it was fantastic, other than this," he said, lifting his bandaged hand. Jason entertained her for the next hour—the bus was late, of course—with tales of his adventures, including a harrowing description of the accident in which he'd injured his hand. He'd rescued one of the Mexican assistants on the dig from a knife-wielding pair of thieves. She shuddered at his dramatic telling.

Lorraine liked Jason. It was impossible not to. He was witty and cheerful, not to mention generous with his help. At one point he bought some melon slices from a street vendor and shared them with her. Lorraine hadn't really been hungry, but the fruit quenched her growing thirst.

She'd never made friends with anyone so quickly. She suspected that everyone responded to Jason this way; his open exuberant personality encouraged confidences and camaraderie.

With billowing exhaust and much grinding of gears, the bus finally pulled into the station. Jason had been right to warn her about its likely condition. The rattletrap of a vehicle looked as if it'd been on the road since the Second World War. Its color was no longer distinguishable and half the windows were missing. In this heat, though, that was probably a blessing.

The bus was one thing, her fellow travelers another. The minute the bus rolled into the yard, people appeared from every direction. Adults and children and caged chickens. One man was hefting a pig under his arm.

"Go and get us the best seat you can," Jason advised, urging her toward the bus. "I'll make sure our luggage gets on board."

Lorraine watched, amazed, as two men climbed

on top of the bus and waited for Jason and another man to throw suitcases up to them. She didn't envy anyone the task of lifting her suitcase, let alone hurling it eight feet off the ground.

After about ten minutes a breathless Jason climbed on board and collapsed onto the seat beside her.

"You mentioned you'd be traveling to someplace near El Mirador," Lorraine said once he'd caught his breath.

"I'm on my way to another dig," he said, shifting a bit to give her more room on the cramped seat. The narrow cushion was barely wide enough for one adult, let alone two.

He'd told Lorraine a little about Mayan ruins earlier, and she'd found it fascinating.

"There's a dig near El Mirador?" She'd researched the tiny coastal town at the library and on the Internet, but hadn't learned much. El Mirador had a population of less than a thousand. The economy of many of these towns along the coast depended, naturally enough, on the fishing industry, but there was little else. She couldn't remember reading about Mayan ruins in the area around El Mirador, but that didn't mean much.

"Actually," Jason explained, "our El Mirador was named after another El Mirador, in Guatemala. It was an important Mayan site—one of the earliest. But there's a Mayan temple a few miles from this El Mirador, too. It was discovered a few years ago, and they've only begun excavating, so I want to spend a few weeks there before I go home."

"Home is Missouri, right?"

"Jefferson City," he said. "Now what about you? Why are you traveling to El Mirador? It's not like the town's exactly a tourist destination."

Lorraine took her time answering, wondering how much to tell Jason. She'd known him slightly longer than an hour. Granted, they'd become virtually instant friends, but still... This wasn't the kind of personal information one generally shared on such recent acquaintance.

"My father lives there," she said without elaborating.

"In El Mirador?" Jason's eyes widened briefly. "What's he doing there?"

"He's a teacher."

"The Peace Corps?"

Lorraine looked out the window. Considering how nervous she was about meeting her father, she should be grateful for someone to talk to. She'd tell Jason the whole story, she decided impulsively. He'd certainly told her a lot about his own background, and she sensed she could trust him. She took a deep breath. "To be honest, Jason, I don't really know. I haven't seen him since I was three—I was told he'd died of leukemia. I only found out a month ago that he's actually alive, and once I did, I couldn't stay away. My fiancé thinks I've gone off the deep end and maybe I have. I don't know anymore.'' She ended up telling Jason about her mother's death, the letter she'd discovered with the items from the safe-deposit box and about Gary.

Jason took a moment to absorb everything. "Does your father know you're coming?"

"Yes, of course," she said, struggling not to sound defensive. Then she sighed. "I'm not sure." Since he hadn't been in Mérida to meet her, she no longer knew what to expect.

"But you've been in touch with him?"

"Oh, yes." Lorraine had grown resentful when Gary asked her these same questions. But Jason seemed genuinely interested and concerned about her, while Gary had been so insistent. So overprotective. "I phoned and left a message at the school, but he didn't return my call. When I didn't hear back from him, I sent a letter. I was hoping he'd be waiting for me at the airport...but he wasn't."

"When did you mail the letter?"

"Beginning of last week."

Jason shook his head. "I hate to tell you this, but he probably hasn't gotten it yet. The mail—" They hit a rut in the road just then. The bus jolted badly and sent both Jason and Lorraine flying upward. Her teeth felt as if they'd been shaken loose, and she heard Jason's cry of pain as his head slammed into the roof. The pig escaped, squealing as it raced toward the back of the bus. Undisturbed by the commotion, the driver didn't even slow down.

After a few minutes, everything was quiet again, and Jason finished his sentence. "The mail in this part of the world is notoriously slow."

"Oh, dear."

"You should probably assume that your father has no idea you're coming," he warned her.

His words sobered Lorraine. She'd traveled thirteen hundred miles, the last part under deplorable conditions. Now there was reason to believe that her arrival would take her father completely by surprise.

Ever since that night the dream had awakened him, Thomas Dancy hadn't been able to stop thinking about Ginny. He realized this probably had more to do with Azucena than Ginny. His common-law wife was due to deliver their third child any day.

He hadn't meant to love Azucena, hadn't meant to start this second family. But along with his other faults, he was weak. Too weak to resist a second chance at love—and life. He usually didn't give in to these occasional bouts of remorse and self-loathing; he was too realistic for that. But occasionally, like now, thoughts of his former life wouldn't leave him alone.

He sat at his desk, his classroom empty, and stared at the test papers he should be grading. Instead, his mind was on Ginny and the daughter he didn't know. Guilt weighed heavily on him for breaking the vows he'd spoken in love. He'd always intended to remain faithful to Ginny. In the early years, after he'd fled to Mexico, she'd met him at prearranged destinations, in Mexico City or Veracruz. He lived for those few brief days together. Then Raine had started school and Ginny's visits became less and less frequent until they finally stopped. Still, he'd spoken vows of love and fidelity. Vows he'd written himself.

He was burdened by more than guilt and regret. He worried about Azucena and this baby yet to be born. He was fifty now, and he'd been with her for only the past eight years. Sometimes he believed he had a right to take whatever happiness he could, the happiness Azucena offered him; other times he prayed Ginny would never know of his weakness for this woman so much younger than himself.

He hadn't wanted more children, but Azucena was stubborn and she'd yearned for a baby. She had a loving generous heart, and he couldn't deny her, not when she'd done so much for him. Soon there would be three children. He wondered if this third child would be a son like the first two.

He loved his children, doted on them and, according to Azucena, spoiled them. Because of Antonio and Hector, he realized how much he'd missed with his daughter. Raine was an adult now, but in his mind she remained a child. She'd been so young when he left! Ginny had brought him photographs during those infrequent visits; the last one was a school picture of Raine, gaptoothed, pigtailed, eight years old.

A knock sounded on his door. "I apologize for disturbing you," one of the older students said in Spanish on entering his classroom. "A man has asked to see you."

"Did he give his name?"

"Jack Keller."

Thomas grinned despite himself. "Tell him I'll be right out." He had little in common with the former mercenary, but it was always good to spend time with another American. Jack didn't visit all that often, but he invariably brought news of home and the world. On the negative side, he tended to have a foul mouth and a quick eye for a pretty face, but both of these faults were easily forgiven. Jack was a good friend to a man who had few.

Thomas shoved the test papers into his leather case and headed for the school office. Jack lounged in a broken-down desk chair, flipping the pages of a year-old magazine. He looked like hell. He needed a haircut, but Azucena would probably see to that. His sun-streaked brown hair brushed his shoulders. Apparently he hadn't shaved in two or three days, either. His jeans were cut off at midcalf, the ends frayed, and he wore tennis shoes without socks.

"Jack." Thomas greeted him with enthusiasm and held out his hand.

"Hey, Thomas." Jack tossed aside the magazine and vaulted to his feet. He gripped Thomas's hand for a firm shake, then slapped him on the back in a gesture of fondness.

"You're beginning to look like an old sea dog," Thomas said.

"Yeah, well, you don't look so bad yourself. Are you a proud papa yet?"

"Any day now." It worried Thomas that there were no medical facilities close to El Mirador, not that Azucena would agree to have this baby anyplace but in their own home with a midwife. Yet he couldn't help being concerned, despite the ease of the two previous deliveries.

"Got time for a cold beer?" Jack asked.

"Of course." Thomas would send word to Azucena via a student. She would want Jack to come to the house for dinner. Not only did she like Jack a great deal, it was a matter of pride to her that she feed their guests like visiting royalty. She'd have Thomas's head if he didn't bring Jack home with him.

He left instructions with Alfonso, then he and Jack strolled over to the waterfront cantina. No sooner had they sat down at a table and tasted their beer than Alfonso was back, breathless from running.

"Señor Dancy!" he cried. "Señor Dancy!"

"What is it?" Thomas's first thought was of Azucena.

"There's a woman at the school asking for you," Alfonso blurted.

"A woman?" Thomas ignored Jack's raised eyebrows.

"*Si.* She says her name is Lorraine Dancy. She says she's your daughter."

Four

Lorraine's nerves wouldn't allow her to wait quietly for her father. She couldn't sit still, and as she paced the school hallway, her heels clicked against the hard stone floor. A framed document on the wall, written in both Spanish and English, stated that the school was financially supported by a group of Texas churches. It listed the headmaster's name, plus the three teachers. And it explained that the children's uniforms were sewn by the Women's Missionary Society. She read the information twice, then paced some more. Lorraine had arrived in El Mirador half an hour ago—it was nearly six now. She'd known her chances of catching Thomas Dancy at the school this late in the afternoon weren't good. Jason had wanted her to check into the lone hotel with him, but she'd decided to look for her father first.

As it turned out, the school building was open, and when she mentioned her father's name to a young man in a school uniform, he'd nodded with enthusiasm and even managed to ask her a few questions in English. He'd suggested she wait inside while he went to get her father.

For a moment Lorraine had felt almost lightheaded with relief—at least her father was there. Then the real anxiety had begun, the jittery nervous fear. The almost sickening excitement.

At the sound of footsteps behind her, Lorraine turned. Thomas Dancy stood in the doorway, framed in bright sunlight.

"Raine," he whispered.

"Thomas Dancy?" she asked hesitantly, then added, "Dad?" He'd called her Raine in his letter, too, but her mother had always insisted that her name not be shortened.

The look in his eyes was answer enough. Deep blue eyes, the same color as hers. He stepped slowly toward her and she could see that he was indeed the man in her mother's photograph. He gazed at her for a full minute, an awed expression on his face. Then he smiled, and his eyes shone with an intensity that suggested tears.

"Raine," he said again. "If only I'd known…"

"You didn't get my letter?" she asked.

"No…no."

"I phoned, too."

He frowned. "I didn't get the message."

"Then you didn't know I was coming?"

"No…but I thank God you did."

They stood only a few feet from each other, and he continued to stare at her. "How like your mother you are," he whispered. "So beautiful…" He raised his hand as if to touch her face, then apparently changed his mind and let his arm fall. The love in his eyes was unmistakable.

At the mention of her mother, Lorraine felt her own eyes fill with tears.

"Raine, what is it?" He stopped short of taking her in his arms.

She stopped short of letting him. "Mom was killed April first," she told him shakily.

Her father looked as if she'd suddenly reached out and stabbed him. His eyes widened with shock and then slowly, as though his legs would no longer hold him, he staggered toward a chair. "Killed? How? Dear God in heaven, tell me what happened."

"She was on her way home from work. It'd been raining that day and no one knows exactly why, but her tires lost traction and her brakes locked—and she skidded into oncoming traffic. She was hit by a huge semi… There was nothing he could do to stop. Nothing anyone could do."

Her father closed his eyes. "Did she suffer?" he asked, his voice so low it was an effort to understand him.

"No. The investigating officer told me death was instantaneous."

Thomas nodded, his face wet with tears that ran unrestrained down his cheeks. "April first, you said?"

"Yes."

He nodded again, reached into a pocket for his handkerchief and wiped away the tears. "I woke up that night." He paused for a moment, apparently deep in thought. "My Ginny is dead," he said as if he needed to hear himself say the words to believe they were true.

Lorraine sat down in the chair beside his. "Mom told me *you* were dead."

"I know. We...we thought it best."

"Why?" Everything Lorraine had endured today would be worth it if he could answer this single question.

Thomas inhaled a deep breath and turned to face her. He took both her hands, clasping them between his own. It was then that he noticed the ring.

"It's Mom's. I put it on the day of the funeral." She told him a little about her engagement to Gary and then paused, needing answers before she continued.

His thumb tenderly caressed the wedding band. "I'll love you always," he whispered—the words engraved inside the ring. His eyes gazed into hers. "I loved your mother and you with all my heart,

Lorraine. First and foremost, I need you to believe that."

"Why would you leave us?" she cried. Now that she was with him, she wanted to know the truth with an urgency that left her trembling. For more than twenty years her mother had lived under false pretenses, and Lorraine had to find out why. She couldn't imagine what would drive her parents to do something so drastic. Honesty had been the very basis of her mother's character. Or so she'd thought.

"Mom loved you, too…all that time. She wouldn't talk about you, especially once I got older. Whenever she did, she'd start to cry."

"I know…I know."

Tears spilled from Lorraine's eyes. "She told me you'd died of leukemia."

The merest hint of a smile touched his mouth, lifting one corner. "We concocted that story together."

"But you're alive!" She needed the truth, and quickly, while she was strong enough to bear it. "Please—tell me…"

"It started in Vietnam," he said, his voice falling to a whisper. "In many ways, the man I was meant to be died there."

"But you were a decorated hero! Mom said the thing she regretted most about the fire was that your medals were lost and—"

Thomas's head snapped up. "She told you that?" His expression was sober. Regretful. "I was far from a hero, Lorraine. I deserted halfway through my tour of duty. I couldn't take the killing any longer, the death...."

Lorraine didn't want to believe what she was hearing. It *couldn't* be true. Any of it. "But—"

"I returned to the States and joined a militant antiwar group. They helped me hide out. From the moment I turned my back on the army, I made it my mission, my goal in life, to keep other young men from dying senselessly on foreign soil. I wanted to save them from watching their friends blown to bits for reasons that had nothing to do with us or our country."

"But surely you could come back now—even if you were a deserter. There was an amnesty, wasn't there?" All her life she'd viewed her father as a hero. This lie her parents had lived made no sense, and she found Thomas's story confusing.

"I did much more than desert." He broke eye contact and lowered his head to stare at their joined hands. "As I said earlier, I joined a militant antiwar group. A number of us decided to blow up the ROTC building at the University of Kentucky. We didn't mean for anyone to get hurt.... The security guard wasn't supposed to be anywhere close to the building."

"He died in the explosion?"

Her father nodded. "Two of our group were picked up almost immediately when they tried to cross the Canadian border. José and I knew it was only a matter of time before we'd be arrested, as well."

"José?"

"José Delgado, a friend, a good one at the time. The two of us made our way into Mexico before an arrest warrant could be issued."

"What happened to him?"

"José? We bummed around the country for a while, then he found another cause. We argued and split up—I haven't seen him in years. The last I heard he was part of a guerrilla group somewhere in Central America."

"But couldn't you come back now? That happened almost thirty years ago!"

"No," Thomas said with a sadness that couldn't be disguised. "There's no statute of limitations on murder. The minute I cross the border, I'll be arrested for murder and prosecuted to the full extent of the law. Raine, I want you to know that I was involved with the group, but I was against the bombing. I never believed violence was the way to get our message across. But I didn't have the courage to stand up to the others. That was my greatest sin and one I've paid for dearly in the years since."

"What happened to the two who were arrested?"

Again her father lowered his gaze. "Rick and Dan? Rick committed suicide in prison, and Ginny told me Dan was paroled after serving six years of a twelve-year sentence."

Questions crowded Lorraine's mind, and she asked the most pressing ones first. "Why didn't Mom join you? Surely after five or ten years she could have done so without anyone suspecting."

"That was what we planned in the beginning," he said. "Your mother moved to Louisville and she visited me every six months or so. We were able to keep in touch through a mutual friend."

"Who?"

"Elaine Wilson."

"Aunt Elaine?" She'd died when Lorraine was nine.

"Everything fell apart after Elaine died," her father said. "Ginny would write that she'd be coming, but each time she'd find some excuse to postpone it. Eventually her visits stopped entirely."

"But couldn't we have moved to Mexico? Then the three of us would've been together."

He hesitated. "Ginny was afraid that if she left the country for more than a few days, she wouldn't be able to return. She worried about her parents. She worried about you, too. Your mother loved you beyond everything, and she wanted you to have the best education and all the advantages America has to offer.''

"But...she told me you were dead." Lorraine didn't know if she could forgive either of them for the lie.

"You were a child and far too young to carry the weight of our secret.''

"But I'm an adult now. I have been for years. There was no reason to continue hiding the truth from me," she insisted. No reason Virginia couldn't have told her and allowed her to form her own judgments, make her own decisions.

"Any blame falls on me, Raine," he said. He raised his hand to her face, touching her cheek. "I was the one who screwed up. I was the one who got involved in a bombing that claimed an innocent man's life.''

"But I needed you," Lorraine said, fighting back tears.

"I needed you, too," he said, and gathered her in his arms. They clung to each other for a long time.

When he released her, Lorraine sat back and tried to collect herself.

"You must be exhausted," he said. "Hungry, too, I'll bet.''

Her stomach growled, reminding her that, except for a few pieces of melon in Mérida, her last meal had been aboard the airplane. Yogurt, a banana and some type of forgettable roll. Her father was right; she was both tired and hungry.

He lifted her suitcase and led her out of the school. While they walked the short distance to his house, Thomas told her how he'd spent his life here in Mexico. Until nine years ago, he'd worked at various odd jobs around the country, not staying in any one place for long. Then the opportunity had come to teach science and math at this private school, a job he thoroughly enjoyed.

"I'm ashamed to admit I didn't find my calling in life until I was over forty."

Already Lorraine could see how easy it would be to love this man. He might have been militant in his youth, but despite the tragic results of his actions, he'd joined the antiwar effort for compassionate reasons. He'd repented his mistakes and was obviously still a good man, but one who'd achieved self-knowledge.

Lorraine was grateful to have found him.

It had been a shock when Lorraine showed up in El Mirador, but one of the happiest of Thomas's life. His daughter was everything he'd hoped she'd be. Intelligent, beautiful, caring. And so much like her mother.

His first look at Lorraine had stopped him cold.

She resembled Ginny in almost every way. In fact, it was like stepping back and seeing Ginny at nineteen.

The news that his wife was dead was a hard blow, and he'd need time to assimilate it. Time and privacy to mourn. He'd told Raine the truth— he had loved her mother. Yes, she'd hurt him; yes, she'd disillusioned him, but he'd forgiven her. He couldn't blame her for the tragic turn his life had taken. He just wished things had been different for both of them. Too late now for wishing, though.

His home was a humble one and Thomas hoped Lorraine would understand that the village was poor. The school couldn't afford to pay him a large salary.

Antonio and Hector were playing in the front yard. Under other circumstances, his sons would have raced toward him, but they were shy boys and unaccustomed to seeing him with strangers. They stopped and stared, Antonio clutching the soccer ball to his chest, as Thomas opened the door for Lorraine.

Azucena was in the kitchen preparing dinner. The scent of garlic drifted through the house. Thomas set Lorraine's suitcase in the living room and tried to find a way to explain that this very pregnant woman was his common-law wife. Lorraine would probably be surprised, perhaps disapproving, but Azucena was his wife in every sense except the legal. Now that he was free to marry her, he would do so.

Azucena stepped into the room, her smile automatic until she saw Lorraine. Her welcome sobered as she glanced at him, her eyes filled with questions. Azucena spoke little English and showed no desire to learn. Because she made no effort herself, their sons knew only a few English words.

"This is my daughter," he explained in Spanish. Her eyes widened, and Thomas could see that she was flustered. He'd told her about his family, about Raine, and sensed that she felt threatened. He wanted to reassure her but wasn't sure how.

"Where's Jack Keller?" Azucena asked abruptly.

"Back on his boat, I assume. I left him when I learned my daughter was at the school."

"You knew about your daughter's visit?" Her beautiful dark eyes were accusing.

"No." He longed to take Azucena in his arms and apologize, but didn't dare. "Her mother died last month, and she only recently found out I was alive."

Azucena nodded, her expression sympathetic. "Introduce me as your housekeeper," she advised with gentle wisdom. "Your daughter has had more than enough shocks."

"I won't lie to her again. It's better if she knows."

"We'll tell her together," Azucena said. "Later. She's traveled a long way and must be exhausted."

He hesitated, then agreed with a short nod.

"Ask her to sit down, and I'll serve you both dinner."

"What about you and the boys?" It didn't seem right not to have them at the table with him. As he'd told Azucena, he didn't like the idea of lying to Raine, but he could see that his daughter was physically tired and emotionally distraught. He didn't want to burden her with still another difficult truth. But he also feared her anger. He couldn't bear to lose her when he'd only just found her again. Although it went against his better judgment, he agreed with Azucena's reasons to delay telling Raine about their relationship.

"Don't worry, we'll eat later," Azucena insisted.

Thomas noticed Raine listening to the flow of words between them. Her eyes revealed her lack of comprehension. "This woman is someone special?" she asked, eyeing Azucena closely.

"My housekeeper," he said, silently adding *and so much more.*

"She's meticulous," Raine said, glancing around the sparse but lovingly decorated home.

Thomas tried to see the house through her eyes and knew it must be far less than she was accustomed to, but he made no apologies. He'd earned his living by honest means.

"Dinner's ready if you'd like to eat now. Azucena's a wonderful cook. She's made a dish called *camarónes con ajo,* which is shrimp with garlic."

"It sounds delicious. Please thank her for me," Lorraine said.

"I will." Thomas showed his daughter to the bathroom, where she could wash up.

She returned a few minutes later. The table was set with steaming ceramic bowls filled with rice, tomatoes and the delectable-smelling shrimp.

Lorraine took a seat. "When is…your housekeeper's baby due?"

"Any day now," he answered as he passed her the rice, hoping to avoid further questions.

"Those were her children outside?"

Thomas nodded.

"Her name is lovely."

"It means lily."

The irony of the situation didn't escape him. At one time Azucena had, in fact, been his housekeeper. The school had hired her on his behalf, and for six months he'd barely noticed her. His house was kept spotless and his meals cooked every night. Beyond that, he was absorbed by the demands of teaching and enjoying his newfound profession. He'd never intended to take Azucena to his bed. He was married, although no one in El Mirador knew about his American wife. Nor did he wish to indulge in behavior that would be viewed with disfavor by the church-supported school.

To date, the headmaster had never mentioned Thomas's living arrangements. He'd eaten meals in this house, so he had to know what was going on. Nevertheless he always referred to Azucena as Thomas's housekeeper. And for those first six months that was exactly what she was. Thomas hadn't made so much as an untoward gesture, and in the end, Azucena, whose name was regarded as a symbol of purity and perfection, had been the one to seduce him.

The meal was excellent. Azucena had chosen his favorite. He could see that Raine was enjoying it, too.

"She really is a wonderful cook," Raine said as Azucena carried a plate of hot tortillas to the table.

It was difficult for Thomas to disguise his fondness for his common-law wife. He knew Lorraine had noticed the smile he'd given Azucena and might have commented, but their meal was interrupted by a loud demanding knock on the door. Both women looked at Thomas.

He set his napkin aside and moved across the

room, unsure what to expect. The knock was not that of a friend. He knew trouble when he heard it.

Two uniformed policemen stood on the other side of the threshold. He'd rarely seen armed police in this town; not only that, he didn't recognize either man, which was unusual in itself. He knew almost everyone in El Mirador, if not by name then by sight.

"Can I help you?" Thomas asked, taking care to pronounce each word distinctly and with authority.

"We're looking for Lorraine Dancy."

"May I ask what this is about?"

"Dad?" Raine said from behind him. "I heard my name."

He ignored her, refusing to break eye contact with the two officers. "Why are you looking for my daughter?"

"We need to ask her a few questions," said the taller and more muscular of the two.

"Questions about what?"

"Jason Applebee," the second policeman informed him. "We need to know what her relationship is to this man."

"Dad?" Raine had joined him. "What's this about?"

"Do you know anyone by the name of Jason Applebee?" he asked in English.

She nodded. "He's an American I met in Mérida. He helped me buy my bus ticket. Is everything all right? Nothing's happened to him, has it?"

Thomas asked the two police officers those very questions. Raine had said nothing previously about meeting this other man, but Thomas could see that she cared about his welfare.

They answered, and he turned back to Lorraine. "They're holding him at the police station. They won't tell me why."

"Oh, no." She covered her mouth with her hand. "Something's wrong. We've got to help him."

Thomas had been in Mexico long enough to know how difficult situations with the police could get. If for no other reason than Raine's endorsement of her new friend, he felt obliged to do what he could to help the guy.

"They want you to go to the station with them," Thomas explained next.

"Me?" Raine looked at him uncertainly.

"I'll be with you."

"Then I'll go," she said. "I'm sure this is just a misunderstanding and everything will be cleared up in no time."

Thomas wished he could believe that. But one thing he knew: he would do everything within his power to protect his daughter.

* * *

The minute Lorraine entered the small building, Jason leaped to his feet, relief at seeing her evident on his face. "Lorraine!" he cried as if she were the answer to his prayers.

"What's going on?" she asked.

Jason glanced at the two officers standing near the door; they gazed back at him impassively.

With three policemen and Jason, plus Lorraine and Thomas, the station was cramped. For the first time Lorraine realized that only one of the men who'd come to the house had accompanied them here. She hadn't a clue where the second man had gone. Not that it particularly concerned her.

"This is my wife," Jason announced in English.

Lorraine barely managed to swallow her denial. Her father glared at her, eyes narrowed. Both policemen immediately glanced at the ring finger on her left hand.

"Is this true?" the older man asked. He was tall and distinguished-looking with a crop of thick white hair.

Everyone present seemed to await confirmation. Jason's gaze begged her to go along with him. She forced a smile and nodded.

The room erupted into shouts and denials from the officer who'd escorted Lorraine and her father to the station. She didn't know what anyone was saying, but it didn't take long for her father to become involved in the heated conversation.

"What's all this about?" Lorraine demanded of Jason under her breath.

"I don't know," he said, looking as confused as she felt. "But from what I can make out, they think I've got some Mayan artifact, which is ridiculous." He appeared frightened, baffled and apologetic. "I didn't mean to drag you into this," he confessed in a low voice, "but I didn't know what else to do."

"Why'd you say I was your wife?"

"I had to tell them something so I could convince them to contact you. I told them you were visiting your father, so you hadn't registered at the hotel yet." He paused, lowering his eyes. "They wouldn't let me place a call or have an attorney present. I didn't know what to do or what the hell's going on. I helped you and I was hoping you could help me."

"Don't worry," she told him, although she hated lying. She supposed there were times it was necessary; now seemed to be one such occasion.

The argument continued between the police and Lorraine's father.

"I still wish you'd told them the truth," she murmured.

"You want me to tell them I was recently on a dig?" He stared at her with wide-eyed disbelief.

"Lorraine, that's crazy. The minute they learn that, they'll be convinced I actually *have* the damn thing."

The white-haired officer walked over to the other side of the room. Jason's backpack was open on a table and his clothes and personal effects littered the top. His bag had been thoroughly searched.

"Dad?" Lorraine stepped closer to her father. "Have you found anything out?"

"Sergeant Lopez is of the opinion that your...husband is guilty of stealing a national treasure. They think Jason's the one who stole the Kukulcan Star." He went on to explain that the Star was an artifact associated with the god Kukulcan. It actually consisted of two separate parts, designed to fit together. One-half of the Star had been discovered in the 1930s and kept in a Mexico City museum. That piece had gone missing a few days after the second half of the Star was found on a new archaeological dig. But it disappeared under mysterious circumstances before its authenticity could be verified. Even worse, one man—a guard at the museum—was hospitalized and not expected to live. Another man, an archaeologist named Raventos, hadn't been seen since the first theft. There was evidence of foul play. It was assumed that the same person was responsible for all of these crimes. And the police suspected Jason of being the culprit," Thomas told them, concluding his explanation.

"That's not true!" Jason shouted. "I swear that isn't true."

"Fortunately for your friend," Thomas said to Lorraine, "Lieutenant Jacinto is inclined to believe him."

"Thank God," Jason whispered, sagging against his chair. "They've searched everything I have. They tore my backpack inside out."

Her father faced Jason and met his look squarely. "If you've taken this artifact, it would be best to own up now."

"I didn't!" Jason said fervently. "I swear by all that's holy I don't know what these men are talking about. I'm just a part-time university instructor."

Lorraine noticed that he conveniently forgot to mention that the subject he taught was archaeology or that he'd been on a recent dig. Not that she blamed him—well, not entirely. She understood the reason he'd given her: just mentioning his background would make him instantly suspect in police eyes. She did wish he was a bit more forthcoming with the truth, but in similar circumstances she wasn't sure she'd be any more honest herself.

"They said they were looking for a long-haired

blond American male with round glasses and a bad cut on his right hand," Thomas said.

Jason shrugged. His own hair was dark and clipped short and he didn't wear glasses. "I don't know what to tell you. It isn't me."

"I'm not sure I'd have made it to El Mirador without his help," Lorraine told her father.

Thomas leveled his gaze on Jason. "Like I said, lucky for you Lieutenant Jacinto believes you."

Jason sighed with relief.

"I've been able to convince them to let you return to your hotel room for the night, but they might want to question you again come morning."

"Of course. I'll do anything I can to clear my name," Jason said eagerly.

"I'll be here if you need me," Thomas added.

"Thank you, sir. I appreciate your help more than I can say."

"Jason won't disappoint you," Lorraine said with confidence. "He'll do whatever he's supposed to do."

"Well, for tonight you're free to go back to the hotel," Thomas reminded him.

"Thank you again," Jason said.

Jason, Lorraine and her father left the police station together. The police had repacked his bag and returned it. Her father insisted on walking Jason to his hotel and stopped to talk to the proprietor, an old man who greeted Thomas warmly.

Although Lorraine couldn't understand what was being said, the gist of the conversation was obvious. The man in the hotel was to keep his eye on Jason.

Thomas didn't refer to her role in this fiasco until they were almost back at the house. "Why'd you lie about being Jason's wife?" he asked her point-blank.

"I...I didn't know what else to do." She knew she'd displeased him, but that couldn't be avoided. "It wasn't something I planned on doing," she qualified. "But when he said I was his wife..." Lorraine gave a helpless shrug. "Anyway, I know Jason's innocent."

"You're that sure?"

"Yes, positive," she returned without further thought. "Yes," she said again for emphasis.

Her father was about to say something else, then stopped abruptly. "Antonio," he called as a youngster raced toward him with an older boy she didn't recognize.

Antonio had been one of the children playing in the yard at the house, she recalled. Something was clearly wrong, because the boy burst into a torrent of Spanish almost as if he couldn't get the words out fast enough.

Her father listened and his body language confirmed her guess. He turned, gripping her arms tightly. "We have to get you out of here."

"Get me out?" Lorraine was nearly too stunned to speak.

"One of the policemen searched through your suitcase while we were at the station."

"But that's not legal!" she cried in outrage.

"Raine," he said, shaking her hard. "They found the artifact."

Five

Jack sat on board *Scotch on Water* watching the sun sink into a friendly pink sky. This was his favorite time of day. Soon the moon would rise over the water, its reflection silver-bright. He propped his feet on the side of the boat and held a bottle of his favorite Mexican beer. A clear sky, a beer in his hand and his mind free of worries. Life didn't get any better than this.

With nothing more than the sunset to distract him, Jack let his thoughts wander back to his friend Thomas Dancy. When Thomas had learned of his daughter's visit, he'd raced back to the school, promising he'd see Jack later. Hell, Jack hadn't even known Dancy *had* a daughter. Her visit sure as hell wasn't expected if Dancy's reaction was anything to go by. He hadn't heard from his friend since, but he would; Dancy was a man of his word. Jack had delayed having dinner, preferring to let Azucena spoil him with one of her specialties. Man, could she cook! His mouth watered just thinking about what she could do with a fresh fish, a couple of tomatoes, peppers and a few spices. Her tortillas hot from the grill were the best he'd ever tasted. If she was feeling up to it, he'd ask her for a haircut, too. He should shave before dinner, he mused, rubbing his hand down his face. The stubble scraped his palm.

It'd been good to see Thomas again, even if their visit was cut short. He'd forgotten how much he enjoyed Dancy's company. Jack had laughed more in the half hour he'd spent with Thomas than he had in weeks. He'd make a point of sticking around until the kid was born. He wanted to be sure he saw lots of Antonio and Hector, too. Those two were pure fun. It didn't hurt any that they worshiped him, either.

His evening plans might have fallen through, but the afternoon hadn't been wasted. He'd filled the boat's 480-gallon fuel tanks with diesel and paid for his supplies. They'd be loaded on board first thing in the morning. Given the option of heading toward Florida or Belize, he'd decided to return to the Central American country and would set his course southward as soon as the mood struck him.

"Jack!"

The urgency of the voice caught him off guard. He dropped his feet and stood, tensing with sudden wariness. Then he leaned over the boat's side, peering toward the dock.

Thomas raced along the waterfront, tugging a blonde in a white pantsuit by the hand. Jack noticed that the woman was having trouble keeping pace. Briefly he wondered if she was Dancy's daughter. Her purse swung wildly at her side and threatened to slip off her shoulder. Both were breathless and appeared to be arguing. As they drew closer, Jack was able to make out their words.

"Antonio's your son, isn't he?" She turned to Thomas and Jack could hear the anger in her voice.

"We don't have time to discuss that now," Thomas said.

"He called you Papa. How many other children do you have? How many wives?" Then, as if she should have realized it earlier, she added, "Azucena's your...lover, isn't she? Why, she can't be more than three or four years older than me!" Shock and outrage sounded in each word. She lapsed into silence as they approached Jack's slip.

Thomas's face was tight with frustration. "I'm here to ask a favor," he said, looking up at Jack.

"It's yours," Jack said, not waiting to hear what it was. Few people in this world warranted such a response, but Jack liked and trusted Thomas Dancy.

"Raine, this is Jack Keller."

Jack nodded in her direction, choosing to disregard the fact that they'd been arguing. "Pleasure to meet you, Raine."

She barely glanced at him. "I prefer to be called Lorraine," she said with all the warmth of a rattlesnake.

La-di-da. "Lorraine," he corrected himself, and resisted rolling his eyes.

Thomas didn't waste words. "I need you to get her back to the States without the authorities here finding out."

Jack read the panic in his friend's voice and eyes. "In other words, you don't want me to take her through customs."

"You got it." And then Thomas said, "You need to leave now. Right away."

"Trouble?" Jack asked, ignoring the woman.

"Big trouble."

"You're overreacting," Lorraine insisted. "Once I'm able to explain the situation, I'm sure—"

"We don't have time to discuss it," Dancy said, cutting her off.

"The last thing I should be doing now is running," she countered. "Taking off like this makes me look guilty. I'd rather face the authorities than—" she paused and cast Jack a scornful look "—be stuck with him."

Apparently Jack didn't meet her dress code.

Truth be known, he wasn't exactly thrilled about sharing her company, either.

"We've got to get you back to the States," Thomas said forcefully. "If the police arrest you, I won't be able to help. They'll be here any minute. Now go! For the love of God, go!"

Police? Arrested? *Her?* Jack couldn't imagine what she'd done to fall into such disfavor with the authorities, but whatever it was had to be major.

"Take her!" Thomas practically propelled her in Jack's direction. "Get her out of here."

"My suitcase...my clothes! I can't just leave like this! Besides, there are things you and I need to talk about."

"The police have your suitcase! Anyway, do you think they'll let you keep it when Sergeant Lopez hauls you off to jail? Do you?" Thomas's composure slipped as his voice rose in fear and anger. "Trust me, you don't want to see the inside of a Mexican jail. Now go, dammit. Get the hell out of here." He was shouting now, gesturing frantically for Jack to take her. Thomas untied the rope from the dock and tossed it onto the deck.

"The American Embassy will help me," Lorraine said as she reluctantly climbed on board. *Scotch on Water* rocked slightly with her entry. "When I explain I know nothing about the artifact," she went on, "they'll square everything with the Mexican government on my behalf."

Even without knowing her circumstances, Jack could see the woman lived in a fantasy world. Once she was in the hands of the Mexican authorities, there was little anyone could do to help her. The willingness—and ability—of the American Embassy to assist her was a matter best left to speculation. Thomas knew this as well as Jack did.

"Please—just go," Thomas pleaded.

"But—"

The boat's engine fired to life with a roar. A burst of exhaust fumes polluted the air.

"But I only just arrived!" she shouted. The high-pitched plea in her voice could be heard over the noise of the engine. "I—there's things I need to know before I leave... This isn't right. None of this."

Jack heard her distress but felt no real sympathy.

"This isn't what I want, either," Thomas said. Slowly, as if it ripped his heart out, he stepped away from the slip. "I'll find a way to reach you," he promised. "You have precious cargo, my friend," he told Jack, his eyes filled with pain. "Get her safely back to the States for me."

The situation was urgent; that much was obvious. Without waiting any longer, Jack climbed to the flybridge. Thomas remained at the far end of the dock and watched them pull out.

Looking over his shoulder, Jack noticed that Lorraine stood at the rear of the cabin cruiser. He pushed the lever forward, easing the craft out of the protected waters of the marina. Lorraine leaned against the gunwale, arms crossed. Even from the back, Jack could tell how furious she was. She might be tempted to leap overboard and swim back to land, but he wouldn't recommend it.

Not long afterward, the empty feeling in the pit of his stomach reminded Jack that he hadn't eaten yet. Furthermore, there was damn little food on board. The supplies he'd ordered and paid for were back in El Mirador on the storekeeper's porch. Not only was he out his supplies, but he was stuck with a woman who was sure to irritate him every time she opened her damn-fool mouth.

No, this certainly wasn't how he'd thought his evening would go. No, sir. Not at all.

Lorraine stayed on the open deck of the boat and watched the lights of El Mirador gradually disappear. She wasn't sure how long she stood there, trying to make sense of what had happened in the past hour. It seemed that only minutes ago she'd been enjoying a wonderful meal with her father, becoming acquainted with the man she'd believed forever lost to her. Her face reddened as she recalled the way she'd complimented his "housekeeper."

This business with the Kukulcan Star was a complete shock—and made her feel even more idiotic. It was entirely clear now that Jason Applebee—if that was his real name—had used her to corroborate his story. He'd tricked her into lying on his behalf, knowing that the authorities were looking for a man traveling alone. No wonder he'd wanted her to tell the police they were married. She groaned at her own stupidity. She'd believed in his innocence right to the bitter end—when she'd learned that the artifact had been found in *her* luggage. That certainly didn't say much for her ability to judge character. As for his appearance, he could easily have cut and dyed his hair. And as for placing the artifact inside her suitcase, he could have done that when she'd climbed on the bus and he'd loaded their bags onto the roof.

How convenient for Jason that he'd come across such a naive trusting American. If there was anything she should've learned from the past month, it was not to trust appearances. Now, because of him and her own naiveté, she was on a boat with this...this overgrown whatever he was. Jack Keller looked like an unkempt surfer who'd spent too much time in the sun. Apparently he lived on his boat. His hair was bleached blond, his body tanned to a bronze hue. Even if she'd just reminded herself that there was no use in relying on appearances, she couldn't help it with this guy. He seemed so shiftless and irresponsible. Her father must've been desperate to have brought her to such a misfit.

They'd been at sea for more than an hour before either spoke.

"Find me something to eat, would you?" Jack called from the flybridge.

His tone of voice rankled—he sounded as if he expected her to be at his beck and call the entire trip. She thought about setting him straight but stifled her irritation. He was, after all, doing her and her father a favor.

"Where would you like me to look?" she called back.

"Try the galley," he said, as though she should have figured that out for herself.

The boat pitched and heaved with the swells as Lorraine made her way belowdecks, which was no easy task because the steps were incredibly steep. Once below, she was in the saddest, smallest excuse for a kitchen she could ever have imagined. She took a moment to glance around and found a toilet and shower, crammed into an impossibly tiny space. The only other room, if it could be considered that, was obviously where

Jack slept. There was a narrow bunk, littered with clothes. Books lined the walls and he'd hung several firearms there, next to the light. Never having been around anyone who owned a gun, Lorraine had no idea what kind or caliber these were, but they didn't resemble any she'd seen in the movies.

Returning to the galley, she discovered a wrinkled orange in the refrigerator, along with four or five beers. She pushed those aside—with a fleeting recollection of Katharine Hepburn in *The African Queen* methodically dumping out Humphrey Bogart's booze. Further investigation netted her a dried-out tortilla and an open can of sardines, the smell of which disgusted her.

With no other choice, she peeled the orange. By the time she'd finished that small task, her stomach was queasy.

"I...seem to be getting seasick," she said when she brought him the orange. "Do you have any suggestions?"

"When you vomit be sure you do it with your head over the side. If you get sick on this boat, you clean it up."

"Thank you for that charming advice," she muttered as she walked carefully back to the main deck. The ocean wasn't calm anymore, the way it'd been when they set out, and it tossed the boat viciously. *Scotch on Water*—ridiculous name for

a boat—surged up and down with the waves, and
with every bounce her stomach heaved. Determined not to throw up, Lorraine sat in the only
chair on the deck, pressing her arms against her
stomach. That didn't seem to be helping. She was
shaking with chills and sweating, both at the same
time.

It wasn't long before she vaulted out of the
chair and raced to the side of the boat. What little
she'd managed to eat at her father's before the
police arrived was soon gone. Still retching, she
closed her eyes. Finally it seemed to be over. She
straightened and moaned loudly, no longer caring
if Jack heard her or not. She was too sick to maintain any pretenses.

"Feel better?" he asked.

"No. Worse." She swore the man sounded
amused. She would ignore him, she decided, wiping her mouth with the back of her hand.

"Go ahead and lie down, but I don't suggest
you do it belowdecks."

She had no intention of sleeping in that horrible
bed and there didn't appear to be anyplace else.
If she hadn't felt so deathly ill, she might have
pointed that out.

Jack disappeared and came back a couple of
minutes later with a blanket and pillow. He threw
them to her in the chair.

"Thank you," she managed to say, rolling her

head from side to side, more miserable than she could ever remember being.

He hunkered down beside her, but in Lorraine's opinion didn't look too sympathetic.

"How long will it take to reach the States?" she asked in a weak voice.

He didn't answer immediately. "Longer than either of us is going to like," he finally said.

Lorraine already knew he was right.

When Jason returned to the hotel—Dancys in tow—he'd recognized that time was of the essence. Thomas and Lorraine had eventually left after interminable cautions and goodbyes, and now he was back in his room, repacking the few things he'd taken out of his bag. He knew it wouldn't be long before the authorities discovered his lie, and when they did, no amount of smooth talk was going to stop them from arresting him. He needed to make his move, and soon.

Damn, but he hadn't expected the police to be this tight on his tail. The bandage on his hand must have alerted the clerk at the bus depot. His mistake, he realized, was believing the bus stations hadn't been alerted. His photograph couldn't possibly have circulated yet—could it? In any event, he'd changed his appearance as best he could. Cut and dyed his hair, discarded his glasses in favor of colored contacts, changed his clothing.

But he could do nothing about the deep cut on his hand. That must be what had given him away.

He'd linked up with Lorraine to confuse the authorities, yet no sooner had he checked into the hotel than the cops arrived. He'd barely had time to do more than sign the register and go up to his room, such as it was.

He stepped quietly into the hallway to check the exits and saw that the proprietor had taken Dancy's words to heart and fully intended to keep a close eye on him. Dancy wasn't nearly as big a fool as his daughter.

Back in his room, Jason stuffed a few scattered things into his pack, including a switchblade he'd hidden under the pillow. The police either hadn't found the knife or weren't concerned about it. When he was finished, he glanced out the small window that overlooked the street. A police car was just pulling up in front of the hotel. With no time to lose, he threw on his jacket and grabbed the backpack, then slipped quietly out the door.

Jason met up with the proprietor on the back stairwell. Their conversation was brief. The old man's mistake was thinking he could stop him. The struggle to silence him cost Jason precious minutes. He would've liked to avoid another death, but this one couldn't be helped. If anyone was to blame, it was Dancy.

By the time Jason reached the rear exit of the

hotel, he could hear police racing up the stairs to his room. That was close. Much too close.

Now he needed to find Lorraine. During the bus ride, he'd done his damnedest to talk her into checking into the hotel; however, he couldn't show his cards by being too demanding. But before he left her that afternoon, he'd learned where Dancy lived.

He hid until night had completely fallen and then found his way down a series of back streets to the schoolmaster's house on the edge of town. Fortunately El Mirador was laid out in a simple gridlike pattern, and the moon was bright. He'd tracked people under more adverse conditions— quite recently, as a matter of fact. Lorraine shouldn't be hard to find.

She was the key. Once he had what he wanted from her, he'd just disappear again.

A dog barked as he crept down the dirt road. Fearing discovery, he ducked around the darker side of a small adobe house.

Then, in a wonderful turn of luck, Jason watched as Thomas Dancy hurried toward the houses shouting for someone named Azucena.

A pregnant woman rushed out of a house directly across the street and fell into Dancy's arms, sobbing.

The two were hugging each other as if they'd spent the past year apart. Jason's patience wore thin until he was able to make out the woman's words. So the police had already been to the house and found the artifact. *Damn.*

"Where is she?" the woman asked in Spanish. Jason was interested in finding that out, as well.

"With Jack."

"You gave her to Jack Keller?"

"What choice did I have?" Dancy asked. "I had to get her out of here before the police arrested her."

Again Jason had to credit the man with some intelligence, unlike his daughter who was as gullible as they came. Dancy was right to send her away. The police would've made mincemeat out of her. He smiled, remembering how easily she'd believed his stories—and how willingly she'd told him all about herself. He almost hated dragging her into this, but there was nothing he could do about that now.

"Jack's a good friend," Dancy said. He drew the woman as close as her swollen belly would allow and kissed the top of her head.

"I trust him to see that your daughter is safely returned to your country."

"Mexico is my country now," Dancy said, but even from a distance Jason could hear the sadness in his voice. "And soon you will be my wife."

The woman lifted her head to look up at Dancy. Jason couldn't see her expression.

"I'm free to marry you," Dancy explained.

"I don't need to stand before the priest to be your wife. In my heart, I am already your wife. My body shelters your child. In this house your sons sleep. I have everything I need."

"I do, too," Dancy said, sliding his arm around her waist and leading her back into the house.

Jack Keller, Jason repeated silently. Now that he had the name, he had everything *he* needed, too.

Lorraine awoke with the sun shining in her eyes. Her body rebelled from having spent the night on a deck chair. Her throat felt dry and irritated from being sick. Her neck was stiff, too. But the physical discomforts were minor compared to the ache in her heart. The events of the previous day ran through her mind, and she started to feel dizzy as she thought about everything that had happened. As little as twenty-four hours ago, she'd kissed Gary goodbye at the air port. And then the flight, the bus trip, meeting her father...and Jason's betrayal. The police. Jack's boat... A single day felt more like a lifetime.

She'd gone to sleep without washing her face and brushing her teeth for perhaps the first time in her life. Her hair was uncombed and her stomach empty. What she'd managed to eat the night before had ended up feeding the fish.

A sound startled her and she glanced up to find Jack standing on deck, hands on his hips as he squinted out at the bright blue water. He didn't look any better in daylight than he had at dusk. If anything, he seemed even more unkempt and unfriendly.

"Good morning," she ventured.

He glared at her and didn't return the greeting. Apparently he wasn't a morning person.

"Would you like me to put on a pot of coffee?" she asked. Despite his grudging manner, she wanted him to know she was grateful for his help. And she was more than willing to do her share.

"Cook up some eggs while you're at it," he snarled.

She hesitated, not understanding the malice in his voice. "All right. How would you like them cooked?"

"Over easy," he snapped. "I prefer the yolks runny."

"Okay." She wasn't entirely sure how she'd manage, but she'd learn that soon enough. "If you'll kindly tell me where the coffee and the eggs are, I'll see to it first thing."

"Where the coffee and the eggs are?" Jack repeated, speaking with exaggerated slowness. "You don't *know?*"

"No." She hadn't seen them the night before

when she'd brought him the orange. Perhaps there was another fridge somewhere, or a cooler.

"My supplies are back in El Mirador."

"But..." It took a while for the implication to register in Lorraine's mind. "You mean to say we don't have any food?"

"That's exactly what I'm saying."

She was ten times hungrier now than before she'd known that. "What are we going to do?" she asked in growing alarm.

"Fish. Sardines make good bait."

She grimaced.

"What's wrong now?" he demanded.

It seemed silly under the circumstances, but he *had* asked. "I have trouble watching anything die, even a fish."

He laughed as if he considered that uproariously funny. "Then do without."

Six

The woman was utterly useless. If he hadn't known that before, Jack would've ascertained it in about two seconds.

"I'll fish," Lorraine finally said after a lengthy silence, "but I refuse to…clean any." She turned her back on him. Disapproval radiated off her like sonar waves. Her nose was so high in the air, he thought with amusement, it was a wonder some bird didn't land and roost on it.

"Do you have a problem with pulling your own weight?" he asked, not that he was looking for an argument. He was more interested in seeing how far he could push her.

"Of course not. I'll pull my own weight."

It was too early in the morning to argue. Besides, he was damned hungry. He missed his morning coffee and was in no mood to deal with an unexpected passenger, especially one who'd inconvenienced him as much as this woman had. Not only that, she didn't seem to recognize that he was doing her a favor by saving her stupid ass from jail.

"I want to know what you plan to do about our predicament," she said next.

Well, excuse me. All he needed now was for Her Highness to start issuing commands.

"I already told you." With his back to her, he worked at rigging up the first fishing pole. He secured the bait—the sardine was nothing he'd seriously consider eating himself—and locked the rod into place. Once he'd finished that, he set up the second pole. With two lines in the water, he doubled his chances of scoring breakfast. Hell, he hadn't so much as caught a fish and already Miss Pull-her-own-weight was letting it be known she wasn't about to bloody her delicate fingers.

"Sight of blood makes you squeamish, does it?" he taunted.

"Hardly," she said in a huff.

He arched his brow and finished with the second rod.

"I find the idea of fishing barbaric."

"You can have breakfast or, as I said earlier, you're free to do without it."

"Fine."

Unlike him, she'd enjoyed a decent dinner—the dinner *he* should've had over at Thomas's place. Whether or not she ate breakfast was entirely her choice. Jack couldn't care less.

"Um, I realize how that must sound," she said, apparently reconsidering. "It's not that I don't appreciate the offer..."

"Hey," Jack said as he moved forward, "you go ahead and do what you've got to do." He started the engines and the boat took off at a slow easy troll.

Lorraine looked as if she was about to be sick again. Her face went from healthy pink to ashen, followed almost immediately by a faint tinge of green.

Jack resisted asking her how she was feeling. That seemed too cruel, even for him. One look said it all.

Her Highness staggered back to the chair and collapsed into it.

Luck was with him, and in less than ten minutes he'd snagged his first fish. A red snapper, which made for excellent eating.

Lorraine didn't move from her throne the entire time it took him to reel in breakfast. Nor did she show any signs of interest when he took his catch below, gutted, filleted and fried it up in a skillet. The scent of the fish frying started his mouth watering. It didn't come any fresher than this. He could have eaten in the galley, and often did. Not now. With a good deal of show, he dragged another chair onto the deck and placed it beside Lorraine's. Then he carried up his plate, along with a cold beer, and settled down. She glanced once in his direction, and Jack recognized the look. Hunger. After insisting that she didn't like fishing, her pride wouldn't allow her to give in and enjoy a damned fine meal—even if he did say so himself.

"I don't mean to be a pest..." she murmured.

"It's a gift."

"A gift?" she repeated.

"Being a pest. You appear to have a real talent for it."

That shut her up for a few minutes, as he'd suspected it would.

"What are we going to do about the lack of supplies?" she asked after a while.

Jack could tell from the forced evenness in her voice that she was having trouble controlling her temper. He figured she probably didn't lose it often; a fine Southern belle like Lorraine had good manners drilled into her the way boot camp had taught him the basics of soldiering.

"I'll answer your question if you answer mine," he said, savoring the last bite of fish and washing it down with a swallow of beer. There was plenty left in the galley, but he didn't mention that. If she wanted breakfast she'd have to ask for it.

"All right," she said with obvious reluctance. The boat bobbed gently, and she'd regained some of her color. A good sign, he supposed. Until she found her sea legs she'd be miserable. Jack wasn't sure which he preferred. Sick as a dog, she still managed to be a damned nuisance. He hated to think how much she'd annoy him when she was a hundred percent herself.

"You wanted to ask me something?" She sounded impatient.

He weighed his thoughts. Teasing her was definitely entertaining, but he felt a little confused about this unaccountable need to learn what he could about her. It must be on account of Thomas; he simply wanted to know what kind of woman his friend had for a daughter. "I realize this isn't any of my damn business," he began, "but I find curiosity has gotten the better of me." He chuckled dryly. "What's your husband like? Is he as tight-assed as you?"

Her gaze fell to the wedding band on her left hand as though she was surprised to see it there. Forgotten Mr. Whoever-he-was already?

"I imagine the two of you are quite the pair," he went on. "Do you ever jump each other's bones?"

"I beg your pardon?"

"You know, get so hot for each other you can't wait to get your clothes off. That's when sex is best, don't you find? When it's hot and sweaty, grinding away against a wall or better yet on top of the kitchen table.''

Her eyes went wide as if she couldn't believe what she was hearing. ''I find you both vulgar and offensive.''

Jack laughed. It was far too much fun baiting this woman. ''You don't like me any better than I like you. That's perfectly fine by me. But you can't blame a guy for being curious about the type of man who'd marry someone as highfalutin as you.''

''I don't know what makes you think—''

''I bet you and your stuffed-shirt husband make love every Wednesday and Sunday nights, regular as clockwork.''

''That's none of your business!''

He laughed again. ''I'm right, aren't I? You do it with your pajamas on, too. And when you're done you make polite little sounds, give each other a peck on the cheek and then roll over and go to sleep.''

''Is there a reason you're so curious about my love life?'' she asked. She was pretending to be bored but not doing a very good job of it. He watched as color seeped up her neckline and into her cheeks.

He ignored the question.

''Are you interested in the love life of every

woman you meet," she asked, still faking disinterest, "or is it just me?"

Jack snickered as if to suggest someone like her would be the last woman on earth to tempt him. "Just curious," he answered. "I'm not doing a survey or anything." However, much as he hated to admit it, she had a point. He didn't normally provoke a woman this intently. There was just something about her....

It was the clothes she wore, he decided. The conservative pantsuit. No one wore white out here. Not that it looked so white anymore. And it didn't help matters that it fit her like a glove. She'd removed the jacket and the short pink top hugged her waist and allowed him to speculate about the soft swell of her breasts beneath. He shook his head. The woman had no sense; if he'd had nefarious designs on her—which he certainly didn't—she'd be in trouble.

"You've asked your question, Mr. Keller, stupid as it was, and now it's my turn."

"Feel free." He gestured toward her.

"You've already started drinking. I don't think that's a good idea."

"You get to ask me a question, sweetheart, not preach a sermon."

"All right," she muttered, casting him a look of pure disgust. "What exactly do you intend to do about the lack of supplies?"

He laughed at the sheer foolishness of her question. "You don't have anything to worry about, Your Highness."

To her credit, she ignored his teasing. "So what are we going to do?"

The answer seemed obvious. "Buy more, of course."

Lorraine had never disliked anyone so fiercely in her entire life. Jack Keller was rude, insensitive and vulgar. It was beyond comprehension that her father had freely handed her over to this... barbarian. Reluctantly she had to conclude that her situation must be far more dangerous than she'd realized.

The morning had seemed interminable. The sun beat down with an intensity that robbed her of strength. All wit had abandoned her. Jack appeared to take great pleasure in ridiculing her and calling her ridiculous names like Your Highness. He spouted insults almost as readily as swearwords. When he wasn't mocking her, he called her Raine. The only person who'd ever called her that was her father. When Jack said it, he made it sound, somehow, as though he was speaking to a disobedient child.

The one positive aspect of the morning was that she'd finally adjusted to the boat's movement on the water. She wasn't sure if it was the lack of anything in her stomach or if she'd found what he referred to as her sea legs. Whichever, she was grateful. She'd never spent any time on a boat before and had no idea what else to expect.

Gazing out at the horizon, Lorraine suddenly saw land—an outcropping of lush green hills far in the distance. It excited her so much she climbed awkwardly out of her chair and shuffled toward the rear of the boat.

"Where are we?" she asked.

"Mexico."

"*That* much I know," she returned, trying not to sound sarcastic. At this point, it was difficult. She sighed, loudly and expressively. "Are we buying supplies here?" she asked.

"That's the plan."

She couldn't quite hide her relief. It was clear to her, if not Jack, that they couldn't continue this voyage without obtaining some food.

As they headed toward land, Lorraine noticed a number of high-rise luxury hotels in the distance. "What city is that?" she asked when curiosity overcame her unwillingness to ask him any further questions.

"Campeche," he said, and didn't elaborate.

Lorraine remembered reading about the town in the information she'd gathered when she was researching the Yucatán Peninsula. If she recalled correctly, the city had a population of more than

250,000 and was one of the fastest-growing tourist spots in the entire region. There were a number of Mayan ruins close by.

"Don't get your hopes up," Jack muttered.

"What do you mean?"

"We aren't going to Campeche."

"We aren't?" She frowned in disappointment. "But—"

"We can't risk it."

In her opinion, they'd probably be safer in a large city where they could get lost in anonymous crowds. Not that he'd given her any say in the matter, nor did he seem at all interested in her opinions. "Well, if not Campeche, where *are* we going?"

"La Ruta Maya," he said. "That means route of the Maya. It's a small village down the coast from Campeche. Tradition says the village was on the main artery for Mayan traders a thousand years ago.

"I've docked there in the past," Jack added, "and I can buy supplies with a minimum of fuss. That way we can be in and out of port quickly."

"I see."

"I don't think you do," Jack said, narrowing his gaze. "We can't risk you being seen. With that suit of yours and that blond hair, you'd stick out like a red flag to a herd of bulls."

"What do you want me to do?" she demanded.

"Jump overboard and hold my breath until you get back?"

"Don't give me any ideas."

Lorraine had to clamp her jaws shut to keep from saying something she was sure to regret later. No one had ever infuriated her faster than this shiftless, worthless, good-for-nothing bum. She wanted as little to do with him as possible and actually felt grateful that he assumed she was married. She could only guess how much more obnoxious he would've been if he'd figured she was up for grabs. Wearing her mother's wedding band had turned out to be a fortunate thing.

"You're going to have to stay out of sight while I'm in town."

The implication didn't hit her right away. Then, "You want me to go down there—belowdecks?" It would be stifling holed up in that dreadful little place.

"You got it," he said. Then, as though he understood her objection, he told her, "I'll be as quick as I can."

"How long?" She supposed she could endure anything provided she had some idea of the time involved. Fifteen minutes? Twenty? Already she could feel the suffocating heat crowding in around her.

"If everything goes smoothly, I should be back in about forty minutes."

"Forty minutes!" she exploded. Just how long could it take to purchase a few necessities?

"Possibly a bit longer."

Lorraine had to bite her tongue. He was doing this on purpose, she knew he was, just to punish her for their predicament. The more she objected, the more time he'd take. She wouldn't put it past him.

He slowed the boat long before they reached the village. "Go on below," he said tersely.

"But..." Lorraine closed her mouth rather than protest further. It would be pointless to mention that they were well out of sight of the village and it wasn't likely anyone could see her. Any argument would only be grounds for trouble with Jack.

Her steps were mutinous as she climbed the few steps into the cabin and slammed the door. The heat hit her like a furnace blast, and sweat immediately dampened her brow.

Jack pounded down the steps and opened the door. A sweet cooling breeze whistled through. "Listen and listen good," he said in a clear, calm voice. "I'm going to close these doors once I've docked. I don't want you to come out until I tell you it's safe to do so. Understand?"

She didn't answer.

"Understand?" he repeated.

"Yes," she muttered.

"Good," he said, still sounding calm.

Five minutes later he cut the engine. She heard footsteps on the dock and then felt the boat bounce against the tire bumper. A rush of Spanish followed between Jack and someone on the pier. It appeared to be a pleasant exchange. The boat rocked slightly when Jack jumped onto the dock.

With the insufferable heat Lorraine barely had the strength to remain upright. The table and benches were filled with papers and an assortment of clothes, which she folded and placed in the drawers. Not that her goal was to be helpful. She simply needed space to stretch out. Books littered the compact area. Bored, Lorraine glanced at a few titles and shook her head. A few sailing manuals. Techniques of war. Weapons updates. Military histories. Almost every piece of reading material had something to do with soldiering and death. For all she knew, he could be a trained killer. Talk about jumping from the frying pan into the fire! And down here, in this intolerable heat, it felt as though that was exactly what she'd done.

Lorraine couldn't help wondering if her father knew about Jack's preoccupation with war and death. If he did, would he have asked Jack to get her out of the country? Lorraine doubted it.

Forty minutes passed. Forty of the longest minutes of her life. She wet a cloth and dabbed her face and wrists. Ten minutes later, she unbuttoned her blouse and fanned herself with a copy of *Soldier of Fortune* magazine. Jack had been gone for fifty minutes now. Every once in a while she'd hear voices; her hopes would soar but then the sound would fade away. Water slapped against the side of the boat, which rocked gently in the protected waters of the marina.

At one o'clock she heard the faint strains of music drifting down from what must have been a waterfront cantina. The emptiness in her stomach refused to be ignored. All she could think about was how hot and miserable she was and how hungry. Visions of salty tortilla chips and fresh salsa tormented her. Served with a tart salt-rimmed margarita... Or was that more Tex-Mex than Mexican? She wasn't sure. But they'd certainly have *something* at this cantina. Maybe a shrimp-and-garlic dish like the one her father's... wife had made. No, she wouldn't think about them. She conjured up the memory of chicken fajitas, instead, with lots of onions and peppers....

The music grew louder. It didn't require much imagination to picture Jack sitting inside the cantina, taking his own sweet time over a big lunch, drinking a cold beer. He probably had a friendly *señorita* on his lap, as well. The image was so real, so believable, she convinced herself of its truth.

Forty minutes he'd said, and he'd been gone longer than an hour. Lorraine couldn't stand it anymore. Not only did she intensely dislike Jack, there was no reason she should trust him. Given what she'd learned about her father and Azucena, how could she trust any of these people? Once again, she pushed all thoughts of her father from her mind. She didn't want to think about him, didn't want to acknowledge that Gary had been right and she'd made the biggest mistake of her life in seeking out this stranger.

She'd lost control of the situation by letting others make all the decisions. Time to rectify that. She hadn't had anything to do with that stupid artifact, and once she was able to explain what had happened, the authorities would believe her. They *had* to. Anyway, she'd rather take her chances with the police than die a slow death at the hands of Jack Keller. And she couldn't stand this heat a minute longer.

Being a conscientious person, she found a pen and paper and left Jack a note.

I appreciate your help, but would prefer to have the American Consulate speak to the authorities on my behalf.

Thank you.
Lorraine

She propped the paper on the table with the saltshaker and reached for her purse. Then she hesitated. Most of her traveler's checks were back in her suitcase in El Mirador and she had only a small amount of cash. She couldn't very well ask a vendor in this dinky town to accept a credit card.

It didn't take her long to discover where Jack kept his cash—although she did feel guilty about rummaging through his things. This was just a small loan, she told herself. Either she'd repay him herself or her father would. She peeled off a few bills and shoved them inside her purse.

Once more she hesitated, then removed her watch and set it in his drawer. Its value far exceeded the cash she'd borrowed, she reasoned. She left quickly before she could change her mind.

When she opened the double doors leading to the deck, Lorraine gulped in deep breaths of the fresh cool air. Cautiously she stuck her head out and looked around.

The village was small, smaller even than El Mirador. A row of ramshackle shops lined the waterfront, but La Ruta Maya didn't seem to consist of much else. The first thing she needed to do was find someone to drive her into Campeche. Surely in a city of that size she'd be able to connect with the American Embassy. Then she'd explain what had happened, how Jason Applebee had hidden the artifact in her suitcase, and the American government would clear her name and get her safely home.

Lorraine didn't blame her father for interceding on her behalf, but his solution had been shortsighted. Once her name was cleared, she'd be free to return to El Mirador in the near future and demand some answers from her father. Then again, perhaps it would be better just to go home and forget all of this.

She realized as she climbed off Jack's boat that she was taking a risk, but that couldn't be avoided. The truth was, he'd be just as glad to get rid of her. This seemed the best solution all around.

Within a few minutes of leaving the dock area, Lorraine noticed that several children had started to follow her. Not wanting to attract attention, she opened her purse, thinking to give them each a new peso and send them on their way. Her ploy didn't work. As soon as she reached for her coin purse, she was surrounded by children of every age. They pressed in around her, crowding her, all eager for a handout.

An older man barked at the children in an authoritative voice and they scattered. Lorraine thanked him with a smile and continued down the street, stopping only long enough to buy some fruit in the village marketplace. She gobbled down the fresh papaya, then purchased a tortilla filled with vegetables and meat. The meat didn't have a familiar taste, but she decided she didn't want to know exactly what she was eating. She understood turtle was popular fare in this area—not a thought that appealed to her. However, at this point she was too hungry to care.

With her helpful Spanish phrase book, she asked a grandmotherly woman about finding a driver who would take her to Campeche. The woman avoided eye contact and shook her head. Lorraine asked a vendor next, but he was far more interested in selling his wares than answering her questions. He held up a number of things—baskets and pottery—he hoped to interest her in buying and explained two or three times in fractured English that he would give her a special rate because she was his first customer of the day. She managed to extricate herself from him, then asked a third person, a young barefoot woman, who pointed Lorraine in the direction of the cantina.

On second thought, perhaps it would make more sense to contact the American Embassy by phone and not worry about hiring someone to drive her.

Lorraine flipped through the pages of her Spanish dictionary until she found the word for telephone. She felt embarrassed by how little she remembered of her high-school language class. *"Teléfono?"* she asked.

The barefoot woman grinned and nodded enthusiastically, then pointed toward the cantina again.

Lorraine muttered under her breath, glancing at the very place she'd hoped to avoid. She supposed she didn't have anything to lose. If Jack did happen to be inside, which she strongly suspected he was, she'd simply explain what she'd said in her note.

When she peered inside the cantina, she found—to her relief, and surprise—that Jack Keller was nowhere to be seen. The place was stark, devoid of any decoration. It had a rough plank floor, a long wooden bar and a number of crude tables and chairs.

Four or five underdressed women glared at her when she walked in. Lorraine nodded at them, certain they could see that they had nothing to fear from her. She had no intention of cutting in on their business.

A greasy-looking man glanced up from a table, where he sat with a bottle of tequila and a shot glass. He was dark and ugly, and a scar ran down one side of his face. He eyed her with the avid interest of a tomcat spying a mouse. It wasn't a comfortable sensation, but she ignored him and approached the bartender, whose frown seemed to suggest she should get out while the getting was good.

Lorraine forced a smile. With her dictionary in hand, she asked about the phone. He shook his head. There was one against the wall, but apparently it was out of order. *No funcióna,* a handwritten sign informed her. Again going through the dictionary, she painstakingly asked about hiring a driver to take her to Campeche.

"I take you to Campeche," the greasy-looking man at the table offered in heavily accented English, his voice slurred with suggestion. His chair made a scraping sound as he stood and carried the bottle and shot glass over to the bar.

Every eye in the place was on the two of them.

"No, thank you," Lorraine said as politely as she could. She continued to look at the bartender.

"You want a driver?" the man persisted. "I get you there."

"I prefer to hire a car, thank you." She reverted her attention to the bartender.

Her unpleasant companion slammed the bottle down on the bar. "We have fun on the way, no?"

"No," Lorraine said, refusing to look at him. He smelled evil. She'd never thought such a thing was possible, but this man was the epitome of the word. The stench about him was nothing compared to the blankness in his eyes, as if he had no feelings, no sympathy, no conscience. The way he stared at her made her skin crawl.

The bartender, who'd said little to this point, spoke to the man in a placating manner. Although she couldn't understand much of what was said, it seemed fairly obvious this man was feared. The bartender then appeared to suggest something involving one or more of the other women, judging by the way he motioned toward them. One thing Lorraine did pick up from the exchange was the man's name. Carlos.

Carlos's reaction to the bartender's suggestion was a blast of foul-sounding words that had the bartender fleeing to the other end of the bar.

"You come with me," Carlos said, and reached for her. "We have fun on the way to Campeche, you and me." He grinned at her as if to say she might as well enjoy it because she had no choice.

Lorraine managed to avoid his grasp. "I most certainly will not."

He lunged for her a second time, but once more she was able to avoid his groping hands. Clearly Carlos was drunker than he'd seemed, which was in her favor. Although he looked to be a mean drunk.

"Kindly keep your hands to yourself!" she snapped.

Carlos's response was to grab a fistful of her hair and yank hard.

Lorraine let out a cry of shock and pain, whirled around and slapped him as hard as she could across the face. "Keep your filthy hands off me, you brute!" The action had been purely instinctive. She didn't know what kind of monster this man was, but she wasn't about to let him or anyone else manhandle her.

A collective gasp went through the cantina. Even Carlos appeared too stunned to react. Then he slapped her, hard enough to send her staggering backward. Her jaw felt as if it'd been dislocated, and the pain brought stinging tears to her eyes.

He laughed, and it was the cruelest sound she'd ever heard. She saw pure undiluted hate in his eyes. Holding her hand over her cheek, she took three small steps back, recognizing beyond doubt that she'd crossed a dangerous line and was about to suffer the consequences.

She wanted to say something, a joke, an apology, anything to defuse the situation, but her mouth had gone dry. She could hardly force out a word.

She'd made one mistake after another, but this was the most desperate yet. Two minutes ago she'd walked into the cantina with a simple request and now she was staring into the eyes of a man who clearly wanted to kill her—and worse. She felt a sudden urge to yell "Time out!" so she could sit down and analyze what had gone wrong…and figure out how to rescue herself.

At the sound of footsteps behind her, she whirled around. Her relief at seeing Jack was enough to make her knees weak.

"Oh, thank God," she whispered, and briefly closed her eyes. The one man she'd been trying to avoid was now going to be her salvation.

The tension between Jack and Carlos could be felt by everyone in the room. Lorraine practically ran toward Jack.

"You know this woman?" Carlos asked, glaring at them through narrowed, menacing eyes.

Jack took one look at Lorraine and shrugged. "Never saw her before in my life."

Seven

Generally speaking, Jack was an easygoing kind of guy. It took a lot to rile him. But Lorraine managed to do it without so much as opening her mouth. He'd returned to the boat with a case of beer balanced on his shoulder and a plate of hot food for her. The way he figured, she'd been fourteen or fifteen hours without anything to eat, and a generous helping of Angelina's special chicken *frijoles* and rice was sure to sweeten her disposition. It had certainly improved his own.

Little could have shocked him more than finding her gone. By the time he read her note, he was so angry his ears burned. Jack didn't often let anyone or anything reduce him to this state. In his previous work, anger wasn't an emotion he could afford to express. When it happened, which was rare, he didn't plow his fist through a wall. If anything he remained stoic. His acquaintances knew well that the calmer he was, the angrier.

He could have pulled out of port then and there with a clear conscience—but he hadn't. Thomas was his friend. Dammit all, though, there was a limit to what he could take. After spending a few minutes cooling down, he left the supplies piled on the dock, where the shopkeeper had delivered them, and went in search of the most irritating, infuriating, ungrateful woman he'd ever run across. When he found her in the cantina, he couldn't deny a certain sense of satisfaction at discovering that she'd gotten herself in a shitload of trouble.

Now he intended to see how she planned to get herself out of it. Rescuing damsels in distress was an outdated business at best, and Jack had long since decided a woman of the nineties was capable of taking care of herself. If Thomas Dancy's daughter needed help, she'd ask for it. On second thought, she'd have to ask *real* pretty for him to give a tinker's damn what happened to her. One thing was certain: he was going to make her sweat it out before he stepped in.

"You're going to pretend you don't know me?" Lorraine shouted. She thrust out her arms in supplication or in anger, he wasn't sure which. A look of astonished disbelief crossed her face.

Jack ignored her and sauntered up to the bar, where he ordered a glass of tequila and a lime. After the day he'd had, he needed a high-potency drink.

"He knows me." Lorraine stretched out her

arm and waggled her index finger at Jack. "He might claim otherwise, but he knows me. We're traveling together."

Jack tossed back his tequila and sucked greedily on the lime.

"Just exactly what kind of man are you?" she raged, disgust written on every feature.

"A thirsty one," Jack answered with a slow, lazy grin. Then, as if to prove his point, he downed a second shot and smiled at her through gritted teeth as the alcohol burned its way down the back of his throat. "As far as I'm concerned, your friend over there is welcome to you."

"His name's Carlos. If you were any kind of a man, you'd see I'm in real trouble here."

"Yeah." Did his heart good to see it, too.

"Aren't you going to *do* something?"

"No." He raised his glass and saluted Carlos. Lorraine certainly knew how to pick 'em. Old Carlos looked like he'd just as soon slit a guy's throat as sit down and have a drink with him.

Apparently Carlos didn't know what to make of the exchange between him and Lorraine. He glanced from one to the other, his head jerking back and forth in an effort to follow the conversation.

One of the prostitutes minced across the cantina toward Jack. The best-looking one of the lot, Jack was pleased to note. He collected a second glass and met her at a table.

Her smile radiated easy sex. Her eagerness for his company was a pleasant change after what he'd been forced to endure with Miss High-and-Mighty. Jack pulled out a chair and sat down. Grinning, the woman sat on his lap and poured them each a drink, making sure her lush breasts grazed his arm.

"You're a rat, Jack Keller," Lorraine yelled. Carlos half rose from his chair, obviously startled by her vehemence.

Jack yawned as though bored. "Sticks and stones, Lorraine, sticks and stones."

"I can't believe you're going t-to take up with that woman when you can see I've got a problem here."

Well, yeah, she did, Jack thought. Carlos was keeping a damn close eye on her. He seemed more than ready to leap up and grab her if she tried to make a run for it.

"Hey, you got yourself into this mess," he said. "It's going to be real interesting to watch you get yourself out of it."

"You're lower than low."

Jack laughed and nuzzled the throat of the woman on his lap. While she might be nice-enough looking, she unfortunately smelled like cheap perfume, stale smoke and sex. Not that he'd let Lorraine know. As far as Her Highness was concerned, the other woman was a breath of fresh air. And tempting, damn tempting.

"Okay, okay," Lorraine said, sounding far less certain now. "If you want me to apologize, then I will. I shouldn't have left the boat."

This was what he'd been waiting for from the first. Jack abruptly set the woman aside and vaulted to his feet. "You're damn right you shouldn't have. I asked a small thing of you. One small thing."

"It was so hot down there—and you took longer than you said."

"It's too much to expect you to follow a simple request?"

"I thought...I hoped..."

They scowled at each other. Jack's expression was as intense and angry as he could make it. His voice was raised, and while he didn't want to attract a lot of unnecessary attention, he hoped to extract her from this predicament and save his own hide in the process. From the cutthroat looks Carlos gave him, it wasn't going to be easy.

"Don't shout at me," Lorraine said, giving a fine impression of royalty.

"I'll shout at you if I damn well please, and right now it pleases me a great deal."

"This wouldn't have happened if you'd had the decency—"

"Enough!" Carlos boomed, and banged his fist on the bar. The sound echoed through the room like a gunshot.

Lorraine gasped and pressed her hand over her heart. For several frightening seconds the entire cantina went silent. Then, before he could react, she whirled around and faced Carlos. "Can't you see we're having an important discussion here? When I'm finished with Jack Keller, I'll take you on. Until then, kindly wait your turn."

Carlos's mouth fell open, and he wore a look of complete and utter confusion.

"Decency?" Jack shouted, doing his best to distract Carlos's attention from Lorraine. "If you want to talk about decency, I've got plenty to say. Let's have this out right here and now."

Lorraine stared at him as if he'd gone mad. She wasn't far off, since his little performance was a good imitation of a lunatic's ravings. Waving his arms, still shouting, he edged her toward the door. With the two of them trading insults he'd be able to confuse Carlos long enough, he hoped, to place himself between them. And give her a way out.

Once she was close to the door, he yelled a few more insulting remarks, using the same tone of voice, hoping she was smart enough to understand what he was doing. "Run," he ordered when she stood in the doorway.

"Run?"

"Get the hell out of here!"

She hesitated, then turned on her heel. Okay, so it wasn't a brilliant plan, but it was the best he could do on short notice.

"What about you?" Jack thought he heard her ask. Answering wasn't a concern just then. Carlos was.

The other man dashed after Lorraine, and seeing there was damn little he could do but stop him, Jack stepped into his path. It'd been a long while since he'd been involved in hand-to-hand combat. This time, however, the odds left much to be desired.

Carlos had a knife and he didn't.

Lorraine was panting and her thigh muscles were quivering from the long run to the waterfront. She raced to the boat, the dock rocking precariously with the sudden movement. Not sure what to do next, she immediately went belowdecks and collapsed on the U-shaped bench that constituted the eating area. She could hear her pulse pounding in her ears.

This episode had been a disaster entirely of her own making. She was to blame for everything— the danger to herself and to Jack, as well. When he got back, she'd bet her last dollar he wouldn't be gracious about it, either. Not that she didn't deserve every comment he could possibly make.

She'd done something incredibly stupid, and she didn't have a single excuse to offer. What could she say—it was too hot and she'd become tired of waiting? At the moment, that sounded pretty lame.

Her pulse still hadn't returned to normal when she realized she couldn't remain down here. Not without knowing what had happened to Jack. She had to find a way to help him; after all, he'd put himself at risk trying to help her. It'd taken her far longer than it should have to figure out what he intended, back at the cantina, what he wanted her to do. All she hoped was that he knew how to protect himself.

He did, she thought, reassured, as she went up to the deck. The evidence was all over the boat. Everything he read was about warfare, self-defense and fighting.

But her confidence in Jack's abilities waned as time passed. She'd thought he'd be close behind her. Two, three minutes. Not so. A good ten minutes had already gone by.

Her relief at seeing him approach was enormous. He wasn't running, but he didn't seem to be taking a leisurely stroll, either. Even from the deck she could see that blood soaked his sleeve and ran in rivulets down his arm and onto his hand. One side of his face was swollen, too.

"Jack...Jack." Lorraine felt sick with regret,

knowing he'd received these injuries because of her.

As soon as he'd reached the dock, Jack broke into a trot, making the dock pitch precariously. When he reached *Scotch on Water,* he untied the rope and jumped onto the deck. Moments later the engines revved to life, churning up the water.

A flurry of Spanish came at them as Carlos and three other men appeared on the waterfront.

Jack didn't bother to translate. Even with her limited knowledge of Spanish, Lorraine caught the drift, and it wasn't anything she cared to repeat.

Jack put the boat in gear, and they roared off with enough force to sink smaller boats in their wake.

They hadn't cleared the marina when Lorraine heard an odd cracking sound, as if one of the engines had backfired. She glanced over her shoulder, but before anything could register, Jack shoved her to the deck and fell heavily on top of her. The shock of his actions left her stunned.

"What's happening?" she asked when she'd recovered her breath.

"That, Your Highness, was your good buddy taking potshots at us."

"Shots? You mean with a gun?"

"That's the weapon of choice for your average

thug these days.'' Jack climbed off her and then helped her to her feet.

Once they were safely in open water, Jack cut the engines to a more comfortable speed. He stood with his hands on the wheel, staring straight ahead.

Lorraine knew the time had come to apologize, abjectly and in full. Unfortunately her tongue refused to cooperate. It shouldn't be this difficult. But Jack had the infuriating self-satisfied look of a man who knew he was right and was waiting for her to admit it.

''You're hurt,'' she said, instead.

He pressed the back of his hand to the corner of his mouth, then glanced at the slash on his upper arm. He arched his eyebrows as if surprised at how deep the injury was. Gingerly he tested the area and winced as his fingers probed it.

''Let me take care of that,'' Lorraine volunteered. She was about to head belowdecks for the first-aid kit she'd noticed earlier.

''Leave it,'' Jack snarled.

''No! It needs attention. I'm a nurse and I should know.''

''Look, I don't want—''

Tempting though it was, she had no intention of wasting time arguing with him. Without waiting for his approval, she went belowdecks and grabbed the kit.

He remained at the helm and grudgingly let her tend to the wound. Lorraine thought it probably should have had stitches, but fortunately the first-aid kit contained a number of butterfly bandages, which served almost as well. Other than a grunt now and again, Jack didn't speak while she bandaged the cut.

"What about your face?" she asked when she'd finished with his arm.

"It's fine," he growled.

An ugly bruise had started to form on his chin. Examining it, Lorraine swallowed her pride. "I'm sorry, Jack."

He didn't respond right away, then looked at her briefly. "I see you have your watch back."

So he knew.

She'd retrieved her wristwatch when she'd gone below to get the first-aid kit.

"Did you put the money back, too?" he asked.

"Yes." She wasn't proud of what she'd done. Her face burned with embarrassment.

It had been a stupid idea—*another* one—and she sincerely regretted it.

"Don't try anything like that again. Understand?"

She nodded. She didn't know if he was referring to her taking the money or leaving the boat. Probably both.

"I hope you realize you're getting to be damned expensive."

"I put the money back," she insisted with ill grace.

"I'm not talking about the money you *borrowed*," Jack muttered. "The supplies. This is the second time this has happened."

"What?" She'd seen the case of beer on the tabletop belowdecks and assumed everything else had already been loaded onto the boat.

"They got left behind on the dock."

She closed her eyes and groaned, vaguely remembering the boxes stacked alongside the boat. "But the beer...there's a case down below. You mean to say the only thing that got on board was the beer?"

Late that afternoon, Jack docked in a freshwater inlet for the night. Rio Usumacinta emptied into this cove, which was a small, sheltered one. Although he was fairly confident Carlos hadn't tried to follow them, he wasn't taking any chances.

As the sun sank in the west, Jack sat with his feet propped up, sipping from a bottle of his favorite *cerveza*. A smile touched his lips at the memory of Lorraine's reaction when she realized that the only thing he'd managed to bring on board was the beer. The look on her face had been priceless. That expression of frustrated outrage had almost been worth the problems she'd caused. Almost.

He closed his eyes, enjoying the sense of calm at the end of a day that had taken one unexpected turn after another. As far as his passenger went, he didn't like her, couldn't trust her and considered her a royal pain in the ass. Nevertheless he had to hand it to her: the woman had pluck. It wasn't everyone who could stand up to a powerful drug lord like Carlos Caracol.

Jack hadn't immediately figured out who Carlos was, but once he did, he realized what a lucky escape they'd had. The name was one he knew well. It amazed Jack that Carlos hadn't landed behind bars before now—or with a bullet in his back. He had a small band of followers and connections to a much bigger drug pipeline bringing in cocaine from other parts of Mexico and Central America. A few months ago Jack had talked to two government agents working in cooperation with the United States. Carlos's name had come up then. He was believed to be responsible for the death of a Mexican official, but nothing could be proved. The man was a known killer, but smart enough to stay out of prison. He certainly wasn't the kind of enemy Jack wanted. What Carlos Caracol had been doing in a cantina in La Ruta Maya Jack couldn't begin to guess.

Remembering how Lorraine had whirled on the

man and primly informed him he'd have to wait his turn had been one of life's more amusing moments. Jack couldn't suppress a chuckle. He would never have left her to deal with Carlos on her own, however appealing the prospect. But it'd given him a few minutes of pleasure letting her think he just might.

He'd spent several years in the Caribbean and the Gulf of Mexico now, lived a life that was the envy of his friends. Plenty of money at his disposal and not a care in the world. Yet he'd felt more aware of life these past two days with Lorraine than at any time since he'd inherited *Scotch on Water*. This annoying, priggish, straitlaced woman. Go figure.

Something else troubled him. She was beginning to look good. Too good.

The sound of a gentle splash startled him. He opened his eyes and sat upright. Lorraine had taken the plunge, literally, and was swimming around in her bra and panties like a porpoise, enjoying the water. She dove under, giving him an excellent view of her nicely rounded derriere. Her legs weren't half-bad, either. Shapely and trim. That led him to consider other parts of her body he had no business thinking about.

"She's married," he muttered just loudly enough to give himself a wake-up call. A fling with Lorraine was a fling with disaster, and he wasn't going to let that happen. No way in hell was he that big a fool.

Getting too involved with *any* woman was a mistake, as he'd already learned, but getting involved with someone else's wife... He shook his head. At least Marcie hadn't been married at the time he'd fallen in love with her.

"Having a good time?" Jack stood and leaned against the gunwale, watching her frolic in the water.

Lorraine jerked around, her hair a froth of shampoo. She treaded water and stared up at him, blinking rapidly when the shampoo dripped into her right eye. "I thought...you were asleep. I didn't think you'd mind if I used your shampoo."

"Not in the least." He crossed his ankles and assumed a more comfortable stance.

"Since you were asleep and...and since we're anchored in freshwater here, it seemed like the perfect opportunity to wash my hair."

"A hell of a good idea." He covered his mouth and yawned. Still, he didn't move away, not when he could see how uncomfortable she was with him staring at her. The way he figured, he deserved some reward for all the trouble she'd caused. Embarrassing her was an entertaining enough activity. He wasn't going to complain about the view, either.

"You're an amazing woman," he said.

"Amazing?" She rubbed her eye, which had to be smarting by now.

"Maybe fearless is a better description."

"Fearless? If you're talking about what happened this afternoon—"

"I'm not." He shouldn't do this to her, but what the hell. "I'm talking about swimming in piranha-infested waters."

A look of sheer terror came over Lorraine. He'd never seen anyone move so fast!

Jack couldn't help it; he burst out laughing.

Thomas paced the small area outside the bedroom. Each time Azucena moaned, he had to stop himself from bursting through the bedroom door. She'd been in labor for twenty hours now, far longer than with either Antonio or Hector. According to the midwife, this baby was breech and the labor had proved to be far more intense. The birth would be complicated.

Exhausted himself, Thomas could only imagine how Azucena felt. He loved her and was grateful to her for giving him back his life. For years he'd gone listlessly from one insignificant job to the next, convinced that something would happen to change his circumstances. For years he'd believed that, somehow, Ginny and Raine would join him in Mexico. In his dreamworld, he'd believed that it was only a matter of time before all would be forgiven and the charges against him dropped. Then he'd moved to El Mirador, been offered not just a job, but one he loved, one that meant something. He'd met Azucena then, too, and his life had been blessed from that moment forward.

He'd loved Ginny, grieved at the news of her death, but Azucena was his future. He'd married her as soon as he could arrange it. She was his wife, the mother of his sons. The thought that he might lose her now overwhelmed him.

Fear seized his lungs and he could hardly breathe. Death was said to come in threes. His legs grew so unsteady they could barely support him. He sat and buried his face in his hands.

First Ginny. Then Ernesto's body had been found at the hotel, his throat slit. The investigation had left Thomas deeply shaken. The more he learned about Jason Applebee, the more outraged he became. To a large extent, Thomas blamed himself for Ernesto's death, since he was the one who'd asked the hotel proprietor to keep an eye on the American.

First Ginny, then Ernesto, and he prayed to God the third death wouldn't be Azucena.

"Papa." Antonio climbed onto his lap and wrapped his small arms tightly around Thomas's neck. Thomas understood his son's need to hold on for all he was worth. In a way he was doing the same thing. He was worried sick about Azucena, and Raine was never far from his mind, either.

He trusted Jack to see his daughter safely out of the country, but there could be unforeseen troubles ahead. Jason Applebee was no novice when it came to using and abusing others. He was probably furious at having lost the stolen artifact, and furious, he'd be even more dangerous. News had come by way of the radio that the half of the Kukulcan Star found in Raine's suitcase had been returned to the museum in Mexico City. If Jason—

Azucena's scream shattered the silence and the blood drained from Thomas's face. In that moment he would have sold his soul for a doctor and a decent medical facility.

"Mama?" Antonio clung even harder to his father.

Thomas slid both arms around the boy and closed his eyes in silent prayer.

When she screamed again, Thomas put the boy gently down and jumped to his feet. He threw open the bedroom door. The midwife, standing at the foot of the bed, glanced disapprovingly over her shoulder.

"Not now. Leave us. This is no place for you."

"Is she all right?" he pleaded.

"Thomas?"

Azucena sounded so weak. "Should I get the

priest?'' he asked. *Dear God,* he thought again, *I can't lose her.* ''Tell me! For the love of God tell me what to do.''

Panic set in, and he didn't wait for an answer but raced from the house, certain he was about to lose both his wife and unborn child. He didn't stop running until he reached the church. He dashed through the front doors to find the parish priest kneeling in prayer at the altar.

''Father, Father,'' Thomas gasped, sprinting down the center aisle.

Father Garcia was well over seventy and incapable of moving quickly. Now that he had the priest's attention, Thomas wasn't sure what to tell him.

''What is it?'' Father Garcia asked anxiously.

''Azucena,'' he said between deep breaths. ''The baby's breech.'' He covered his face with both hands, terrified of the future without her, and slumped to his knees at the altar.

The priest accompanied him back to the house. When Thomas opened the front door, the first thing he heard was an infant's wail. The overpowering relief that followed brought tears to his eyes.

''Azucena,'' he sobbed. ''Azucena.'' Uncaring what the midwife thought, he rushed into the bedroom to find the older woman attending to the infant. Azucena lifted her head from the pillow.

''We have a third son,'' she whispered.

Thomas grabbed her hand and kissed it. Father Garcia walked slowly into the room, and seeing mother and child alive, he crossed himself and looked toward heaven.

"My love," Azucena murmured so quietly he could barely hear. She wiped the tears from his face and pressed her palm to his face.

Thomas glanced over his shoulder at the midwife. "Is she...will she be all right?"

The woman nodded. "You have a fine healthy son."

"Thank God," Thomas said, fighting back emotion. "Thank God."

Eight

Jack threw back his head and howled with laughter at the sight of Lorraine thrashing through the water in her eagerness to reach the boat. His amusement increased as she sputtered at him, her head full of shampoo with bubbles dripping onto her face.

The last laugh, however, was all hers.

Madder than a mean-tempered wasp, she agilely heaved herself out of the water and into the boat. Her wet underwear left precious little to the imagination. Jack's humor quickly faded, and his throat went dry at the sight of her. He'd been too long without a woman, he decided, if Lorraine was affecting him like this.

With a wedding band on her finger, she was strictly off-limits. He wasn't interested in an affair, however brief. His love life had been robust and healthy for a number of years, with only one hard-and-fast rule.

No married women.

Ever.

Jack was a good-looking cuss and he knew it. Girls had started flocking to him from the time he was in junior high. There'd never been a shortage of single women, and frankly, he wasn't interested in creating unnecessary enemies. Like husbands. In addition, this was the daughter of a friend. A good friend, who trusted him to get her safely back to the United States.

One look at Lorraine's full breasts and the shapely curve of her hips glistening in the light from the setting sun, and the hard-and-fast rule was becoming merely a guideline. He couldn't make himself turn away. Damn, she was beautiful. It wasn't that he hadn't noticed earlier. Anyone could see that, despite her prissy attitude, she was easy on the eyes. But Jack had forced himself not to respond...until now. He'd done a damn good job of pretending he wasn't aware of her, hiding the attraction behind a barrage of insults. The questions about her love life had been an ill-advised attempt to remind himself that she was off-limits.

The problem was she had a body that would stop traffic in Vegas. Long shapely legs that tapered down to delicate trim ankles. She wore bikini underpants, pale blue nylon ones. The waistband hugged her slender hips, and her stomach was smooth and flat. While her legs and hips were striking, her full breasts were quite possibly her most incredible asset. Even ensconced in a lace-trimmed bra, they were the most luscious-looking breasts he'd seen in years. Even worse—or better, depending on your perspective—her nipples had beaded and seemed to be pointing directly at him. He'd had automatic weapons aimed in his direction and experienced less dismay than he did at that moment.

Then it hit him. Hard. *He wanted her.* Without any trouble whatsoever, he could envision her in his arms...and his bed. It was so easy to imagine her smiling up at him as he hurriedly shed his clothes.

A cold sweat broke out on his brow. He rubbed his eyes to dispel the image of Lorraine in his bed while he struggled to breathe evenly. He instructed himself to remember the nameless woman in Belize and Catherina Efrain, a woman he'd had a brief fling with a year or two earlier. He'd met her when she was on vacation in Campecho and was later surprised to learn she worked for the Mexican government. Thinking about Catherina helped— but not enough.

Being trapped with Lorraine in the close confines of the boat wasn't going to make things any easier. Jack had to forcefully—and repeatedly—remind himself of something that, until now, had been instinctive.

Lorraine was hands-off.

Squinting and muttering, she swept her shampoo-coated hair away from her face and glared in his direction. The effect was somewhat undermined by the rapid blinking of one eye. "There aren't any piranhas here, are there?" she demanded.

She stretched out her arm, groping for a towel. Apparently she'd brought it from belowdecks before she entered the water.

"How'd you guess?" he returned, his voice whiskey-rough. Whatever wit he'd once possessed had vanished while he struggled to disguise the effect she'd had on him.

"Oh-h-h," she groaned, stumbling blindly around.

He couldn't figure out what she was doing. It took all his self-control not to stare openmouthed while she paraded half-nude in front of him. He finally realized she was searching for a bucket. Now that she'd found one, she leaned over the gunwale, presenting him with yet another blood-stirring view of her buttocks.

Jack slammed his eyes shut while she lowered the bucket over the side, then opened them just in time to watch her pour the water directly over her head. Lather and suds cascaded down her delectable body.

"I hope you're happy," she shrieked. She reached for the towel, burying her face in it.

"Ecstatic."

Furious, she whirled around and in her rush stubbed her toe. She gasped in pain, then grabbed her foot, hopping madly around on the other, her breasts jiggling with her movements. "Damn, damn, damn!" she cried between small intermittent groans.

"Damn?" Jack couldn't believe his ears.

"Is something wrong with *damn?*" She scowled at him as if he'd purposely dropped an anvil on her precious foot.

"As a matter of fact, there is. You stubbed your toe, right?"

She nodded, biting down on her lower lip. She leaned against the side of the boat and carefully examined her big toe for damage.

"*Damn*'s the best you can do?"

She looked up at him, her eyes questioning. "Do?"

"That's your strongest swearword?"

She stared at him.

"Sweetheart, I'm gonna have to give you lessons."

"I don't need you to teach me anything," she said furiously.

"*Damn?*" He didn't know why he found this so hilarious. Probably because he needed something to take his mind off how incredibly sexy she looked. She continued to stare at him. The longer she stared, the more amused he became.

His laugh started off as a small sarcastic chuckle.

Lorraine's eyes narrowed with outrage. "You're incredibly rude, do you know that?"

He laughed harder. *"Damn?"*

"In fact, you're impossible." She wrapped the towel around her waist and walked away from him.

"Don't worry, I'm a good teacher," he called after her. "We'll start off easy with the basic four-letter words, then work our way up to the more complicated phrases. By the time you're back in the States, I'll have you saying things that would make a longshoreman blush."

"I hope you enjoy making fun of me."

"More than you'll ever know." Still grinning, he wiped the mirth from his face. His reaction was way out of proportion, but it was either laugh or risk kissing her—which was the one thing he couldn't do.

Lorraine paused and glanced at him over her shoulder, then sadly shook her head and disappeared belowdecks.

Jack heard her rummaging around. Convinced he'd made a narrow escape, he settled down in his chair and congratulated himself on his restraint.

* * *

Lorraine didn't understand Jack Keller. Furthermore, she had no intention of trying. As far as she was concerned, he was a Neanderthal. She waited until her underwear was almost dry before she put her linen suit back on. Then she ran a comb through her tangled hair, wincing as she encountered one snarl after another. The man was impossible. Impossible! He'd purposely terrified her with that comment about piranhas. Like an idiot, she'd believed him.

Apparently it wasn't enough just to scare her. He'd taken great delight in ridiculing her, as well. And then offering to teach her to swear! Her mother had claimed swearing was the sign of a poor vocabulary; Lorraine herself considered it in bad taste.

The way he'd laughed made her clench her hands and yank the comb hard enough to bring tears to her eyes. Just when she was beginning to have kind thoughts about him, too. She had to admit she didn't know what would've happened if he hadn't intervened with that horrible man. He'd helped her even knowing she'd taken his money.

Jack, being Jack, had made sure she knew that *he* knew what she'd done. But he hadn't gone on and on about it. She almost wished he had; it would make hating him easier.

One moment she was feeling warm and generous toward him, the next she felt outraged by his obnoxious behavior. The man was puzzling, and her reactions to him equally so. She hated him, despised him, and yet she'd deliberately flaunted herself in front of him, making sure he got a good look at her body. Her skin went hot, then cold, as she owned up to the truth of what she'd done. She'd actually wanted him to kiss her. Touch her. She disapproved of flirting with a man this way, and it really wasn't like her. While she wasn't married as he believed, she *was* engaged and she owed her loyalty to her fiancé. Lorraine didn't understand her own behavior any more than she understood Jack's. Perhaps it had something to do with what had happened back at the cantina. He'd saved her in a situation that might have been life or death. A shiver ran down her spine whenever she thought about it.

Had she been able to find a means of making herself comfortable, Lorraine would have remained below. Spending any additional time in Jack's company was too risky, in too many ways. But once she'd gathered her courage, she climbed back to the main deck to discover Jack poring over sea charts by the light of a gas lantern.

"Where are we headed next?" she asked.

"Pucuro."

Lorraine glanced down at the table, hoping to find the place Jack had mentioned.

"Here," he said, pointing his finger at the notation on the map. "We need supplies. Remember?"

Seeing that he'd already purchased supplies twice, this probably wasn't a good time to complain that he never consulted her regarding their plans. If it hadn't been for his rather unappetizing leftover fish and the plate of food he'd brought on board in La Ruta Maya, they'd be starving by now.

"We'll leave at first light and reach Pucuro around noon tomorrow. I need your word of honor that you'll do exactly as I say when we get there. I want you to stay out of sight this time."

"All right," she muttered.

"I'm serious, Lorraine. I can't have you sneaking off again. Not in Pucuro."

"I already gave you my word. What more do you want?"

"I want you to spell it out."

He sounded as if he distrusted her, which offended Lorraine—but then again, she'd given him ample cause. Speaking slowly and clearly, she said, "I promise I will stay belowdecks. I will not come up until you tell me the coast is clear." *Literally,* she thought. For the first time in her life, that expression described the actual truth.

"Pucuro isn't like La Ruta Maya. I've been

there once before and..." He paused, leaving the remainder unsaid.

"And?" she urged, wanting him to continue. She needed to know what they were letting themselves in for.

He shook his head. "It's dangerous there. Pucuro is the last place I'd normally take a woman," he confessed, "but we don't have any choice. We're going to need to stop somewhere, and soon." He sounded none too pleased by that fact.

"How long will it take you to get what we need?" she asked.

"Shouldn't be long," he replied, then tagged on a question of his own. "Have you ever fired a weapon?"

Her breathing went shallow at the thought. "You mean...a gun? No, never."

His response was an irritated sigh.

"There's no need to get mad about it. I've never even held a gun."

"That's what I was afraid of."

"I have no desire to learn, either."

Jack's eyes were cold and serious. "You're going to have to learn."

"This is a joke, right?"

"I might make light of a great many things, but I don't joke about guns."

He hurried belowdecks, returning a moment later with a small gun. "This is an automatic

Glock .22. You might need to defend yourself when we're in Pucuro. I want to leave the boat knowing that if anything goes wrong, you can take care of yourself. Understand? When we finish with that, I'll show you how to run the boat on your own.''

"You're overreacting," she insisted stiffly. "First, I don't need a gun to defend myself, and second—"

"You need the gun." His voice left no room for argument.

"Jack, this is ridiculous!''·

"You're going to learn how to fire this weapon, and that's all there is to it.''

"Fine," she said, looking distastefully down at it.

Under protest, she listened dutifully while he explained the inner workings of the gun. When he'd done that, he demonstrated how to load the thing. Then he expected her to do it herself.

Lorraine finally complied, but not happily. He ignored her complaints, making her repeat the procedure until he was satisfied she'd learned what he wanted her to know.

"Next I want you to fire it.''

"No way!" The idea of actually shooting was repugnant to her. Besides, she didn't even have a target to aim for.

"Raine, this matter isn't open for discussion.''

"Oh, for heaven's sake," she muttered. She stepped back and waited for him to reveal the finer techniques of handling a gun.

"Hold it," he insisted.

"I already did."

His jaw tightened and, sighing heavily, she reached for the weapon.

"I want you to get the feel of it," he explained. "Balance it in your hands, get accustomed to the weight of it."

"I did that earlier." She hadn't, not really. She wasn't usually so disagreeable, but Jack seemed to bring out the worst in her. The fact that he was standing this close bothered her, too. Her heart beat a loud thudding tattoo; she was sure he could hear it. Lord, she was hot. Even with her hair piled on top of her head, sweat trickled down the back of her neck. Jack was sweating, too. His skin glistened with it in the moonlight. She found him far more provocative than she wanted. Now that he'd shaved she recognized that he was far too attractive for his own good—or hers.

"You ready to fire?" he snapped, cutting off her musings.

"Oh, all right, if it'll make you happy." She stretched out both arms and took aim at the dark ocean.

Jack moved directly behind her. His arms came around hers and his hands supported her wrists.

Lorraine drew in a deep breath at the way her body reacted. For one mad second she actually forgot about the gun in her hand. Instead, she felt the warmth of his body against hers, his taut muscles and solid strength. She had to struggle to pay attention to what he was saying. He seemed to be losing patience with her, because his directions became clipped and short.

"Now," he said, "pull the trigger."

Lorraine gently squeezed.

Nothing happened.

"Harder," he said close to her ear. Too close.

She shut her eyes and squeezed the trigger again.

"Keep your eyes open," he barked.

She opened them at precisely the moment the automatic fired. Lorraine reeled with the unexpected force of the discharge. She might have toppled onto her backside if not for Jack, who stopped her fall. His hands caught her sides, shockingly close to her breasts—and lingered far longer than necessary.

"I...I did it," she announced breathlessly. She cleared her throat and spoke again. "That wasn't so bad."

"Do you want to fire it once more just to be sure you're comfortable with it?" Jack didn't sound like himself, either.

"No...I've got the hang of it."

"You're sure?"

Lorraine nodded and had the inexplicable feeling that she'd had more than one lucky escape.

It was almost noon the following day when they approached Pucuro. Jack ordered Lorraine belowdecks long before they reached the harbor. He didn't want to take the slightest chance of anyone's seeing her. He hadn't come right out and said it, but Pucuro was full of cutthroats and thieves. However, it was either stop here or waste another day searching for some other little out-of-the-way port.

"Jack?" Lorraine stood on the steps below, the wind tousling her hair. Jack was hard-pressed to remember any woman looking more beautiful than she did right then.

"What?" He forced himself to sound short-tempered.

"Would it be possible...for you to pick me up a few clothes while you're in town?"

"Any particular color?"

"Yellow's my favorite."

"I'll do what I can."

"Thank you." She disappeared, closing the door behind her.

Jack maneuvered the boat toward the docks, which were old and in disrepair. A number of small boats were tied there. He noticed a couple of disreputable-looking young men who studied him as though trying to estimate how easy it would be to take him on. Jack met their stares until both glanced away. An edgy feeling came over him as they hurriedly left.

With no one in the vicinity to hear, Jack knocked lightly on the bulkhead and told Lorraine, "I'm going now."

"Be quick, okay?"

"I shouldn't be gone more than thirty minutes." He was well aware how uncomfortable it was for her belowdecks. Soon it would be stifling.

He was about to leave, then decided to give her one last warning. "You need to be quiet."

"I know that. Just go, okay?"

He hesitated. The feeling was back, and experience had taught him not to ignore his gut instincts. Unfortunately he had to go into town; there were few other alternatives. It'd been a long time since they'd eaten and they couldn't go much longer without supplies.

"Is something wrong?" Lorraine's loud whisper came up from below.

"Not a damn thing. Just sit tight." He didn't like leaving her, but he had no choice. "One final reminder. Don't fire the gun unless it's absolutely necessary. Understand?" The last thing he needed was her using it as a signal to remind him to pick up coffee.

When he'd jumped onto the wharf, Jack had to watch where he stepped. The wood had rotted in quite a few places. As quickly as he could, he headed in the direction of the town's only store. Supplies were outragcously priced, but for once Jack wasn't going to quibble. He wanted in and out of Pucuro, no questions asked.

It went without saying that he wasn't fond of the town. His first and only visit to Pucuro, a number of years ago, had nearly gotten him killed. He'd been part of Deliverance Company, and Murphy had sent him on a fact-finding mission. Fool that he was, Jack had gotten the information he needed, then lingered in the cantina. That had been his first mistake.

He'd decided to stay for a glass of beer when he noticed a woman across the room. The look she gave him wasn't unfamiliar. She was interested and frankly, after several months of celibacy, so was he. Cain had insisted that when his men were on a mission, they keep their pants zipped. Only Cain wasn't in charge anymore, Murphy was, and so Jack had made a classic mistake. He'd gone home with the pretty *señorita*.

Not until it was too late did he realize he'd walked into a trap.

Jack shook his head, hoping to rid himself of

the memory, although he carried the scars of that mistake on his body. By the time Deliverance Company found him, he was half-dead. The half that was still alive wasn't pleased.

Now he kept his eyes focused straight ahead, talked to no one and hurried down the dirt road to the store. He finished buying his supplies in record time and paid an exorbitant amount to make sure they were immediately loaded onto the boat. That done, he walked into town to visit the open-air market. Instead of purchasing clothes that were expressly female, he bought a couple of shirts and a pair of pants. He had to guess at size.

Jack was beginning to feel downright smug. Perhaps Lorraine was right and he was overreacting. The entire venture had taken all of fifteen minutes. He was returning to the waterfront when a youngster of seven or eight raced to his side.

"*Señor*," he said, looking up at Jack with wide brown eyes. "Your lady friend sent me to find you." He spoke in Spanish.

"What?" Jack was going to kill Lorraine with his bare hands.

"She needs you."

"She's going to need me, all right," he muttered.

"Come, I'll take you to her." The boy slipped his hand in Jack's. "This way," he said, steering Jack down a narrow lane.

One request—that was all he'd asked of her. The woman couldn't follow the simplest instruction. By the time he got through with her, she'd— His thoughts came to an abrupt halt.

The sensation he'd experienced earlier—the bad feeling—recurred. Except that it was far stronger than it had been before.

Slowly, with care, Jack turned around.

Carlos stood at the far end of the street. "Hello, amigo. We meet again."

Nine

The heat belowdecks was intolerable, but Lorraine was determined to prove to Jack that she was capable of following instructions. Under no circumstances was she to leave the boat; he'd made her promise. Not that he had anything to worry about. Lorraine had learned her lesson in La Ruta Maya.

Despite the heat and discomfort, she would prove to him once and for all that she was a woman of her word.

The waiting was as unbearable as the suffocating heat. The first hour was the worst, holed up in this tomb with only her thoughts to occupy her—and those were of little comfort. Her mother had lived a lie and her father... Lorraine didn't know what to think. She felt angry every time she thought about the way he'd passed off the Mayan woman as his housekeeper. When she wasn't brooding about her parents and the mistakes they'd made, her thoughts took a natural path to Gary. Their relationship had undergone a change in the weeks since her mother's funeral. Gary sensed it, too.

Lorraine loved him, planned to marry him, but after her mother died, all she'd wanted was to be alone. Gary had yearned to comfort her; he'd wanted her to *need* him. She hadn't.

Then there was this awful attraction she felt for Jack. Of all the things tormenting her right now, that was perhaps the worst. Her face burned with humiliation as she recalled how she'd flaunted herself in front of him. Not since high school had she worked that hard to get a member of the opposite sex to notice her.

She glanced at her watch. The waiting seemed to go on forever and she felt listless and weak. Jack had promised he'd be quick. Thirty minutes. Wasn't that what he'd said?

Then it occurred to her that something had happened to him. He'd been gone well over an hour at this point, despite his insistence that Pucuro wasn't a port where he was inclined to linger. She imagined all the horrible possibilities—he'd been attacked, accidentally injured, arrested—until she was convinced something had gone dreadfully wrong.

Then it occurred to her that maybe Jack wasn't coming back at all. He didn't like her. He'd let her know it, too. Nor had he restrained himself from telling her, at every conceivable opportunity, that he considered her a pain in the butt.

Even now, she remembered his look of disdain when her father had brought her down to the waterfront. His attitude hadn't changed much.

No, she mused, reasoning away the fear. Jack might consider abandoning her, but he wouldn't leave his boat. He'd be back. Unless—her imagination kicked in again—unless he'd run into trouble.

The panic rose in the back of her throat, nearly choking off her breath. If something *had* gone wrong, he might need her help. Not knowing what to do, she paced his cramped living quarters, more convinced with every passing minute that she needed to take some sort of action on his behalf.

Her hand was on the door, ready to pull it open, when she hesitated and considered yet another possibility. This might well be a test to prove that she could be trusted. It'd be just like him to force her to demonstrate her dependability. For all she knew, he could be sitting on the wharf this very minute, just waiting to see how long she'd keep her promise.

Well, if he wanted proof, she'd damn well give it to him.

Determined not to act on her instincts, she sat back down. Hell could freeze over before she'd leave this boat.

Her determination lasted all of ten minutes.

Fears followed doubts, and with the doubts came the questions. Just how long should she wait for Jack to return? What if she passed out in the heat? What if he was injured and had no way of letting her know? Maybe he was in jail. Or the morgue. The inventory of less-than-comforting possibilities began to mount again.

Just when Lorraine was sure she'd go mad, she heard voices. Faint at first, then louder and more distinct. Listening carefully, she realized there were two, possibly three men, speaking in Spanish. They were on the dock right next to the boat. A minute later the boat tilted and there was the sound of footfalls on the boat itself.

Could Jack be with them?

She was about to call up and ask, then remembered that Jack had specifically told her to stay belowdecks until he personally came for her. Then and only then was she to show herself.

She couldn't tell exactly how many people were on the boat—two men or three. It was difficult to distinguish voices. Two seemed to do most of the talking, but she thought she'd heard three separate sets of footsteps. The two who did the talking were having some kind of argument.

The door leading belowdecks rattled. Lorraine froze and thanked God she'd had the sense to lock it earlier.

The argument escalated. The men argued back and forth, but as far as she could tell nothing had been decided.

She continued to listen and to wait. There was movement above; the boat swayed repeatedly as the men climbed on and off. She heard boxes or containers set down heavily—they must be carrying the supplies on board. One question remained, though: Where had Jack gone?

Then there was silence, but she didn't think they'd left the boat. Her breathing grew shallow as she listened intently. After a while, she heard the sound of bottles being opened. They'd probably found Jack's stash of beer and were helping themselves.

The boat pitched sharply to one side as the men clambered off and trudged down the dock. Their loud boisterous voices slowly faded.

Lorraine wasn't sure which was worse—not knowing what had happened to Jack or the waiting. Feeling weak and disoriented, she laid her head down on the table and closed her eyes.

She might have drifted off to sleep, but she didn't think so. The next thing she heard was footsteps. A single pair this time.

Jack.

She bolted upright as relief rushed through her. Everything was fine. He was back. Almost immediately her exhilaration turned to anger. Keeping her waiting like this had been a rotten thing to do. He'd done it on purpose, too; she just knew it. He was punishing her for what had happened in La Ruta Maya.

Well, she had every intention of letting Jack know exactly what she thought of that kind of behavior. By the time she finished with him, he'd be more than happy to get rid of her—but no happier than she was to get rid of him.

Opening the door, she paused long enough to drag a breath of fresh cool air into her starving lungs, then climbed out. She marched purposely onto the deck. She could hear the sound of the boat's twin engines purring contentedly in the background. That Neanderthal was about to pull out of port without letting her know he'd come back! Why should she be surprised? This was typical of everything else he'd done.

"It took you long enough," she raged—then nearly swallowed her tongue in shock.

It wasn't Jack who'd come on board, but Carlos.

Lorraine gasped and remembered too late that she'd left the gun belowdecks.

Gary Franklin was worried. He hadn't heard from Lorraine since she'd gone on this crazy trip to Mexico. To his way of thinking, there was something strange about the entire business.

She'd been so desperate to find out everything she could about her father she'd refused to listen to reason.

At one time Lorraine would have heeded his advice, but everything had changed when her mother died. Now he sometimes felt he didn't know her at all. He tried to be patient, although it was increasingly difficult. At her mother's death she'd withdrawn completely into herself, blocking out the world—and that included him. Frankly it had hurt; he'd wanted to comfort her, to hold her in his arms and help her through her grief. But she wouldn't allow it. He'd finally realized it wasn't anything personal. Lorraine might not have wanted him, but she hadn't wanted anyone else, either.

Virginia's death had devastated her, but it had been a shock to him, too. He'd heard all the mother-in-law jokes and laughed with the rest, but Virginia wasn't like that. Wouldn't have been like that, he corrected himself. She was gone now. The wedding was still set for late autumn, and he figured the sooner they were married, the better.

Lorraine needed him more than ever, and he loved her. At thirty-six, he'd waited longer than most men he knew before deciding to make the leap into matrimony. He'd been looking for the right woman; at least that was what he'd told his parents. It wasn't a lie, but it wasn't the full truth.

Unlike his peers, he hadn't felt any urge to settle down. To put it like that made him sound immature, which wasn't the case, either. He happened to enjoy his freedom. But he felt it was time he got married, and he and Lorraine were compatible in the ways that mattered. They liked the same things, believed in the same causes. Both were sensible and not easily swayed by popular opinion. He liked an orderly world; so did she.

Gary leaned back in his office chair and clasped his hands behind his head. Lorraine had given him the phone number where she could be reached, with the understanding that she preferred to contact him and not the other way around.

This was one of the traits that irked Gary about his fiancée. She could be uncompromising. Occasionally she seemed a little too quick to form an opinion and cling to it. While he admired her straightforward manner, there were times he wished she'd been more willing to bend. Still, he had faith in her common sense. Despite his uneasiness, he supposed she'd manage all right, even in some out-of-the-way Mexican village.

His phone pealed, and Gary reached for the receiver. "Hello."

"Gary, it's Marjorie Ellis." The woman hesitated as if she expected a reaction.

Gary didn't give her one.

"I'm on the road right now, but I've got a couple of questions for you, if you have the time."

Marjorie was new on the job and needed some guidance. A whole lot of guidance, if the truth be known. Their company, Med-X, sold medical supplies and equipment to hospitals, doctors' offices, nursing homes and the like. Gary had been in the field for ten years and had recently accepted a management position.

Marjorie, who'd been hired as his replacement, lacked almost every skill he considered crucial to the job. She was disorganized. She wasn't punctual. Her computer skills were nonexistent, and he had to explain things three and four times before she grasped them. What redeemed Marjorie Ellis was the fact that Med-X clients loved her. That was a shock, but he couldn't argue with success. Two months on the job, and she'd outsold every other trainee in the company. Now that was impressive.

"What do you need to know?" Gary asked, keeping his tone friendly and helpful.

"It'd probably be best if I came into the office and we talked about it. That is, if you have the time," she said again.

Time was something Gary had plenty of, now that Lorraine was away. "Not a problem." He glanced at his watch. "When?"

"Is this afternoon at four convenient?"

He flipped noisily through the pages of his appointment calendar, doing his best to make sure she heard it. He already knew the slot was open. No use letting Marjorie think he wasn't a busy man, though. "Does four-thirty work for you?"

Gary heard the rustle of papers in the background and suspected she'd dropped a file. "Sure," Marjorie said. "I'll see you then." Her voice was faint, as though she'd turned her face away from the telephone receiver. Gary could picture her with the cell phone tucked under her chin while she bent to retrieve the spilled paperwork. Typical.

"I'll look forward to it." As he replaced the receiver, Gary realized how true that was. Marjorie was a ditz with plenty of...well, ditzy moments, but she was also likable and had a delightful easy laugh.

Without Lorraine, he was actually lonely. He missed her and somehow doubted she missed him with the same intensity. An hour in Marjorie's company—even if he had to explain the same computer program half a dozen times—would at least be a distraction.

Carlos intended to kill her. Lorraine knew it the minute she saw him. She looked wildly around, hoping someone would see her plight and help or at least send for the police. There was no one, and even if there'd been people nearby, she wasn't sure they would have risked becoming involved.

Slowly, as if he enjoyed the anticipation, Carlos advanced toward her. For every step he took, she retreated one until her back was against the bulkhead. His breath made her want to gag, but she refused to show her terror, refused even to flinch.

"What are you doing here?" she demanded with false bravado.

"I come to teach you a lesson." His smile vanished, and using both hands, Carlos ripped apart her blouse, sending the buttons flying.

Lorraine gasped at the unexpectedness of his action and attempted to knee him but missed. Her knee wasn't her only means of defense, and recovering quickly, she clawed her long nails down his face, leaving bloody streaks.

Carlos backhanded her with enough force to split her lip. Blood filled her mouth and she spit at him. He might rape and kill her, but she wouldn't make it easy.

A shout came from the dock and she caught a glimpse of Jack. *Jack.* Thank God. It hadn't registered at first, but if Carlos had reached her, he must have either killed or injured Jack.

At the sound of Jack's voice, Carlos glanced over his shoulder and cursed loudly. He grabbed for a gun tucked in his belt behind his back and would have fired if Lorraine hadn't acted quickly. Using the full weight of her body, she threw herself against his side.

The gun fired, then flew out of Carlos's hand, landing on the deck. The bullet went wild, and Jack leaped aboard *Scotch on Water,* fiercely rocking the boat.

Without hesitation, the two men dove at each other like wild beasts tearing into a fresh kill. Lorraine nearly tripped over the boxes of supplies in an effort to get out of the way. Arms and legs flailed and barely escaped hitting her. She danced a complete circle around the men, looking for a chance to assist Jack.

Not knowing what else to do, she jumped on Carlos's back and wrapped her arms around his neck as tightly as she could in an amateurish attempt to strangle him. He tossed her off almost effortlessly. She hit the side of her head when she landed, and for a moment saw stars.

Stunned, she sat and waited for her vision to clear, then struggled to her feet. Refusing to stand by and do nothing, she reached for the bucket. If she could clobber Carlos over the head with it, or better yet put it *on* his head, she might actually help. Unfortunately he refused to hold still and she ended up chasing him around the deck, pail in hand, ready to act once the opportunity presented itself.

Jack proved an able-bodied combatant, but Carlos outweighed him by forty or fifty pounds. He, too, seemed to be an expert at hand-to-hand combat.

"The gun," Jack shouted at Lorraine. "Get the gun."

Of course. That made perfect sense and would be a great deal more help to him than chasing after Carlos with a yellow rubber bucket. Adrenaline pumping through her, she hurried below for the Glock .22 he'd given her.

As she disappeared she heard Jack curse. Frantic, she grabbed the weapon from its hiding place and checked to make sure it was loaded. Then, her hands trembling so badly she could barely manage it, she released the safety and climbed back to the main deck.

It didn't dawn on her until a shot rang out that Jack hadn't been referring to the gun belowdecks but the one she'd knocked away from Carlos. The one that had just been fired.

The sound was like an explosion that echoed in her ears long afterward. She prayed with all her might that it was Carlos who'd been hit. Not Jack, please, not Jack.

But God hadn't heard her desperate plea. When she reappeared on deck, she found Jack lying in a pool of blood. He stared sightlessly up at the sky, unmoving.

Jack, who'd put himself in harm's way to protect her.

"No!" she screamed. She didn't hesitate as she leveled the weapon she held at Carlos. "You dirty son of a bitch," she sobbed, thinking Jack would be proud of her. Because she'd advanced beyond *damn*.

Blindly she fired the gun. Once, twice. Again and then again. The first bullet knocked the weapon out of his hand. He roared in anger and sprang back. The second shot grazed his shoulder. The next two went wild.

Lorraine paused and aimed more carefully, figuring that if she'd hit him once she could do it again.

Her calm determination must have frightened him. With a cry of outrage, Carlos leaped overboard. Lorraine would have shot him in the water if not for the men racing toward the waterfront, shouting and waving guns. A bullet bored into the wood next to her head as two men pointed their weapons at her from the wharf.

Acting purely on instinct, she reached for the boat's throttle and shoved it forward. The powerful engines heaved and roared, but refused to budge. Groaning with frustration and fear, she pushed them into full power as Jack had showed her earlier. Again nothing happened. Then, all at once, the boat surged forward with such force she was nearly hurled overboard. Her grip on the wheel was what saved her.

Something didn't feel right, but she didn't have time to discern what it was until they were safely at sea. As they headed out, she looked back and realized what had happened.

She hadn't untied *Scotch on Water*. Behind her, she towed the entire dock and every other boat in town.

Ten

Rather than deal immediately with the problem of the attached dock, Lorraine set the course of *Scotch on Water* toward open sea. Leaving the helm, she raced over to Jack. His blood slicked the deck. Falling on her knees, she searched frantically for a pulse. Relief and gratitude surged through her at the strong steady beat she could feel against her fingertips. He was alive.

"Thank God," she whispered as tears stung her eyes. "Thank God."

Her medical training had been extensive, but she'd never had to deal with a gunshot wound. She trembled, mentally reviewing emergency procedures.

The bullet had entered his shoulder, and when she tore aside his shirt, she realized the wound still bled profusely. She also saw that Jack was close to going into shock. Scrambling to her feet, she raced below and grabbed a pillow, blankets, clean towels.

She settled the pillow beneath his shoulders,

wrapped him snugly from stomach to feet in the blankets, then pressed a towel to the wound, holding it firmly in place. Once the bleeding had slowed, she was able to examine the wound more carefully. Fortunately the bullet hadn't struck his chest, so she didn't have to worry about his lungs. Nor had it severed an artery.

One step at a time, she reminded herself. One tiny step at a time. *You can do this. You can do this.* She repeated the words like a mantra, hoping they'd bolster her confidence. The last thing Jack needed now was for her to panic.

"Oh, Jack," she sobbed, brushing the unruly hair from his brow. She blamed herself; if she'd gotten the right gun, none of this would've happened. She could have saved Jack. Instead, he might die and it would be all her fault.

She refused to dwell on her own fears and regrets. What she had to concentrate on now was helping Jack, following the right procedures…not failing him again. Blessedly he was unconscious; at least now she could do whatever was necessary. She forced herself to think. Closing her eyes, she sat back on her heels and continued to stroke his face while she considered her options. She decided to start by probing the wound to determine exactly where the bullet was and how deep it lay. She hated to use something as crude as a filleting knife, but what else was there? That was when she remembered the compact sewing kit she carried in her purse.

She lingered for a moment, not wanting to leave him, then hurried belowdecks.

After setting a pan of water on the stove to boil, she dumped the contents of her purse on the mattress. Her wallet, passport, a pen and her cosmetic bag tumbled out, together with the miniature sewing kit. She yanked open the snap and extracted the small scissors. What she really needed was a pair of tweezers.

She had a pair, she remembered, experiencing a sense of exhilaration. Her cosmetic bag. She kept one there, or had in years past. Grabbing the zippered bag, she pulled it open and emptied it onto the bed. A wrapped tampon, her compact, lipstick and blush bounced on the mattress and scattered among her other things. When she shook the bag, her eyebrow pencil, lip liner and something round and gold followed, along with the tweezers.

She took the tweezers and the small scissors, and set them both in the pan of boiling water, leaving them there for several minutes to sterilize. While she waited, she rummaged through the cupboards, certain she'd seen a bottle of scotch in an earlier search.

"Yes!" she cried in triumph when she found it.

Tucking it under one arm, she carried the pan of boiling water in both hands and returned to Jack.

Feeling relatively confident that no one was chasing them—it seemed unlikely, since she'd towed every boat in town—Lorraine shut off the engines. She stared in dismay at the bobbing dock and the string of boats. Actually, her lack of forethought had been a godsend. She'd inadvertently deprived their pursuers of any way to follow them. She didn't know whether to laugh or cry as she leaned over the side and untied *Scotch on Water*, leaving the dock and its attached boats to drift away of their own accord.

When she'd finished, she readied Jack as much as possible and prepared herself for the coming ordeal.

"I'm going to check to see where the bullet is," she told him, then explained that it might be necessary to leave it inside if she couldn't remove it easily. Again she touched his face. For whatever reason, touching him comforted her and calmed her frazzled nerves. Her mouth was dry and her throat thick with fear.

As gently as possible, she lifted the blood-soaked towel from his left shoulder and poured a liberal dose of alcohol on the wound. Then, feeling she needed a bit of fortification herself, she took a deep swig and gasped. The scotch burned through her, but the jolt was exactly what she needed. She secured the top and set the bottle aside.

Inhaling a shaky breath, she studied Jack's pale expressionless face. She tried to imagine what he'd say if he could speak to her. No doubt there'd be a few curses, an insult or two—and gruff reassurance. Biting her lower lip, Lorraine prayed for guidance and a sure hand.

The hot tweezers burned her skin, but she forced herself to grip them tightly, afraid they might slip. She dug carefully into the open wound. Blood gushed from his shoulder the instant she did. She dabbed it away with a folded towel. As she wiped the injury clean, she noted once more how raw and red the torn flesh looked. If he lived through this—and dammit, he would!—Jack was going to have an angry scar.

The tweezers scraped against the bullet, and just as she'd feared, it was buried deep in the flesh. Blood flowed more rapidly from the wound as soon as she pulled the tweezers away. Sweat beaded her brow. It soon became apparent that any attempt to extract the bullet would do more harm than good. He'd already lost a lot of blood.

"It's going to be all right, Jack. I'm going to leave the bullet and pack the wound with a tampon because that's the best I have in the way of medical supplies. I'm not going to let you die. Understand?''

Unexpectedly Jack moaned and rolled his head to one side. It seemed that, even unconscious, the man was going to argue with her.

"Don't worry, you won't get PMS." Her laugh was mildly hysterical. He'd never know what she'd done, and that was just as well or she'd never hear the end of it. From now on, she'd need to boil gauze and pack the wound with it until healing had begun. For the rest of his life, Jack Keller would carry a bullet in his shoulder as a reminder of her foolishness.

She discarded the tweezers and scissors, returned belowdecks and grabbed the tampon. By the time she'd finished bandaging him, knotting the gauze as tightly as she could, reaction had set in and her hands trembled fiercely. She stroked his brow and pushed back his hair. His skin no longer seemed as clammy, she thought, assessing his condition in as detached a manner as she could. His respiration was better, too, not as shallow.

It was then that the first drop of rain hit. Intent as she was on her task, Lorraine hadn't noticed the darkening sky. The wind had picked up, as well. Moving Jack belowdecks would be impossible.

A second drop hit her and then more. Many, many more.

She had no choice but to wait out the storm here on deck and shelter Jack as best she could.

Jack was in hell. At least, he assumed that was where he was. He felt as if he were on fire, then realized that the pain was more localized. His shoulder seemed to be responsible for the greatest part of his discomfort.

His mouth was parched, and all he could think about was a drink of cool, refreshing water. No, he had to be in hell—otherwise he wouldn't be this thirsty.

As if he'd spoken the request aloud, he felt something cool against his lips. But only a drop, as if God intended to torture him by granting just a hint of relief. Just enough to remind him of the intensity of his thirst....

"Drink," a soft feminine voice whispered.

Marcie? Here? Now? That was all he needed to convince him he was indeed being punished. Everything he wanted was offered, then withheld. He'd ventured into the lake of fire. His heart ached at the sound of her voice, so soft and loving.

He felt his head being gently lifted. A glass of water was pressed to his lips. As soon as he recognized what it was, he drank greedily, gratefully.

Heaven, he decided. He'd been routed toward a more angelic resting place—although he couldn't imagine what he'd done to warrant such exalted treatment. But, hey, who was he to question an executive decision, especially one that leaned in his favor?

Content now, Jack fell into a deep and peaceful sleep.

In his dream he was visiting a Mexican village. He glanced around at the sun-baked adobe houses, the small church, the cantina. So far, so good.

Then Marcie appeared. Sweet Marcie, the plumber's wife. Marcie and her children. Marcie and her husband.

Jack watched her and admired what a terrific mother she was to her twins. Every once in a while, she looked in his direction and smiled. She couldn't see him, though; he knew that. Because Jack stood apart, gazing in. He felt a deep sadness. The kind of sadness that left him in little doubt of his own failings and imperfections.

Watching the dream-Marcie with her family, observing their love and happiness, was like seeing how his own life might have gone had he been a different kind of person. Had he made other choices through the years.

Caught up in his regrets, Jack didn't realize another man had joined the small party. He blinked, certain there must be some mistake. The man was

Carlos. Jack called out a taunting remark, but the dream-Carlos couldn't hear him.

Then Carlos grabbed Marcie by the shoulder and shoved her against the wall. Jack bolted upright. "What the hell do you think you're doing?" he shouted.

Knowing it wouldn't do any good to yell since no one seemed able to hear him, Jack waited for Clifford to step in. But Clifford was nowhere to be seen. The children had disappeared, too.

Turning his attention back to Marcie, he watched helplessly as Carlos shoved her hard. As sure as anything, Carlos was going to rape her. Jack had to stop him. There wasn't time to let her find her own way out of the scrape. There wasn't time. Dammit, he'd told her to stay out of sight, warned her again and again.

Fists clenched, Jack entered the fray. The other man's head snapped back with the first punch. Jack was beginning to think he'd outmaneuvered him when a gun appeared in Carlos's hand. Only, it wasn't Jack he pointed the pistol at but Marcie.

"No!" With a cry of outrage, Jack leaped in front of the other man and took the bullet. He felt its impact, the searing pain and the instant knowledge that he'd really done it this time. After all those lucky escapes, eluding death, it seemed his luck had run out. He was too late. This time he would die.

Ah…now he understood. It was all plain to him now. His death, giving up his life so someone he loved might live, was what had secured him a place in heaven. The throbbing pain in his shoulder didn't seem nearly as intense anymore. He'd saved Marcie....

"Jack, oh, Jack, you're burning up with fever."

He opened his eyes, expecting to find Marcie gazing down at him. Instead, it was Lorraine. He blinked, confused.

"Where am I?" He wasn't sure he'd said the words aloud until she answered.

"In the middle of the Gulf of Mexico. Oh, Jack, I don't have a clue where we are. We're just drifting—the engines are off. I haven't seen land in two days.... But at least it's not raining right now."

Despite his determination to keep his eyes open, they slowly closed. He yearned to tell her not to worry, everything would work out, but the ability to speak had been taken away. He could rest easy now. Marcie was back with her husband and children, and Lorraine was safe, too. Safe from Carlos and safe from him.

The torrential rain beat down on them with a vengeance. Sitting on the deck beside Jack, Lorraine held a vinyl slicker over their heads until the muscles in her upper arms cramped in protest.

The slicker offered little protection, but at least it kept the rain off Jack's face.

The storm had raged on and off for two days. Every time the downpour slackened, she'd thought it was over—and then it would start again. Lorraine had never experienced such misery. She didn't know which was worse, the weather or their predicament. Without land in sight, she hadn't any idea where they were or how to find out. If Jack died, Lorraine didn't know what her own fate would be.

She wanted Jack to live—and for a whole lot more than his navigational skills. She owed him so much, more than it was possible to repay. Every time she thought about his being shot, saving her from Carlos, her chest tightened with emotion.

She was afraid he'd die.

She was afraid she'd killed Carlos. And afraid she hadn't.

She was afraid she'd gotten them so completely lost even Jack would never find the way back and they'd die at sea. If someone did manage to rescue her, she feared no one would believe in her innocence and she'd spend years rotting in a Mexican prison.

Throughout the storm, Lorraine remained constantly at Jack's side, refusing to leave him as they drifted aimlessly out to sea.

For a few hours she entertained herself by trying to remember the plots of her favorite classic movies, scene by scene. *Brief Encounter. It Happened One Night. The Bishop's Wife. Sabrina.* And of course *The African Queen.* Movies she and her mother had loved.

She thought about her mother, too, and tried to hate her, then discovered she couldn't. She went over what she knew of her parents' marriage again and again until it made a crazy kind of sense. Her parents had loved each other, but unchangeable circumstances had led to their separation. From what her father had told her, he'd been in touch through the years, yet after a while Virginia had stopped responding. Stopped visiting. Lorraine remembered her mother taking what she said were business trips. Lorraine had stayed with Aunt Elaine for as long as a week. These trips seemed to make her mother sad, she recalled. She herself had been so young.

At some point in her childhood, her mother must have made a conscious decision not to move to Mexico. Since she was a devout Catholic, divorce was not an option for her. She must have made peace with herself and her past, and for whatever reason eased herself out of Thomas's life.

None of this explained why she'd never told

Lorraine the truth. And now Lorraine would never know, could only speculate.

Thoughts of her mother were complicated enough, but what she felt toward her father was completely confusing. All those years her mother had remained faithful. But Thomas hadn't. For all Lorraine knew, he could have fathered dozens of children. She didn't want to think about him, didn't want to dwell on his infidelities. Didn't want...

Lorraine wasn't sure when she fell asleep. Next thing she knew, it was morning and the sun shone down like a blessing from heaven. She opened her eyes and blinked at the brightness—and noticed that Jack's eyes were open, too. For a long time they simply looked at each other, as if taking in the fact that they were both alive. The urge to touch his face the way she had earlier was almost overpowering. She longed to wrap her arms around him, hold him close. She wanted to tell him how desperately afraid she'd been that he'd die and how she couldn't have borne the guilt of it. She wanted to tell him that beneath his disreputable exterior, he was a good man. What higher praise was there than that? A man who was honorable and good. *A man she was beginning to love.* But she told him none of these things.

Instead, she whispered "Good morning," in an unsteady voice as she struggled to conceal her relief and the accompanying rush of emotion. "How do you feel?"

"About what you'd expect."

"That bad?"

His grin was brief. "That bad. What about you?"

"I'm okay." She ached in places she didn't know it was possible to ache. But then, she wasn't accustomed to sleeping in an upright position.

"The gunshot," he said hoarsely. "How bad is it?"

"Bad enough." She wouldn't lie to him. "But not nearly as critical as it could have been. The bullet's still there. Removing it would've done too much damage. You'd lost a lot of blood as it was."

"The bullet's still there?" He arched his brows. "Does this mean I'm going to set off airport metal detectors?" He gave her an infectious grin.

"I guess you'll have to find out."

His eyes held hers. Then he reached up and pressed his hand to her cheek. "Thank you," he whispered. The gesture was one of tenderness and unspeakable warmth. Her hand joined his and she blinked back tears, wishing she knew how to tell him that she admired his courage and his honor. That she was grateful he'd taken it upon himself to help her when it would have been just as easy to refuse. She closed her eyes, wanting to savor this moment, hold on to it forever. Her pulse steadied. Reality returned.

During the worst of his fever, he'd called for another woman, someone he obviously loved and cared for deeply. A woman who was—or had been—an important part of his life.

Briefly she considered asking about Marcie. And she considered correcting the impression that she was a married woman. But for his sake, as well as her own, it was better to let him believe she had a husband back in Louisville.

The feelings between them were too intense. And the situation was far too difficult. This relationship had no hope of any future, and rather than allow it to follow a path that would only bring them pain, she regretfully removed her hand from Jack's. He seemed to realize what was happening and lowered his arm to his side.

"I shot Carlos," she told him, thinking a bit of good news would cheer him up.

"Did you kill the son of a bitch?"

"No, but not from lack of trying. I got off six shots," she added proudly.

He grinned at that.

"Best I can figure, though, I only grazed his upper arm."

"I hope he's in more pain than I am."

"Me, too."

"How'd you get us away from Pucuro?"

She turned away. "You don't want to know."

"Ah, but I do."

"It's a story for another day," she said firmly. Suddenly tears blurred her eyes again, no matter how hard she tried to blink them away. "Let me see about making you more comfortable."

"Raine."

"Don't call me that." She sniffled and wiped her cheeks with one hand.

"You're crying," he said, ignoring her protest.

"Am I?"

"Yes."

"Then these are tears of...of joy."

"Joy?" His question was accompanied by a frown.

"You're going to live, Jack. You're going to be okay."

Carlos Caracol cursed and gritted his teeth as Camelia cleaned the blood from his upper arm. "Stop," he commanded. He jerked with the pain. He'd gone three days without medical care, and infection had set in. The throbbing in his arm was bad enough to bring him to Camelia, a woman he knew he could trust.

"I said stop," he growled.

"Do you want to lose that arm?"

"No."

"Then let me finish," she said with perfect calm.

This was what he liked most about Camelia—he didn't intimidate her. He'd known the first time he met her that this was a woman worthy of his attention, and he'd been right. It was of little concern to him that she was married. As it turned out, the fact didn't bother her, either. Her youngest son, a three-year-old, looked a lot like him. Carlos didn't want any family responsibilities, but it pleased him to know he'd fathered a child with her.

Squirming on the chair in her kitchen, he submitted his arm to her again. He closed his eyes and concentrated on the tantalizing scent of meat and spices simmering on the stove. It'd been the better part of a week since he'd enjoyed a decent meal. Longer since he'd enjoyed the pleasure a woman could give.

He grimaced as Camelia dabbed some sort of stinging liquid on his arm. The throbbing was worse than ever. But the pain Carlos felt was more than just physical sensation. That American bitch had done it to him again. Whenever he found her, her male friend wasn't far behind. Those two were becoming a nuisance, but what they didn't realize was that no one made a fool of Carlos Caracol and lived to tell about it.

"Be still," Camelia said, her voice sharp.

His eyes flew open.

"You're tense. Relax."

"Give me something to take away the pain." He eased his free hand under her blouse and reached for a plump breast.

"Not now," she said, and slapped his wrist.

Carlos frowned. To hear her talk anyone would think she was married to him. "Do you have a headache?" he scoffed.

Her saucy grin was enough to assure him that wasn't the case. "With you? Never."

His mood lifted. "Good."

"Later, after your arm is clean."

"And I've eaten."

She continued to dab at the wound. He swore she used straight whiskey. Every place she touched him, his skin burned.

"Are you going to tell me who did this?"

"No."

"Man or woman?"

Carlos hesitated before answering. "Woman."

Camelia's reaction told him he should have lied. She broke into a hearty laugh and shook her head. "I always thought a woman would be the end of you, except I thought it would be me. Did you want her?"

"No," he growled, deciding to lie. He did want the bitch, but only to show her what it was like with a real man. And to punish her.

"You lie."

The problem with Camelia was that she knew him too well. He grabbed a thick swatch of her hair, twisted it around his fist and yanked hard.

"Ouch." Her eyes widened with surprise.

"That bitch is going to regret the day she ever laid eyes on me." Each word was distinctly pronounced.

He was gratified to see that Camelia got his message. "I pity her," she whispered.

He grinned, his ego bolstered by her words. "I'll make sure that when she dies, she's most grateful."

Eleven

"What's this?" Jack demanded as Lorraine spoon-fed him broth.

"Soup." Jack wasn't a good patient, but she'd expected that. He was impatient with the time it took to regain his strength. His complaints were constant. He hated being incapacitated. Hated relying on her help. Hated being weak.

"Pretty sorry excuse for soup if you ask me," he muttered, opening his mouth for another spoonful.

"You appear to be eating it."

"Do I have a choice?"

"Nope." She grinned, and to her surprise he did, too. Their eyes met, and neither seemed willing to look away. It had been like this from the moment he'd regained consciousness. This awareness, this appreciation. Countless hours she'd remained at his side, nursing him, lending him her will, her strength...her heart. He didn't need her determination to survive; his own was strong enough. But her heart—that he kept, and although they never mentioned the growing awareness between them, they both knew it was there.

Jack's eyes roamed her face, and Lorraine started to tremble at the warmth in his gaze. She made herself return to the task of feeding him, but her hands shook too badly and she had to stop for a moment.

"When can I have real food?"

"Soon," she promised. Without antibiotics to help combat infection, his body required more time to heal. He needed a great deal of sleep, too, and it frustrated him that he only seemed able to stay awake an hour or so before drifting off again.

Time lagged for her while he slept. In the past few days she'd read every piece of printed material on board. Twice. She'd laundered all his clothes and appropriated a couple of shirts and a pair of drawstring cotton shorts for herself. She'd cleaned, scrubbed and reorganized the entire living quarters. It was apparent from certain things she'd found while cleaning—small gifts, cards she shouldn't have read but did—that Jack maintained a number of ongoing relationships with women around the Caribbean. This confirmed the decision she'd already made: it would be best to let him continue believing she was married. Besides, she couldn't come up with an easy way to tell him there really wasn't a husband, after all. He'd assumed it—she let him—and now she preferred to leave things as they were. And Gary…well, she'd agreed to marry him. She loved Gary, she truly did. She had no business contemplating for even two seconds any kind of liaison with another man. She'd taken to wearing his engagement necklace outside her shirt. Jack's shirt.

Jack would have been more comfortable below-decks in his own bed, but he'd rejected that idea, choosing to soak in the sunshine and fresh salt air. Lorraine made a bed for him on a chair that partially reclined, and he spent his time there.

"You forgot to untie *Scotch on Water* from the dock!" He chuckled.

Lorraine knew it had been a mistake to tell Jack how she'd managed to escape from Pucuro. He'd teased her about it more than once. Those were the only times his face showed signs of color. He'd lost a great deal of blood and was still deathly pale and very weak. She supposed she ought to be grateful that Jack seemed to find the tale of their escape so amusing.

He finished the soup, and Lorraine watched as he fought to keep his eyes open. "Sleep, Jack," she urged, ready to retire for the night herself. She slept belowdecks in his bed.

"I want to talk," he insisted, and clung to her wrist to keep her from leaving.

"Later," she promised.

"Don't leave for a few minutes, all right?"

"All right."

"I'll just rest my eyes for a little while and then we can…"

Whatever he was about to say was lost as he fell asleep. She didn't know what he wanted to talk about, and in some ways was grateful he'd been too weak. Her fear was that he'd bring up something better left unsaid.

The subject of her assumed marriage was like a lit fuse thrust between them. At times Lorraine wished she'd set him straight the first time he'd mentioned her "husband." But then she'd remember Gary, or something would happen to remind her how far removed Jack's world was from hers. There could be no future for them.

She should leave now, she realized, and go down below. Still she stayed at his side, watching the moon's reflection on the water. She might simply be rationalizing her feelings, but really, it made perfect sense, under these circumstances, that she'd be attracted to Jack. He'd saved her life and she'd saved his. Such a bond between two people couldn't be ignored.

They'd created a genuine friendship in the days he'd been so terribly sick. Or so Lorraine believed, anyway. They'd talked about many things, and he'd given her glimpses of his life before *Scotch on Water*. It didn't surprise her to learn he'd been a mercenary. He'd worked with a group of men who'd called themselves Deliverance Company. Apparently he'd had deep friendships with these men.

Lorraine did her share of talking, too. She told him about her childhood, growing up without a father, and about her mother. But describing her life with Virginia made her sad, and she quickly changed the subject to her favorite movie plots. He hadn't seen many movies in the past few years, and she delighted in recalling the ones she treasured and watched again and again. She'd thought about some of them recently, so retelling *The African Queen* and *Casablanca* was—admittedly—a chance to show off. His reactions were everything she could have asked for. These movie sessions were the most fun she'd had since before her mother died. She particularly enjoyed narrating the plot of *Romancing the Stone*, which he'd never seen. It wasn't hard, somehow, to imagine the two of them in the lead roles....

There were more personal stories, too. That very afternoon, in fact, she'd asked him about his scars. He explained his injuries from the years he served with Deliverance Company and then wanted to know if *she* had any. Only one, she'd told him, from a broken arm that had required surgery. She'd been horsing around with friends, demonstrating her skill sliding down a staircase railing. Unfortunately she'd toppled and tumbled down an entire flight, landing on her right arm. The experience had taught her a certain caution.

Lorraine waited, watching him sleep. His breathing evened out and she started to ease away from his side and slip belowdecks. To her surprise his grip on her wrist tightened.

"Don't go," he whispered, but his eyes remained closed.

The night, with moonlight glowing on the water, was almost unearthly in its beauty. "Lie with me a while," he urged. He slid over to give her space.

Resting her head against his good shoulder, she lay beside him. Jack wrapped his right arm around her and she draped hers across his middle.

This quiet intimacy between them was exquisite. Without speaking of it, they both seemed to recognize that this was time set apart. Even when she was certain Jack had fallen into a deep sleep, she didn't leave. She hadn't been this content in days. Weeks. She'd found a haven in this stranger's arms.

Except that he wasn't a stranger anymore....

Lorraine awoke and the world was dark. The boat pitched aimlessly about the gulf, going wherever the currents took her. Stars glittered in the inky sky—more stars than she'd ever seen.

She'd lain there for some time, soaking in the beauty and peace of these moments, before she realized Jack was awake, too. His arm was around her and her head was tucked beneath his chin, which he rubbed softly against her hair. It was the kind of thing a lover would do. Tilting her head back, Lorraine looked at Jack. Their eyes met, and the way he stared at her filled her with longing. She wanted him to kiss her.

He wanted it, too. She saw it in his eyes, in the avid way he studied her mouth. She swallowed, almost groaning with the need to feel his lips on hers. His hand, which lay gently against her ribs, rose slowly until it reached her breast. Earlier that evening she'd removed her bra and donned one of his clean shirts as a nightgown, and now Jack's hand encountered bare skin. His eyes widened as his knuckles grazed her nipple, and he paused. Held his breath. So did Lorraine.

Neither pretended that touch hadn't happened. Neither looked coyly away. He did nothing to disguise his own body's reaction. He wanted her, and her heart rejoiced.

He lowered his head as if to kiss her, but stopped himself just before their mouths joined.

"Tell me about your husband," he whispered.

Lorraine wasn't sure how to answer him. If she told him the truth now, she feared the temptation would be more than either of them could resist.

He'd kiss her and she'd welcome his touch. Before long, they'd be lovers and that would be a mistake she couldn't afford. There was too much she didn't know about Jack. Too much she didn't *want* to know. He had a wild and dangerous side, like the heroes in her favorite movies. A relationship with Jack could never last. She'd end up being just another of his women. Nor would she betray Gary....

"What...do you want to know?"

"His name."

She hesitated. "Gary. Gary Franklin."

"You kept your maiden name? Dancy?"

"Yes," she whispered.

"Does he call you Lorraine or Raine?"

"Lorraine." She didn't want to discuss Gary. Her fiancé seemed far removed from these weeks with Jack. Out here in the middle of the Gulf of Mexico everything about her life in Louisville, including Gary, seemed unreal.

"What does he do?"

"He's a manager for a medical-supply company." She recognized what Jack was doing. He was trying to create a sense of Gary as a man, as a real person and not merely a name, in an effort to stem the potency of their attraction. It wasn't working. Had she offered him her lips just then, he would have kissed her. It was what they both wanted, their hunger so strong it seemed to pulse between them.

"Does he love you?"

She had trouble forming the word, and it came out sounding scratchy, uncertain. "Yes."

"Enough?"

It hadn't been easy for Gary to stand aside and let her search for her father on her own. He'd wanted to travel with her, but she'd discouraged that. As it turned out, she wished he *had* come, then none of this would have happened.

"Does he love you enough, Lorraine?"

"Yes," she whispered, and her voice broke.

Jack eased his hand away from her breast, slowly, as if he knew he'd never touch her again.

Lorraine worried her lower lip. There was no going back now. Continuing the lie had sealed their future.

Lorraine refused to make the same mistakes her mother had. In a way, it was that simple. When the time came, she'd return to Louisville and go through with the wedding. She'd have Gary's children and live a good honest life. It was what she wanted. What she needed. Her mother would have approved.

Jack awoke to find Lorraine no longer at his side. It was just as well, he acknowledged, but he couldn't quite make his heart believe it.

Ever since Marcie, Jack had avoided emotional entanglements. There were a couple of women he saw on an occasional basis, but both were the type who neither wanted nor expected any kind of commitment. Jack was content with his life-style. He didn't know why he found it necessary to keep reminding himself of that. Until recently he hadn't even *liked* Lorraine. He'd considered her prissy, stubborn and self-righteous. Furthermore, she was married.

Lorraine hadn't changed. And she was still married. The difference was in how he viewed her. In the days since they'd left El Mirador, he'd come to know her and realize she was caring, generous, amusing, brave, beautiful—with each day the list grew longer. But she was the same person she'd always been.

The physical differences were the more noticeable. Her fancy linen jacket had been replaced by one of his shirts, the ends tied at her waist, revealing tantalizing glimpses of midriff. The linen pants were gone, too. Instead, she wore a pair of his shorts and walked barefoot. Half the time it was all he could do to keep from staring at her legs.

Her hair, once so perfect with every strand in place, was gathered into a ponytail. Over the past few days she'd acquired a rich golden tan. Rarely had he seen any woman more physically appealing.

While he'd been drifting in and out of consciousness, she'd remained continually at his side. Jack couldn't remember any time he'd awakened and not found her there. Her smile was gentle, her words encouraging, her touch tender. The truth was, in all his life, Jack had never had anyone care this much about him.

And sometime during the past few days, he'd fallen in love with her. In love with a woman already married to another man.

In a different situation, he would have made his escape. Fled temptation. Gotten the hell out of her life before he screwed it up beyond hope. But now there was no place to run. They were trapped on this boat together.

One other option was to make her hate him, freeze her out, be cruel. Say or do something that would keep her at arm's length. But Jack discovered he couldn't. He was half-inclined to credit his lack of resolve to his weakened condition, but that was a lie, and he knew it. He was in love with Lorraine, and loving her prevented him from saying or doing anything that would bring her pain. That included what he wanted most, which was to touch her the way a lover would. Kiss her, make love to her, cherish her.

He cursed his weakness the night before, when

he'd touched her breast. He'd wanted to do a hell of a lot more and was fully aware that she would have let him. He also knew that in time she'd come to regret it. When she returned to her husband, he vowed she'd go undefiled, without remorse, free of guilt.

What made his love for Lorraine beautiful, Jack reflected, was its purity. His relationship with Marcie and every other woman in his life had found its existence primarily in the physical.

Not so with Lorraine. Their relationship had a physical dimension, but more than that, it had an emotional depth, even a spiritual one. He was a man who'd lived his life on the edge, emotionally distant; now he found himself in unfamiliar territory.

"Morning," Lorraine greeted him as she stepped onto the deck with breakfast. It was ten days after the shooting. "How are you feeling?"

"Better." The first thing he noticed was that she didn't sound quite like herself. He couldn't stop looking at her. Sunlight surrounded her, giving her an angelic appearance. He wondered wryly if God planned to teach him a lesson and had sent Lorraine to torment him with all the might-have-beens.

Carrying the tray, she stepped out of the sunlight. Jack's gaze narrowed when he saw her face. Something wasn't right. She wasn't good at hiding her emotions. It was one of the traits he found so wonderful about her.

"Raine." He always called her that when he wanted a reaction.

She either ignored it or didn't hear him. "I brought your breakfast."

"What's wrong?" He favored the direct approach.

She frowned at him as if she wondered how he knew.

"Tell me," he ordered. He moved over, making space for her on the chair.

He read her hesitation. Then with a deep sigh, she sat down next to him. "Remember I told you I first tried to remove the bullet with tweezers?"

He nodded.

"Well...the tweezers were in my makeup case. I was in a hurry and I dumped out my purse on the mattress. I remember seeing something odd then, but didn't take time to examine it. And afterward I just scooped everything up and put it back."

"Something odd?"

"A...gold object. I didn't know what it was or how it got into my bag, but it didn't seem important at the time. I'm constantly putting things in my purse for one reason or another. Earrings, that sort of thing. I thought it might be a broken earring or a pin I'd forgotten. I didn't think twice about it.''

"What is it?''

Lorraine reached for his hand and squeezed his fingers hard. "I...can't tell you for sure what it is, but I can guess. And I have a strong suspicion about how it got there.''

"How?'' he urged.

"Jason Applebee. I'm afraid it's another artifact. Another of those star things.''

It'd been over a week now, and no one had seen or heard anything of Jack Keller or Lorraine Dancy or *Scotch on Water*. Jason had run the risk of capture and worse in his efforts to locate the woman—or more important, her purse. He was afraid she'd discovered the Mayan artifact he'd hidden inside the small zippered bag. If she hadn't already found it, then it was only a matter of time.

At least he'd been smart enough not to plant both pieces in her luggage. That would have been disastrous. To lose one half of the Kukulcan Star was bad enough, but both would be unthinkable. Intolerable. Too many people had died already. Mostly by his hand. Jason had put himself at risk time after time and refused to be thwarted now.

This penchant for killing had come as a surprise. Jason hadn't realized he had any appetite for it. He'd prefer to avoid it, of course, but he'd learned that when it was a matter of getting what he wanted murder came easy. Easier than he would have dreamed possible.

From the time he was a kid, archaeology had fascinated him, especially anything concerning the Maya. He'd studied it exhaustively, obsessively. As a teenager he'd come to believe—to know—that he was the Mayan god Kukulcan reincarnated, waiting for the right time to reveal his true identity. Kukulcan was, among other things, endowed with a huge penis. Unlike him, though, Jason hadn't taken a vow of celibacy. Hey, why should he deprive himself of sexual pleasure? Frankly he couldn't see any reason not to indulge. In the end Kukulcan had broken his own vow and was overwhelmed by guilt. He'd set out on a snakeskin raft and sailed toward the east. According to myth, the raft had then burst into flames that consumed him. His heart rose heavenward and eventually merged with the sun. One day, it was said, Kukulcan would come back, and Jason had found the key to his promised return. He'd stolen the archaeological find of the century.

He felt his anger rise as he remembered that he'd already lost half the Star; he'd learned from the press and the radio that it had been returned to the museum—which meant it was more crucial than ever that he get the other half back.

But that half was in the possession of a woman,

an imbecile who hadn't a clue what she held in her hands.

Jason had called upon every resource available to him, to no avail. It was as if *Scotch on Water* had disappeared off the face of the earth, as if Lorraine and Jack Keller had vanished. Perhaps they'd been engulfed in a fiery plume themselves and drifted toward the sun. But they would resurface one day, and when they did, Jason vowed he'd be waiting for them.

"Let me see it," Jack said. He resisted the urge to touch Lorraine, to reassure her. He noticed that a strand of hair, so neatly tucked behind her ear, had escaped, and finding the impulse too strong to withstand, he replaced it.

Her eyes met his and she reached up to clasp his hand. Their fingers entwined and she leaned forward and braced her forehead against his good shoulder.

"Hey, what's got you so worried?" he whispered. "Your friend isn't going to find us. Hell, *I* don't even know exactly where we are."

Lorraine's only response was a tremulous sigh.

"Get the artifact for me," he said, "and I'll take a look and tell you what I know." Living in Mexico, Jack had learned a fair amount about Mayan mythology and culture.

Lorraine left him with obvious reluctance and

returned a couple of moments later. "Here," she said, and handed him a three-pointed gold object about the size of a silver dollar.

Jack turned it over in his hand and felt his excitement growing as he began to understand the significance of what he held. "Good God," he whispered.

"What is it?"

"Let me ask you something first. Did you see the artifact the police found in your luggage?"

"No."

"Did anyone tell you anything about it?"

Lorraine paused. "Jason was talking to me at the time, and everyone else was speaking Spanish. But I do remember them mentioning a Mayan god." She paused, as if going over the conversation in her mind, then shook her head. "I can't recall the name."

"Was it by any chance Kukulcan? Or Quetzalcoatl?"

She frowned. "That might have been it—the first one. Why?" She stared at the gold piece in her hand.

"If this is what I think it is, you're holding the lost half of the Kukulcan Star."

"A star," she repeated. She turned it over in her hand. "I see where it could be a star—I guess."

"Each half has three corresponding points," he

explained, taking it out of her palm, "and the two halves link together."

"Who was Quetzalcoatl?" she asked, the name stumbling awkwardly over her tongue. "The other one you mentioned."

"In most of Mexico he's known as Kukulcan, and he's half man and half myth. There's a lot of conflicting information about the Plumed Serpent, as he's also called. And it seems there were two Mayan leaders who took on the name Kukulcan, as well, and were looked on as gods. In any event, the Mayans believed this deity, the original one, descended from heaven and presented their society with the concepts of love and patience. He was said to have united them into a confederation of tribes.

"Unfortunately this state of utopia didn't last long. He was tricked into breaking his vow of celibacy. Filled with guilt and regret, he set sail, promising one day to return. Only this time he promised to come back as the Morning Star, the symbol of regeneration and hope."

"Is this the Morning Star, then? Why is it in two connecting parts?"

"That I can't say, but if what I understand is correct, it solves the mystery of his supposed return. See these symbols?" He reverently handed her the artifact. "I don't know what they mean, but I do know that when the halves are linked, the secret is supposed to be completely revealed. I don't think the pieces ever *have* been linked. One half of the Star has been kept in a museum, since it was found in the 1930s.''

"Oh, my goodness!" Lorraine murmured, her hand to her mouth. "When I arrived in Mérida, I waited forever before I was able to clear customs. Someone said all the available agents were checking everyone departing the country, looking for a stolen museum piece.''

"Half of the Kukulcan Star," Jack said.

"You think this is the other half?" Lorraine asked.

"It has to be, if they found one in your suitcase.''

"You're right.''

"Once locked together and read," Jack went on, "these two pieces will open up all kinds of new discoveries into the culture of the ancient Maya." He shook his head. "Incredible, isn't it?''

Lorraine frowned, her fingers folded protectively over the half-star.

"Hey," he said. He lifted her chin until their eyes met. "What's wrong?''

"Oh, Jack, don't you know what this means?'' There was no disguising her fear. "Jason will do anything to get this back.''

"True." Jack wouldn't mislead her. But Jason wasn't their only worry. He knew any number of men and women who would kill for a mere glance at the missing half of the Kukulcan Star. "We have the advantage, though."

"How's that?"

"First of all, we've actually got it in our possession—and we're going to hand it over to the Mexican government."

"But, Jack—"

"And while we're doing that, we'll clear your name of any wrongdoing."

Twelve

Thomas Dancy was close to panic. He'd been absolutely sure Raine would be safely back in the States by now. He'd learned otherwise that afternoon after speaking to a man named Gary Franklin, who identified himself as Raine's fiancé. Something had gone wrong; he was convinced of it. But there was nothing he could do until he heard from Jack. Franklin had been full of questions and was justifiably concerned. The conversation troubled Thomas, but he couldn't put his finger on exactly what bothered him.

Now, as he walked home after a day of teaching, his steps were slow and heavy. His distress over Raine's seeming disappearance had sapped any strength he had left. His two oldest sons played outside in the yard, happily racing their toy trucks around hills of dirt. When they noticed Thomas, they gave a shout of joy and ran toward him.

He caught Antonio in his arms and lifted him high above his head. The boy squealed with delight. Hector waited impatiently for his turn, but Thomas lacked the energy to lift him, too. Instead, he held his son tight against him and bent to kiss his brow.

Inside the house Azucena was nursing the baby. Alberto sucked vigorously, his tiny fists clenched tight. Thomas gazed on both of them with love. He kissed first mother, then child.

"What's wrong?" Azucena asked, studying him.

Thomas lowered himself into the chair beside her and sighed deeply. "A man phoned today looking for Raine. He said he was her fiancé. He's worried. She'd promised to contact him and hasn't."

"She isn't home yet?" Azucena's surprise was evident.

"Apparently not." Depressed and more than a little worried, he leaned back in his chair and closed his eyes.

"Is there any way you can get in touch with Jack?"

Thomas had already given the matter considerable thought. "No."

"What about his friends from Deliverance Company? They might know something."

Thomas mulled that over.

"You did all you could to help her," she reassured him in that gentle way of hers. "The matter is in God's hands now. Tomorrow I'll go to church to light a candle and pray for your daughter and Jack.''

Azucena could say her prayers and light her votive candles, but Thomas put no trust in religion. He'd turned his back on God in a Vietnam rice paddy; for him it was too late. All he could do for Jack and Raine was worry.

Later, it seemed to him inevitable that the dream would return to him that night. Thomas awoke bolt upright in bed, screaming.

''Thomas. Thomas.'' Azucena wrapped her arms around him. ''It's a dream, my love, only a dream.''

''Not this time.'' His voice still shook. ''This was so...real.'' He clung to her and buried his face in her neck. Eyes closed, he savored her loving hands caressing his bare back.

''Tell me what it is,'' she urged. ''Tell me.''

He could barely say the words. ''Someone's about to die. I can feel it. I've felt it for a long time. First Ginny. Then Ernesto. Death comes in threes. It happened that way in Vietnam. I remember we lost two men within a day and we all feared we'd be next. Instead, it was my friend David....'' He paused. ''All that time, I was so damn scared it would be me. I didn't want to die. All I wanted was to go home to my wife and daughter.''

"The war's over. You have nothing to fear."

"It's Raine," he whispered. "Something's going to happen to Raine. I can feel it, Azucena. In here." He carried her hand to his heart and pressed her palm there. "Dear God in heaven, I may already have lost her and I don't even know her yet." He covered his face with his hands and wept helplessly as his wife murmured consolation and whispered prayers.

Jack could barely stand up without keeling over, but he insisted on starting the engines. No amount of arguing would persuade him otherwise.

As Lorraine had already discovered, Jack Keller was by far the most stubborn man she'd ever known.

With the wind beating against her face, she carried a cup of coffee to the flybridge. He sat there, intently studying the charts and comparing them to the readings on the boat's navigational equipment.

He smiled his appreciation when she gave him the mug. "Best I can figure, we're two days from land." He looked back at the chart and made a line with his finger. "See? We're about here, and we're heading straight through the Bay of Campeche to Alvarado. Then..." He glanced up. "Hey, what's that frown about?"

Lorraine didn't know. She realized she should

be happy, overjoyed. In a few days, three at the most, the artifact would be handed over to the authorities. Once that was done, Jack's friend in the government would help clear Lorraine's name. Before she knew it, she'd be back in Louisville with Gary.

"Lorraine?"

"I...I'm not sure."

He slowed the engines. With the utmost tenderness, Jack touched the side of her face and looked deeply into her eyes. His touch stirred her, as it never failed to do, and she lowered her lashes. Since the night they'd lain together, they'd avoided touching, both afraid it would lead to more. A caress. A kiss. It was as if an invisible line had been drawn, and they'd both agreed never to cross it.

"I won't let anything happen to you."

She nodded, trusting him as she'd never trusted anyone.

"No one's going to arrest you, either."

Rather than explain the truth, she let him think she was worried about meeting the authorities. But her fears had little to do with that...and everything to do with Jack.

All the promises she'd made to herself—to avoid her mother's mistakes, to return to her simple well-planned life—didn't seem to mean much anymore. Gary and her life in Louisville were a world away. And she had to force herself to remember she was engaged to marry him.

She couldn't leave Jack, she *couldn't*. The thought was intolerable. Maybe they could be together. Make it work. They were opposites in every way and their lives were completely different, but maybe... As soon as the idea occurred to her, she realized it just wasn't possible. It hadn't worked for her parents, and it wouldn't for her and Jack.

Then another idea sprang, fully formed, into her mind. A plan. She'd return to Louisville and give it a month or two, test her feelings, make sure that being with Jack was the right thing to do. She owed Gary that much—to return home and explain. He loved her and she'd loved him. When she felt certain that this was what she wanted, she'd go back to Mexico and find Jack. If he felt the same way, they could go on from there. Then and only then would she tell him the truth about Gary. He might be angry with her— she wouldn't blame him if he was—but he'd get over it soon enough.

"Lorraine?"

She stared at him blankly.

"Lorraine, what is it?"

"Nothing. Don't worry."

"You sure?" He tilted her face upward and looked closely into her eyes.

She managed to smile. "Positive."

"Okay." But he didn't seem convinced.

"You want me to steer for a while?" she asked, knowing he'd never admit he was tired, although she could see he looked pale and shaky. She tried to make the offer sound casual.

"All right," he said, but his reluctance was obvious. He set the course and turned the helm over to her.

She bit her lip to keep from suggesting he lie down and rest, knowing the mere notion might offend his stubborn pride.

But Jack lay down, anyway, which told her how exhausted he must be. He climbed down the ladder leading to the flybridge and nearly fell into his chair on the deck. Two minutes later he was asleep.

With nothing but open sea around her, Lorraine had plenty of opportunity to study Jack. Some color had returned to his face now. Damn fool. She suspected he'd been near collapse.

Jack's estimate of how long it would take to reach land was accurate. On the evening of the second day, they neared the town of Alvarado. Their supplies of fuel and freshwater were low; they couldn't have stayed out at sea much longer. Lights sparkled on the harbor waters, and the port had a welcoming festive appearance.

Jack eased *Scotch on Water* into a wide berth, and Lorraine heard him chuckling to himself as he secured the boat to the dock. She could guess all too well why he was laughing—because of what'd happened the last time he'd tied up to a dock. It wasn't something *she* planned to mention again.

"I'm leaving now," he announced as he came belowdecks.

Lorraine sat at the table with her arms crossed. She shook her head in disgust. "I can't believe you're doing this to me again."

"I will admit it's brave of me considering previous experiences."

Lorraine struggled not to smile. "You shouldn't be cracking jokes."

"I'll be twenty minutes. Half an hour at the most," he promised.

"That's what you told me before!"

"Lorraine, all I'm going to do is make a couple of phone calls. I'll talk to Dr. Efrain and—"

"I swear, Jack, if you're not back in twenty minutes, I'll come looking for you!"

His smile faded. "No, you won't."

"Be reasonable, Jack."

"No. It's too dangerous." His voice was steely. "And that's all there is to it."

"It's dangerous for you, too," she muttered.

"For the love of God..." He raised his eyes to

the ceiling. "All right, I *guarantee* I'll be back within thirty minutes."

And he was.

She'd glanced frequently at her watch while she waited. Exactly twenty-eight minutes later he returned to the slip. The boat rocked as he climbed on board. Painful experience had taught her to remain belowdecks until she knew with certainty that it was Jack. Smiling jubilantly, he hurried down the steps to join her.

"Everything's set," he told her. "A plane'll fly us into Mexico City first thing in the morning."

"We're leaving here?"

He placed a cloth bundle on the tabletop.

"Catherina is seeing to everything."

"Dr. Efrain is Catherina?" He'd mentioned his "friend" Dr. Efrain a number of times, but hadn't said a first name. A coldness seeped into her blood. In the process of cleaning, she'd found envelopes addressed to Jack in a woman's flowing hand. The return address had read simply *Catherina*. Some friend!

They'd been lovers. Lorraine knew it as surely as if he'd shouted the words. Anger burned through her. Anger and jealousy. She had no right to feel either of those emotions. None. Still...it hurt. She felt as though he'd cheated on her, been unfaithful. What nonsense, and yet she couldn't help it. Lorraine turned away, not wanting him to see her reaction.

"While I was in town, I picked up a few clothes for you. I made sure they're yellow."

"Thank you."

"Lorraine?"

Her voice must have betrayed her. "I thought you loved Marcie." The words were as sarcastic and belittling as she could make them.

He didn't answer for a moment. Long enough for Lorraine to regret her outburst.

"When did I mention Marcie?" The question was soft, close to her ear. He stood directly behind her and she squeezed her eyes shut to keep from turning into his arms.

"You thought I was her during the fever." She'd never asked him about Marcie. Nor had he asked her about Gary after that one night. Whoever Marcie was, Lorraine knew she'd been special.

"Did I mention anyone else?"

"No," she answered coldly.

"Catherina's...an old lover."

"So I gathered." She reached for the bundle of clothes and hugged it against her stomach.

"Lorraine, it's not the way it seems."

"You don't need to explain anything to me. Your love life is none of my business."

"You're right, I don't and it's not—but I *want*

to tell you. I loved Marcie, really loved her, but she married someone else. I came down to Mexico to forget. Not long afterward, I met Catherina.''

Lorraine longed to cover her ears. She didn't want to hear about his past lovers, not when *she* loved him.

''It was a fling...stupid, really. By mutual agreement we parted two weeks later.'' His tone was matter-of-fact, dispassionate.

''It's none of my concern. I'm sorry... I should never have said anything.'' Averting her eyes, she concentrated on unfolding the clothes and found she was pleased with his choices. He'd bought her a bright yellow peasant blouse with a scooped neckline and a matching yellow and turquoise skirt.

''I thought you might be more comfortable meeting Catherina in a dress.''

''Thank you,'' she said again. He'd even remembered shoes, a pair of rope and canvas espadrilles.

''I talked to your father, too.''

''Good idea,'' she said, thankful he hadn't expected her to speak to Thomas.

It was ending; she could feel it already. In a couple of days she'd be on her way back to Louisville. Soon their time together would be little more than a memory to Jack. This was all happening too fast.

"My name will be cleared?"

"Yes. Apparently when the first half of the Kukulcan Star was found and returned, they recognized that it was unlikely you'd been involved, considering when—and how—it was heisted. Applebee used you. And seeing that you now have the second half and you're surrendering it to the authorities, all is forgiven."

Once again she reminded herself that she had reason to be grateful this whole experience was coming to an end.

"There's more," Jack said. "If we hadn't been drifting at sea all this time we would've heard the news."

"What news?"

"Apparently the Kukulcan Star was discovered at an archaeological site. One of the Mayan temples near Mérida. The archaeologist who found it was murdered before he could hand it over to the Department of Antiquities."

"When did this happen?"

"A few days before you got to Mexico. And the museum theft occurred the night before. A guard was critically injured in that robbery. But they didn't find the archaeologist's body until last week."

"You don't need to tell me who the suspect

is," Lorraine murmured. She already knew the police were interested in Jason. And he'd told her himself that he'd been on a recent dig. He'd told her some complicated lie, too, about rescuing another worker to explain his injured hand. Another lie she'd been naive enough to believe... He'd managed to obtain both halves of the Kukulcan Star, but only had them long enough to pass off to her.

"What about Jason?" she asked. "Where do you think he is?"

"With half of Mexico on his tail, my guess is he's long gone."

Long gone, Lorraine mused. Like she would be herself. "By this time tomorrow I'll be free to return to the United States."

"So it seems."

Jack went quiet, as if he, too, had suddenly realized the implications of all that was about to take place.

"Within a month you'll have trouble remembering my name," she said, attempting a joke. One that fell decidedly flat. She turned her back to him and busied herself pouring coffee.

"I'll remember." All at once he was behind her, his hands on her shoulders. "I'm not going to forget a single moment."

"Sure you will." She tried to sound light, funny, but her words were more like a whimper.

He increased the pressure on her shoulders. "I'll remember. I swear it." His voice was husky with emotion.

Lorraine closed her eyes and leaned back against his chest. "I...I'm not going to forget, either."

"Swear it," he demanded.

"I swear it."

They stood together like that for a long time. Minutes? She wasn't sure. Long enough, in any event, to feel his love, its certainty, and yearn to share hers.

Lorraine didn't dare speak. She knew the instant she opened her mouth she'd reveal the truth. But she couldn't do that yet, couldn't tell him. Later it would all come out. Later she'd explain everything. But not now. Not when so many situations were still unresolved. Gary, her father, her problems with the Mexican police.... She needed a clear head. Distance. Time. She had to be very sure before she gave this man her heart. Because when she did, it would be forever.

Frustration was making him crazy. Jason sat in the corner of a dimly lit cantina in Campeche and nursed a glass of whiskey. He'd followed every lead, tracked down every rumor about a blond American woman traveling with Jack Keller, and each time he'd run into a dead end.

None of his bribes had paid off, either. He'd put the word out on the street, notified every contact and offered a large reward. Nothing. It really was as if they'd disappeared off the face of the earth.

His only hope was that she hadn't found the artifact, and that if she had, she'd been smart enough not to hand it over to the Mexican government. His jaw tensed as he thought of the Star being out of his reach again.

Once he retrieved the half in Lorraine Dancy's possession, he'd have to make another attempt to steal the original piece from the museum. They'd no doubt increased security, making his task that much harder. He *would* triumph, though; that was fated. Meant to be. When he got both pieces back, he'd read the Star for the first time. No one else. Him. His entire life had been building up to this moment. When he'd learned the god's secrets, he'd declare himself Kukulcan III. The living promise fulfilled at the beginning of a new millennium.

Under his leadership, the Maya would recover their former glory, and pilgrims from around the world would flock to his temples once again. Excitement blasted through him at the thought. Oh, yes, it was going to happen! He was so close....

Music swirled around him, and a couple of whores eyed his table, encouraging an invitation.

In other circumstances, Jason would have been interested. But not now.

"*Señor?*" A buxom woman strolled toward him. Jason had noticed her earlier. She placed her hands on the edge of his table and leaned forward, giving him a glimpse of her wares.

"I'm not looking for company," he muttered.

"I'm not offering."

Jason glanced up from his drink. "Then what do you want?"

"I've heard that you want to find an American woman traveling by boat. She's with a man by the name of Jack Keller."

She had his full attention now. "I'm listening."

"A...friend of mine had a run-in with them recently."

Well, well. This could be promising. "How recently?" he asked without emotion. Enthusiasm would cost him more than he was willing to pay a whore.

"Ask him yourself," she suggested, nodding toward the bar.

A lone man sat at the end, his arm in a sling. He was big compared to the other men around him. Ugly and mean-looking, to boot. In the States Jason would have taken him for a biker. Certainly he was the kind of man you crossed the street to avoid.

Jason peeled off a few new pesos and stuffed

them inside the woman's blouse. "Thank you, sweetheart."

"You can thank me again later if you like." She arched her brows, letting him know she might consider a quick lay.

"Sounds good, sweetheart," Jason lied. There were younger, better-looking hookers around. He might even see if he could find himself a blonde. He'd been smitten with Lorraine Dancy; it was a shame things didn't work out between them.

Whiskey bottle in hand, Jason walked over to the bar and claimed the empty stool next to the man with the sling. Tattoos covered his naked arms.

"I understand you ran across a couple friends of mine," Jason said in a conversational tone.

"Friends?"

"Let's just say I'm looking for them."

"So am I," the other man said. "You had better pray you locate your friends first, *señor*, because they'll both be dead if I find them before you."

"Really?" Jason murmured. "Any particular reason?"

"I got plenty of reason." He slammed the bottle down on the bar.

"Carlos." The older whore strolled to his side and slipped an arm around his waist. "You promised not to cause problems."

He glared at her, then laughed.

"The American woman shot him," she told Jason.

"The woman will die for it," Carlos snarled.

Lorraine Dancy had more guts than Jason had credited her with. He refilled Carlos's glass from his own bottle. "I don't have any fondness for the bitch myself."

Carlos stared at him, his look an open challenge. "And Keller?"

Jason shrugged. "He's disposable, too. Perhaps we could help each other, after all."

Carlos raised his glass in a silent toast. "Perhaps we can."

Dr. Catherina Efrain was a flawless beauty, perhaps thirty years of age. The much older Director of Antiquities, Dr. Marcos Molino, had joined her. Lorraine sat in the large government office in Mexico City with Jack beside her and tried not to stare at the other woman with her classic features and elegantly styled hair. Tried to push away all thoughts of Jack and this lovely Mexican woman.

"When I received Jack's phone call yesterday afternoon, I immediately talked the matter over with Dr. Molino and arranged for your flight to Mexico City," Catherina was saying. "Our government is very pleased and excited that you have given us this artifact."

"I'm grateful for your help." Lorraine noted that Dr. Molino was content to let Catherina do most of the talking. His English wasn't particularly good, while hers was nearly perfect.

"Our government is most grateful to you, Ms. Dancy."

"I'm relieved that I've been cleared of all charges." It was a heavy weight off her shoulders. Whether or not they believed her innocent was no longer a factor. The Mexican government had what it wanted.

"You have nothing to fear. Everything's been taken care of."

"Her plane ticket," Jack prompted.

"Oh, yes, I almost forgot." Catherina reached for an envelope on her desk. Dr. Molino nodded and smiled.

"I've booked you a flight out of Mexico City first thing in the morning. First class, naturally."

"Thank you, but that isn't necessary. I'm more than happy just to know the Kukulcan Star is where it belongs."

"And?" Jack was looking at Catherina.

Catherina's eyes met his. "I've also made arrangements for you to spend the night at one of the city's finest hotels. A suite has been reserved in your name."

"Oh, my." Lorraine pressed her palm to her heart. "Thank you. But that's far and above—"

"No, it isn't," Jack argued. "You returned one of this country's rarest treasures. You deserve a bit of star treatment. No pun intended."

"I've taken the liberty of ordering a limousine to drive you to the airport tomorrow. The driver will escort you directly to your gate." She hesitated, then turned to Jack. "Was there anything else?"

"The guard."

"Ah, yes, the armed guard."

"I'm going to be guarded?" Lorraine looked from Catherina to Jack and back to Dr. Molino. Once again the older gentleman merely smiled and nodded.

"There's no reason to take any unnecessary risks at this point," Jack told her.

"You'll have protection for the remainder of your stay in my country," Catherina assured Lorraine.

"Good," Jack said approvingly.

Catherina sighed and leaned forward. "Now for a bit of unpleasantness. I'm afraid news about the discovery of the second half of the Kukulcan Star has been leaked to the newspapers. It hasn't appeared in print yet, but..."

Jack muttered a four-letter word and added in a louder voice, "Dammit, how did this happen?"

"Such news is of significant interest to the people of my country. I apologize, but I'm afraid that holding back the story for more than twenty-four hours is impossible now.''

"We're safe," Lorraine said. "Actually, the sooner it's published, the better." It would no longer be worth Jason's while to come after them, since the artifact had already been handed over to the authorities. And if he hadn't learned that already, he would within a day.

Jack caught her gaze and they smiled at each other.

Catherina looked pointedly at Lorraine's wedding band, then glanced at their faces. She seemed to adequately size up the situation. "So, you two have had quite an adventure."

Neither commented.

"There'll be no mention of Lorraine's name in the news?" Jack asked.

"None," the other woman promised.

"Good." Jack relaxed.

"Nor the hotel," Catherina said as she stood and extended her hand to Lorraine. "Again, my country and my government are most grateful for your assistance. We regret the misunderstanding that occurred earlier and pray that you'll accept our sincere apologies."

Dr. Molino stood, too, and they exchanged handshakes all around.

Lorraine was overwhelmed by the Mexican government's generosity. The first-class air ticket was wonderful, but what she was really going to enjoy was that hotel suite. The first thing she intended to do was take a long hot shower. Then she was ordering a steak from room service, plus a glass of wine and the biggest dessert on the menu.

"I'll be in touch," Catherina promised, and Lorraine wasn't sure if she was talking to her or to Jack. She could only believe Catherina meant Jack.

The three of them left the administrative building together. "I'm glad that's over with," Lorraine said, heaving a deep sigh of relief. All night her dreams had been filled with potential disasters. So much had happened already that she couldn't help thinking something else would go wrong.

Jack didn't say anything.

Catherina summoned the cab that waited for them outside the building.

Lorraine climbed into the backseat, waving goodbye to Catherina. "Where to now?" she asked, almost giddy with happiness.

Her relief died at Jack's sudden change of attitude. He sat as far away from her as possible. "I'll ride with you to the hotel." The crispness of his tone told her this was the end. Deep in her heart she'd known that. She could already guess what Jack would do once they arrived. He'd see her to her room, make sure the guard was in place and then, with a brief farewell, he'd take his leave.

Neither of them said a single word during the entire cab ride.

Jack waited while she filled out the necessary paperwork at the front desk of the luxury hotel.

"I hope you enjoy your stay with us, Ms. Dancy. Oh, and there's a message for you." The desk clerk handed her a sheet of paper. She glanced at it and saw her father's name, then slipped the note in her pocket. She'd deal with this later.

"Thank you," she said, the words flat and lifeless. All at once she felt incredibly tired. Clutching the key to her room, she rejoined Jack.

"I'll just go up with you to confirm that the guard's where he's supposed to be," Jack said stiffly.

They were alone in the elevator. Emotion seemed to thicken the air until Lorraine found it nearly impossible to breathe. It really was over now. In a few minutes Jack would say goodbye.

Suddenly Lorraine knew she couldn't let it happen, couldn't let him walk out of her life. Not without telling him how much she loved him.

"Where will you go?" she asked.

"I have a hotel room."

"Here?"

"No." He didn't elaborate.

The elevator doors glided open on the fifth floor and Jack stepped out in front of her, his stance protective. The hallway was empty. Not until they approached the suite door did the man in uniform reveal himself.

Jack and the guard exchanged a few friendly words in Spanish. Jack hesitated a moment, then took the room key from her hand and unlocked the door. Apparently he preferred to speak to her alone.

Once inside, Lorraine waited. She knew what was coming, knew what he planned to say. They faced each other, but he seemed incapable of saying it. Silently she pleaded with him to kiss her. Just once.

As if reading her thoughts, he lifted one hand and touched her cheek. She closed her eyes and heard the unevenness of his breath—or perhaps it was her own.

"Don't go," she whispered. "Stay here with me. Tonight, just tonight."

"Raine, don't. This is hard enough." Even as he spoke he reached for her, hauling her roughly into his arms.

With a glad cry she parted her lips as he fiercely possessed her mouth. He pinned her against the door, the kiss raw and urgent. Lorraine clutched his shirt, needing to anchor herself. His tongue ravaged her mouth and still it wasn't enough to satisfy either of them.

Again and again he kissed her until all reason vanished. Then, abruptly, when she least expected it, he stopped and pulled away. His eyes roamed her face as if to gauge her feelings.

Lorraine boldly met his look and smiled. There was no turning back for them now and she knew it. So did Jack.

Thirteen

"I'm sorry to trouble you again, Mr. Franklin," Marjorie Ellis mumbled, her expression embarrassed.

Gary stepped into her office and sat down at her desk in front of the computer. He'd explained the basics of this program no fewer than five times and she still didn't get it.

"I realize I've been nothing but a bother to you since I took over this position," she went on, clenching her hands tensely.

"It's no problem," he said, trying not to sound exasperated. Then he smiled. She might be a technophobe and totally disorganized, but she made up for that with a multitude of other talents. Her order numbers were phenomenal. For the past two months she'd helped break the all-time sales records for his division. The truth of the matter was, Gary felt thrilled to have her on his team. She made him and the entire division look good.

"I'd like to repay you for all your help," she

said as she stood behind the chair, watching him correct the problem.

Hitting a couple of keys, he cleared her screen.

"Do that again," she cried, leaning closer to the computer.

She wore a light rose scent, he noticed, that was actually quite lovely. He wasn't fond of women's perfumes, but this fragrance seemed to fit her perfectly, without overpowering the senses.

"Here," he said, reaching for a notebook. He wrote out the sequence of commands. "If this ever happens again, you'll know exactly what to do."

"Great. Thank you so much, Mr. Franklin."

It seemed silly for her to call him Mr. Franklin. None of the other associates did. "Call me Gary."

A smile lit up her eyes. "I was serious about wanting to repay you for your patience. I mean, if you'd think it'd be appropriate and all."

"No thanks necessary."

"I knew you'd say that. You're one of the kindest, most thoughtful men I've ever met. LouAnn told me your fiancée's been out of town and I was thinking maybe you'd be interested in joining my son and me for dinner this evening."

Gary hated to admit how lonely he'd been with Lorraine gone. It disturbed him that he hadn't heard from her yet—but he wasn't phoning and checking up on her. No sir. Not after the way she'd reacted to his earlier concern. Still, he did, all too often, have to set aside niggling worries about her. Where was she? Was she all right? But the rest of the time he was convinced that she was just being stubborn, asserting her independence and her need for privacy.

"Sure," he said, accepting Marjorie's invitation before he could change his mind.

"My son's nine, and I'll have to warn you, he's real gung-ho about baseball."

"I like baseball myself," Gary told her. That was putting it mildly. He knew every major-league statistic for the past ten seasons.

"At the mere mention of baseball, Brice is likely to talk your ear off."

"I won't mind in the least." Gary had never been particularly interested in babies, but he happened to get along well with kids. Especially ones who liked baseball. "I'd be delighted to join you and your son for dinner."

"Great," Marjorie said happily. "I'm so glad you can come." She made it sound, somehow, as if he was doing *her* a favor. Not a bad feeling, he mused. Not bad at all.

His days were full here at the office, and he'd been dating Lorraine for the better part of a year now. Generally they spent some time together every day. With her in Mexico, a giant hole had opened up in his life. He'd tried to keep busy, but had run out of after-work projects within a week.

"Is six-thirty all right?" Marjorie asked, cutting into his thoughts.

"Perfect."

"All right, I'll see you then."

Smiling, Gary returned to his office. He sat down at his desk and pulled out the phone number Lorraine had given him. Once again he toyed with the idea of calling this place in Mexico, leaving a message inquiring about her. And yet he didn't want his future father-in-law to think he was the type who overreacted. Thus far, he'd resisted calling, but he wondered again if he should make some effort to reach Lorraine.

He released a long-drawn-out sigh and decided he'd give it a few more days.

That evening Gary arrived for dinner at Marjorie Ellis's place at precisely six-thirty. Grateful for the invitation, he'd brought a small bouquet of flowers and a bottle of wine.

Marjorie met him at the door, wearing black leggings and a long gray top. It was the first time he'd seen her outside of work. Dressed this casually, she took him by surprise; he hadn't realized quite how attractive she was.

She held open the screen door and he stepped inside. Her house looked a lot like her office—

definitely lived-in, unmistakably personal. Despite the clutter of books, plants and artsy objects, he was impressed with the welcome it exuded. "I hope you like lasagna," she said.

"Love it." His favorite. She couldn't have chosen a better meal.

"Great!"

A lanky boy in a baseball cap ambled into the room, wearing a glove on his right hand.

"You must be Brice," Gary said. "Your mom says you like baseball."

"Are you Mr. Franklin?"

"That's me," Gary said. "So what position do you play?"

"Shortstop."

"I played shortstop in college." Gary liked the kid already.

"You did?" Brice's eyes widened admiringly. "So did my dad, but he died."

Gary remembered hearing that Marjorie was a widow. Her husband had drowned in a boating accident three years earlier, but he couldn't recall who'd told him that. Marjorie had done a great job with the boy, that was easy enough to see.

"Would you like me to throw you a few balls?" Gary asked.

The boy beamed. "Can we, Mom?"

"I just put the lasagna in the oven so you have plenty of time," Marjorie said.

Her expression told Gary it wasn't necessary, that he didn't need to entertain her son; what she didn't realize was that he actually enjoyed this sort of thing.

"I'll call you when dinner's on the table," she said as Gary headed out the door with Brice.

Gary and the boy spent nearly an hour playing catch and talking sports before Marjorie called them in for dinner. In addition to lasagna, she served a garlicky Caesar salad, another of his favorites, and crusty French bread.

"This is one of the best meals I've had in months," Gary said with genuine enthusiasm.

To his amazement, Marjorie blushed, which struck him as quite endearing.

Brice disappeared with friends as soon as the table was cleared. Gary realized it was time he made his excuses, but found himself looking for a reason to linger.

Impulsively he tied an apron around his waist and insisted on helping with the dishes. "My mother always said those who cook shouldn't have to wash dishes."

"Nonsense," Marjorie protested. "It'll only take a few minutes."

"It's the least I can do." He plugged the sink, and before she could argue any further, filled it with hot, sudsy water.

"Gary..."

She started to protest again, only this time he plopped a handful of bubbles onto the end of her nose. Her eyes grew huge with shock. Gary couldn't seem to stop laughing. Nor could he stop himself from kissing her.

He hadn't intended it. But for one crazy second, he forgot about Lorraine, forgot he was going to be married in October. Forgot everything but the warm, wonderful woman in his arms.

He eased his mouth from hers, certain that she'd be upset. She had every *right* to be upset.

Marjorie stared at him, her lips moist from his kiss. Then she blinked a couple of times, looking bemused...and utterly charming.

"Should I apologize?" It was probably the most asinine thing he could have asked.

"I...I don't know."

"Let's pretend it didn't happen," he suggested. He dropped his hands from her shoulders.

"Okay," she said, and managed a weak smile. "Although I would like to say one thing."

He wasn't sure he wanted her to, but nodded, anyway.

"You're a hell of a good kisser, Mr. Franklin."

Somehow Marjorie had done it again. He'd acted on impulse, stepped out of character. She should chastise him, yell at him, throw him out on his ear. Instead, he left her home whistling, feeling better than he had in weeks.

* * *

Jack didn't know what had happened to break his resolve. He'd had every intention of saying his farewells and walking away. But when the moment came, he discovered he couldn't do it. His plan had been to see Lorraine safely to the suite, say a few words and be on his way. Even as he ran through all the familiar arguments about why they shouldn't make love, he was kissing her wildly.

Acting purely on instinct, Jack continued the deep slow kisses. He knew very well that these few hours would have to sustain him through all the lonely years ahead.

She whimpered.

Moaning, he dragged his mouth from hers. He'd dreamed of this endlessly, ever since the night she'd lain in his arms. They stared at each other and his breath rasped through his lips. He traced his index finger along her mouth, swollen now with his kisses.

She smiled sweetly and he was lost. He buried his face in her neck and filled his hands with her breasts. They felt hot and heavy in his palms, her nipples hard. He kissed each one in turn. Her head fell back and she slumped against the door. Her fingers were thrust deep in his hair.

Jack's first thought as they entered the bedroom was that this shouldn't be happening. *Couldn't* happen. If he loved Lorraine, he wouldn't allow it to continue.

"Lorraine, no."

She looked at him, her eyes wide and full of despair.

He broke away from her and sat on the edge of the bed. This was hard. Too hard. His body throbbed with the need to accept what she was offering. He couldn't bear the thought of turning away from her now. *But he had to.* This was the only way he had of letting Lorraine know how much he loved her. If he loved her any less, he'd be writhing on this bed with her. Any more, and it would kill him.

"Please…don't do this," she choked out. "Stay…"

"We can't."

She'd endured so much, been so strong. She'd fought off Carlos's attack, engineered a risky escape, nursed him through the effects of a gunshot wound. But she looked fragile just then, as if his refusal was the one thing she *couldn't* endure. Didn't she know? Didn't she realize? Walking out of this bedroom now was the only way he had of proving his love.

He moved away, heaving a deep sigh in an effort to regain his composure. When he turned around, he noticed that Lorraine had used the time to straighten her clothes. She stood at the foot of the bed and watched him.

"You're going to leave now, aren't you?" she asked, close to tears.

He nodded.

"Just like that?"

He hardened his heart. "Just like that," he said.

Her shoulders sagged with resignation. Jack knew firsthand how brave she could be. He loved that about her. He loved everything about her.

"Goodbye," he whispered. He'd taken one step when she hurled herself into his arms.

He knew he should leave while he had the strength. Instead, he closed his eyes and hugged her to him, savoring these final moments together, loving her so much it felt as if his heart would die without her.

She held him tightly and hid her face in his chest. "I can't let you go," she cried, clinging. "Not like this. I need to tell you about Gary and me."

"Don't tell me." His voice was harsh. This was exactly what he didn't want to happen. "Don't," he said again.

"But you need to know!" Her arms tightened with the urgency of her emotions.

"No."

"But—"

He gripped her upper arms and shook her once, hard. "No."

She went still. She looked down and her hair fell forward, blocking her face from his view. "This isn't the end," she promised in a broken whisper.

It had to be. Jack wouldn't allow it to be anything *but* the end. She had a husband who loved and cherished her, and Jack wouldn't allow either of them to betray that trust.

He released her. Then he turned and walked out of the room, his pace fast as he closed the suite door and headed for the elevator.

He was half a block from the hotel when Lorraine came running after him. "Jack, wait!"

He pretended not to hear her. The streets were chaotic, thronged with traffic. Cars honked, people yelled, buses spilled heavy exhaust fumes into the air.

"Jack! Please." Her frantic cry followed him. Jack walked faster.

"It isn't over," she shouted. "All I need is time. I'll be back. As early as next week. I'm coming back. Listen to me, I'll be back. Please listen."

He didn't turn around, just walked away as fast as he could.

Lorraine stood in the middle of the congested sidewalk and watched Jack disappear into the crowd. Her heart told her to race after him and make him listen to the truth, make him understand.

He loved her. He had to, or he would have taken her to bed. She couldn't have made her feelings or her desire for him any plainer. Physically she was frustrated, hungering for sexual completion. Emotionally, she was in mourning—and in awe. His actions told her more about the kind of man he was than anything else he could have done.

Jack was right to go. Out of fairness to Gary, she had to let him.

She needed a few minutes to regain her composure before she reentered the hotel lobby.

A shower first and then bed. Feeling emotionally drained, exhausted to the bone, she stepped into the elevator.

On the ride to the top floor, she reviewed a list of things she had to do. By this time Gary must be worried sick. She'd phone right away. She'd return her father's call later, she thought, pulling the message slip from her pocket. There was nothing on it but his name and the time of his call—this morning, at 9:45. But Jack would— She stopped, refusing to allow her mind to dwell on Jack. This was merely a short interlude apart. In a few days, she promised herself, she'd be back.

She rubbed her eyes tiredly as she inserted the key into the security lock. Pausing, she glanced over her shoulder, surprised to note that the guard was nowhere in sight. So much for the promised protection.

The door clicked open and she walked inside.

"It's about time you got here."

Jason Applebee sat in the living area eating grapes from a beautiful fruit basket.

The key fell out of Lorraine's hand and landed silently on the luxurious carpet.

"I hope you don't mind, but I helped myself. A very nice gift from your friend Catherina, by the way. You weren't going to eat all this fruit yourself, were you?"

"What are you doing here?"

He laughed at her question and slowly shook his head. "Come on, you're smarter than that, Lorraine. Why do you think I'm here?"

Fourteen

The shock of seeing Jason Applebee in her hotel suite left Lorraine stunned. It took her a long moment to recover.

"How'd you know where I was?" she asked with unreal calm. That was probably one of the less important questions, but the first to surface in her confused mind. "What about..." She swallowed her inquiry about the armed guard rather than alert him to the fact that there was one on the premises. She sincerely hoped the guard had gone for a sandwich—and that he'd return any minute. Jason had killed at least once and she didn't think he'd hesitate to do so again.

"Your father was quite informative," Jason told her before popping another juicy grape into his mouth.

"My father would never speak to you."

Jason's grin mocked her. "He would if he thought he was speaking to Gary Franklin, your *dear* fiancé who's so terribly worried because he hasn't heard from you." He mimicked a Southern accent. "We've had several *lovely* chats. He told me all about Jack Keller taking you to Mexico City. He even gave me the name of the hotel."

"You told him you were Gary?" The idea of him pretending to be her fiancé infuriated her. But she directed the brunt of her anger at herself. How she regretted that chatty bus ride from Mérida to El Mirador. What a fool she'd been to spill out the details of her personal life!

"Actually I thought I was quite clever," Jason said smugly. "Your father bought right in to that cornpone Southern bit."

"How'd you get my room number?"

"I have my ways." He glanced around and gave a low whistle. "Pretty expensive digs you've got."

"I want you out of here," she demanded, putting on a brave front. "You've done enough damage as it is."

"No problem," Jason said, and sprang to his feet. "Just give me what's mine."

Lorraine's heart sank. "I can't do that."

"Sure you can."

"How'd you get both pieces of the Kukulcan Star in the first place?" She had to find a way to distract him. The phones were out of reach; he'd grab her before she could get to one. Her only hope was to make a run for the door and pray the guard had returned. There was a chance, a small one, if she kept her wits about her.

"You know about the Kukulcan Star?" That appeared to surprise him.

"I have my ways, too."

He nodded approvingly. "So it seems."

"Really, I'd like to know," she said, pretending to be curious. A man as self-absorbed as Jason would delight in bragging about what he'd done. "You couldn't possibly have managed such a feat on your own," she murmured. She wondered if she was overdoing it.

Apparently not. "Ah, but I did. Suffice it to say I'd been studying Professor Raventos's books for years. When I wrote, he was impressed by my knowledge of the Maya and my appreciation of Kukulcan. The two of us struck up a friendship and he invited me along on the dig. He trusted me."

Lorraine had trusted him, too.

Jason shrugged. "Unfortunately, after he found the Star, my esteemed colleague became...redundant."

Lorraine shuddered, and he laughed.

"Some people assume it's luck, being in the right place at the right time. But it's not. It's careful planning. However, even the best-laid plans sometimes go awry. Sometimes another person interferes...." He advanced menacingly toward her. "Give it to me, Lorraine."

She backed slowly toward the door, arms behind her.

"I've killed for it before. I'd hate to hurt you, but if I have to, I will."

"What happened to you?" she asked. "You're smart. Why would you murder people? Why would you rob a country of its heritage? Is it greed?"

"You don't know, do you?" he asked, shaking his head. "You really don't understand."

"No. Explain it to me. Murder, Jason? *Murder?*"

He shrugged again. "Actually, the first time was the hardest."

"Oh, Jason."

He stretched out his hand. "Give me my Star. It's mine, and when I have it I'll reveal myself to my people. Glory will return to the Maya."

He was crazy. He had to be.

"I already told you, I can't." She was close to making her move.

Jason released an exasperated sigh. "I was afraid you were going to say that. Lorraine, you're a sorry disappointment to me."

"*I* am? You're the one who tricked me into lying on your behalf." She had to keep him talking. "You planted both artifacts on me. You knew

I hadn't seen my father since I was a child, and yet you purposely destroyed our visit. You're despicable. You—''

"Yeah, well, there are worse things. Like what's going to happen to you if you don't give me back my Star." He shook his head, his expression sorrowful. "It would be a pity. I've actually grown quite fond of you. In other circumstances we might have been very good...friends."

"I don't think so."

He chuckled, shaking his head once more. "Trust me, Lorraine, you want me to have the Star. The alternative isn't pleasant."

"Trust you?" She laughed incredulously. And then she ran out the door, slamming it in her wake. The first thing she noticed was that the guard was still gone. With no time to lose, she didn't even consider waiting for the elevator. Instead, she sprinted for the stairway. At the top of the stairs she caught sight of the guard's lifeless body. His throat had been slit.

Lorraine gasped at the sight. Fear and horror propelled her into action. She had to do something drastic or she'd soon be as dead as that guard.

Jason was directly behind her, but she had an advantage. Back in high school she'd learned how to slide down a stairway railing. It was quite a balancing act—and it was how she'd broken her arm. She hadn't tried it since then, but now...

What other choice did she have? She eluded Jason long enough to hop onto the metal railing. The difficulty was in maintaining her balance. Perched sideways, with her arms held straight out, she slid down the first railing.

Jason was quick; the sound of his feet bounding down the stairs echoed in the narrow stairwell. He could shoot her, she realized, but she was no good to him dead. He wanted the Star; what he didn't know was that she no longer had it.

The instant she started down, she screamed for help at the top of her lungs. Unfortunately she'd long since lost her travel dictionary and didn't know how to say it in Spanish. Not that it seemed to matter. No one heard.

She was a full staircase ahead of Jason when he shouted, "Don't make me do something I don't want to."

For all the racket she made, anyone might have thought she was being murdered right then and there. Still no one came. No one seemed to hear. She didn't want to believe that Jason would actually kill her, but after seeing the guard, she had no doubt he'd do it. He was insane. Completely and dangerously insane.

Lorraine stopped thinking after that, concentrating, instead, on her escape. Balance, slide, run across the landing to the next set of stairs. She did it three times, four. And never did she see or hear even a single person. Except Jason, who pounded remorselessly after her.

The stairwell came out by the pool. The area was filled with beautiful, tanned men and women lounging with grease-slicked bodies in reclining chairs, sipping tropical drinks and listening to a mariachi band.

Lorraine burst onto the scene, took a second to assess the situation and raced in the direction of the hotel lobby. She was shocked that Jason was so close behind her.

She had to hand it to him, he was quite the athlete. And quite the actor. He laughed and called after her in Spanish, words she couldn't understand. Most people weren't listening or paying attention, though, focused, instead, on the band.

Jason caught up with her between the pool and the entrance to the hotel. With almost no effort he threw her, kicking and screaming, over his shoulder and carried her off. His strength astonished her. He handled her as if she weighed next to nothing.

She started pounding his back like a madwoman. "Help!" she screamed, frantic to have someone, anyone, notice what was happening. "I need help! He's going to murder me!"

"If you ran up my credit cards, I would, too," a man, obviously half-drunk, yelled back.

"This is no joke," she screamed.

"It never is," the same man shouted.

All Lorraine's struggles accomplished was to tire her. After a while she gave up, convinced it was useless.

"The time for fun and games is over. Where's the Kukulcan Star?" Jason demanded once more through gritted teeth. His hands tightened painfully around her legs.

"I don't have it."

"All right, who does?"

"The Department of Antiquities."

"Lorraine, you don't know how this disappoints me."

"I'm sure it does. Are you going to kill me the way you did that guard?"

"Nope." He continued walking toward the street. "I'm afraid I like you too much for that." He set her feet back on the pavement. "Besides, I've already promised your friend here the pleasure."

When he put her down, she whirled around to see Carlos. The man's smile was as ugly as his face.

"Oh, did I forget to tell you I'd run into a friend of yours?" Jason asked ever so sweetly.

He was going to drown his sorrows in a bottle of good tequila, Jack decided. But once he sat down at the sidewalk restaurant, the desire to get drunk left him. He ordered a beer, instead. Drinking heavily would only compound his misery.

He recalled the last time he'd been in a cantina. La Ruta Maya. That was where Lorraine had left the boat and gotten herself into a mess of trouble. He'd been lucky to find her when he did. Relieved, too—not that he'd let her know it.

Then he thought about Pucuro, that nasty little town with its nasty little dock. Or rather, *without* it. He laughed outright at the image; he was only sorry he'd missed the actual experience. Several people turned in his direction, openly curious about what he found so amusing.

His last bottle of finely aged scotch had been used for medicinal purposes, more specifically to cleanse his shoulder wound. Lorraine had painstakingly nursed him back to health. He remembered their many conversations, about their lives and experiences, about movies, and the night they'd lain together and stared at the reflection of the moon in the water.

What Lorraine had taught him during their time together was his own capacity to make himself vulnerable to someone. He'd told her more about his background and soldiering experiences than he'd ever told anyone.

He wouldn't lie to himself about the pain he felt. It was as agonizing as anything physical.

Walking away from her had been the most difficult, dangerous thing he'd ever done. Dangerous because he wasn't sure he could become again the man he used to be. Without Lorraine and without his old beliefs, his old attitudes—where did that leave him?

He held up his glass and stared into the amber liquid, suddenly craving oblivion. All he could think about was Lorraine. Sitting in a sidewalk bar this close to her hotel made his thoughts inevitable.

Finishing his beer, he decided to catch a cab to his own hotel when he strolled by a telephone. Two steps past it, he stopped, turned and went back.

He dialed the operator and put the call on his credit card, then waited for the connection to Boothill, Texas, to go through.

His best friend's wife answered on the third ring. "Jack, is that you?" Letty shouted.

The connection wasn't the best. "It's me. Is Murphy around?"

"He's vaccinating calves, but listen, I'm glad you phoned. Someone by the name of Thomas Dancy called for you today."

"Thomas?" he asked in surprise. "I spoke to him last night." But, in retrospect, he realized that he hadn't given Thomas a number, a place to reach him. He'd only mentioned the name of Lorraine's hotel, not where he himself was staying. And Thomas would've been able to track down Murphy easily enough; on more than one occasion, Jack had mentioned Murphy and the cattle ranch he owned in the Texas hill country.

"What's this I hear about you escorting his daughter out of Mexico?" An infant wailed in the background. Their third in four years.

"I'll tell you about it later."

"Are you coming for a visit? Murphy would love to see you. So would I."

"I'm thinking about it," Jack admitted. One thing was certain: he had to leave Mexico for now. Get away from the memories and the pain. Reestablish his emotional equilibrium. "Give the kids each a kiss from me," Jack said, forcing himself to sound as if he hadn't a care in the world.

"Hold on just a minute," Letty pleaded. "I've got more news for you."

Jack heard a clank as she set the telephone aside. Almost immediately the baby's cries ceased. News? The last time Letty had something to tell him it was about the third addition to the family.

"Are you still there?" Letty asked when she got back on the line.

"I'm here," he said. He thought of joking that it was costing him five bucks a minute for her to burp the baby, but in reality he wouldn't have cared if it was ten times that amount. Letty and Murphy were as close as Jack had to a real family, and right now he needed them. Needed to know that couples in love could find happiness in this world.

"Okay," Letty said, "getting back to that call from your friend Nancy…"

"Dancy," Jack corrected.

"As long as you know who I mean. He was quite concerned about his daughter."

"There's nothing to worry about."

"Do you know anyone named Gary… Darn, I can't think of the last name. Anyway, he's connected to this Dancy's daughter, but I don't think he told me how. Not that it matters."

Jack stiffened. "I know who you mean. What about him?"

Her voice seemed to be fading, and then it grew loud again. "Dancy said he'd been getting phone calls from this Gary guy, and then today someone entirely different contacted him and claimed to be the same person. Your friend seemed rather concerned about it."

Jack's hand tightened on the receiver. "Go on."

"There's not much more to tell you. Dancy left a message at the hotel you mentioned, but you weren't registered and his daughter hadn't checked in yet. He didn't have any way of getting in touch with you, and he seemed pretty upset about all this. He told the first guy everything he knew about the two of you in Mexico City. Now he's worried, and rightly so, it seems.''

Jack's mind raced. It could only be one person. Jason Applebee.

''I've got to go,'' he said in a rush.

''Don't be a stranger, okay?''

''I'll visit soon. I promise.'' He replaced the receiver, then stood there thinking about what he'd just learned.

This adventure wasn't over yet.

Gary knew the minute he drove onto the freeway that he was going to Marjorie's house, even though his ostensible destination was the mall. He had the perfect excuse to stop by—a signed Ken Griffey, Jr., rookie card that Brice had been dying to see.

He intended to say something along the lines of dropping over because he was in the neighborhood. A stretch and certainly not very original, but he didn't care. He had to know.

Since their kiss, he hadn't been able to stop thinking about her. She dominated his every waking thought, and while they'd agreed to put the whole thing behind them, it hadn't happened. As a result, their working relationship was strained.

Their co-workers would soon guess, and to Gary's way of thinking, it was time to clear the air.

Saturday morning had found him restless and at odds. His original intention had been to do a little shopping...but then, why had he taken the baseball card with him? He didn't know who he was trying to fool. He enjoyed shopping about as much as he enjoyed paying taxes.

When he headed toward the freeway entrance, he admitted that seeing Marjorie was what he'd planned to do all along. Granted, his method lacked finesse. Stopping by unannounced and uninvited wasn't the most brilliant idea he'd ever come up with. On the other hand, maybe she approved of spontaneity.

He parked on the street, walked up to the front porch and rang the doorbell.

Marjorie came to the door. He could tell she was surprised to see him. "Gary...hi."

"Hi." He resisted the urge to say he'd made a mistake and hightail it back to his car. "Is Brice here?" He sounded like a kid, he thought irritably. "I have that baseball card I mentioned and I thought he'd like to see it."

She opened the screen door to let him in. "The signed Ken Griffey, Jr., card? I heard him talking about it to his friends."

She'd done it again—put him at ease. It seemed to be a specialty of hers.

"Brice has baseball practice on Saturday mornings."

Gary supposed he should have thought of that since Brice *had* mentioned it. But then it wasn't really Brice he'd come to visit. He knew he was staring at Marjorie and he couldn't stop. Even in a faded pair of jeans and a sleeveless top she was lovely. For the first time he noticed she had on a pair of yellow rubber gloves. One hand held a can of cleansing powder, the other a sponge.

"I was just about to take a break and have a cup of coffee," she said. "Would you care to join me?"

Gary nodded enthusiastically and followed her into the kitchen. "I didn't mean to interrupt your cleaning."

"I should thank you for dragging me away from it," she told him, peeling off the rubber gloves. "It's my least favorite thing to do."

He moved a stack of newspapers from one of the kitchen chairs and sat down. She poured them each a mug and sat across from him. She frowned, staring into her coffee as if she'd discovered something floating there.

He took a deep breath; it was time to speak honestly. "Showing Brice the baseball card was only an excuse," he said.

She glanced away from him.

"I know we agreed to forget about the kiss..."

"And I think we should," she said, still not looking at him.

"I can't." He couldn't be any more honest than that.

"Me, neither." Her voice was so soft he had to strain to make out the words. "But you're engaged."

"I know that." He didn't need Marjorie to remind him. But he hadn't heard a word from Lorraine, and when he'd finally broken down and called her father early this morning, the conversation had left him more confused than ever. Her father seemed to think Gary had phoned the night before. He hadn't, and said so. Then Thomas Dancy had gotten excited and insisted he had to get off the phone.

"Gary, it isn't a good idea for you to be here."

"I know that, too," he muttered. "I shouldn't have come...and yet I couldn't stay away."

"My lasagna's good, Gary, but not that good."

He smiled, and the tension between them eased. He reached across the table and took hold of her hand. "You're wonderful."

Pulling free, she walked over to the sink and stared out the window.

"Marjorie?"

She whirled around. "You're *engaged*—to someone else. I like you, Gary, more than I should, but I—"

"You like me?" His heart reacted with a surge of joy.

"Don't tell me you didn't know!"

"I didn't." He'd hoped, but that wasn't the same thing.

She closed her eyes and shook her head.

Gary used that moment to his advantage. He got up from the table and went over to her. He was tired of all this talk, all this craziness. The incredible kiss they'd shared earlier had been a fluke, or so he'd convinced himself. Nothing had ever been that good before. Not with Lorraine, not with any woman. He had to kiss Marjorie again, had to see if it was possible to experience this feeling more than once.

"Gary?" Her eyes widened as he pulled her into his embrace.

"Once more," was all he said, and then he lowered his mouth to hers. She groaned in welcome and that was all it took. Soon they were kissing with an urgency and need normally reserved for the bedroom.

Leaning against the sink, Marjorie clutched his shirt with both hands, as though she needed help to hold herself upright. By the time they broke apart, she was making soft whimpering sounds and his knees were weak. They stared at each other.

Marjorie's lips were swollen from the explosion of sensuality between them. Because he felt the need to touch her, Gary traced his finger down the side of her face and along her mouth. He didn't know whether he was doing it to apologize or to entreat her for another kiss.

She looked at him and smiled. Slowly, softly. It was his undoing. This time, however, the kiss was as gentle as the previous one had been uncontrolled. To his shock, it was no less sensual...and perhaps even more so.

"No more..." Marjorie broke off the kiss and leaned her forehead against his chest.

He longed to argue with her but didn't have the breath. If the kissing was this fabulous, he thought, still dazed, what would their lovemaking be like? She must be wondering, too.

Ignoring her protests, feeble at best, he unfastened her blouse and bra. Her breasts were full, and she whimpered anew when he drew one pouting nipple into his mouth.

Her hand stopped him when he moved to unsnap her jeans. "No."

It was a "no" that sounded more like a "yes." He gazed at her, questioning. "You don't mean that."

"I do." She seemed surer this time as she rebuttoned her blouse. "I think you should go now."

He blinked, certain he'd misunderstood. But

when she hurried to the front door and held it open for him, he was left in little doubt.

"Marjorie?"

She looked close to tears.

"Listen, I'm sorry."

"I'm sorry, too, Gary, more than you'll ever know."

"We need to talk." Leaving was the last thing on his mind.

"I can't... We're incapable of communicating any longer."

"That's not the way I see it." They'd been doing one helluva good job a couple of minutes earlier.

"Please go." She unlatched the screen door.

He had no choice but to walk out. Standing on the other side of the threshold, he tried to reason with her one last time.

"My letter of resignation will be on your desk Monday morning," she whispered, her eyes bright with unshed tears.

She gently closed the door.

Fifteen

The murderous look in Carlos's eyes told Lorraine the pleasure he anticipated in killing her. She knew with certainty that he intended to torture and rape her first.

Jason had shoved her into the backseat of a car and bound her hands, almost before she realized what he was doing. "Don't," she pleaded. "Don't do this."

Jason shrugged indifferently. "You brought it on yourself when you handed over my Star. Come on, you had to know I'd be looking for you."

"The Kukulcan Star didn't belong to you."

"Ah, but it does. The person it didn't belong to is you, but despite that you gave it away. You had no right."

Carlos jumped into the front seat and started the car, revving the engine loudly. The two men exchanged a few gruff words in Spanish before Jason reluctantly shoved back the seat and got into the front next to Carlos. No sooner had he slammed the door than the vehicle sped off, accelerating wildly. Lorraine was thrown from one side to the other as the car barreled around corners.

The traffic was horrendous. The hotel was actually situated on the outskirts of the city, closer to the airport. Tossed around as she was, all Lorraine could see were the tops of high-rise buildings, many with bright neon names and logos.

Once, when she did manage to sit up and look out the car window, she thought she might have seen Jack. Her heart instantly soared with hope, which faded almost as quickly. What she'd seen, she decided, was a man in a shirt similar to the one Jack had been wearing. The faint hope that he'd come to her rescue died a sudden death. It wasn't going to happen. He'd said his goodbyes and had no way of knowing the trouble she was in. If she survived this ordeal, it would be by her own wits. Ruthlessly hurled around the backseat of a fast-moving vehicle, hands bound, she had few options. But that didn't prevent her from planning her escape.

"Isn't there a way to negotiate myself out of this?" she asked Jason, thinking she'd appeal to his sense of decency, if he had one. That was highly questionable, of course, but anything seemed worth a try. They'd been on the road about thirty minutes. "I don't have any argument with Carlos," she began.

"You embarrassed him."

"Not on purpose. Tell him how sorry I am."

Jason relayed her message, to which Carlos responded with a hearty laugh.

"The only thing Carlos wants at this point is revenge."

"Where's he taking me?" She could see that they'd left the city proper and were now driving through a sort of shantytown, desperately poor, that went on for miles. At least an hour passed before they reached a two-lane highway that was freshly paved and seemed to lead directly toward the jungle.

Surely Jason had some idea what Carlos intended. She asked him.

"I wouldn't know," Jason said, as if it was of little concern to him.

"I…know who has the Star."

"Too late, Lorraine," Jason continued, sounding bored. "The time for deal-making is long past." His gaze darkened as he glared at her. "You gave away my Star. It was mine."

"Jason, please."

Carlos pulled off the main road onto a dirt one. A plume of dust followed them. They hadn't gone more than a couple of hundred feet when he slammed on the brakes. The sudden stop propelled Lorraine forward until her face struck the seat in front of her. Pain exploded in her face, and her nose started spurting blood.

Jason yelled at Carlos—obviously something about his lack of driving skills—and Carlos yelled back. Lorraine couldn't understand most of it, although *bastardo* was a word she had no difficulty recognizing.

Blood dripped profusely from her nose. Carlos climbed out of the car and shoved back the driver's seat, then caught her by her arm and jerked her roughly out. With no way to maintain her balance, she stumbled, falling onto the ground. This clearly angered Carlos; he reached for her a second time and backhanded her across the face. The pain stunned her, and it wasn't until her mouth filled with fresh blood that she realized her recently healed lip had split open again.

"Hey!" Jason shouted. He bent down and helped her up.

Lorraine pressed her tongue to the corner of her mouth. "Please," she whispered, her eyes imploring him. A bloody nose and split lip were minor injuries compared to what they planned for her; she was sure of that much.

"I'll help you get it back," she said next. "The Star..." By now she was trembling with fear. Her only hope of surviving this ordeal lay with Jason.

Carlos pushed Jason aside and came at her again. The force of his blow sent her back to the ground. Dammit! Lorraine thought. She wasn't going to let him use her as a punching bag! She bounded to her feet with a dexterity she hadn't known she possessed and ran at him with her shoulder lowered, the way she'd seen linebackers charge on a football field. He hadn't expected her to defend herself and was caught off guard.

Carlos stumbled backward. He scrambled up again, fists swinging. Lorraine ducked in the nick of time, then kicked him in the groin. Hard. As hard as she could.

Leaning against the car, Jason roared with laughter. "You're a little hellion, aren't you?"

She didn't waste time answering. Nor did she give Carlos, who'd doubled over, more than a passing glance. This was the perfect time to make a run for it. If she got back to the road, she might find someone driving by, someone who could help her. Having her hands tied was a definite hindrance, but she still managed to run.

Jason's laughter echoed from behind her. At least he wasn't planning to chase her. For that she was grateful.

Carlos shouted something at him and then she heard the distinct sound of a weapon fired. She glanced over her shoulder and gave a spontaneous cry of horror and shock.

Carlos had shot Jason in the head. Blood had sprayed across the hood of the vehicle and he'd slumped to the ground in a sitting position, his eyes open and staring in her direction.

The next bullet whizzed past her ear.

Lorraine screamed in terror and veered off the dirt road and into the jungle. Thrashing through the undergrowth, she blundered forward, one foot at a time, not stopping, not thinking, running for her life. One wrong step and it would all be over.

She had to hurry. Had to find a way to think clearly, to outsmart this maniac and save herself. She knew that if he shot and killed her on the run, she wouldn't face the torment of rape, wouldn't have to endure his sadistic revenge.

But she wanted to *live*. That instinct overpowered everything else. She refused to give up, refused to let Carlos win, refused to die. Not without one hell of a fight first.

Splinters flew from a nearby tree as a second bullet narrowly missed hitting her. Adrenaline surged through her and she ran faster than she'd thought possible, struggling to maintain her balance as she crashed through the tangled undergrowth and jumped over exposed roots.

The paved road was within sight, not that it would help her now. She had to stay hidden as much as possible. If Carlos wanted to use her for target practice, he wouldn't find her racing down an open highway.

The moment her feet hit the smooth pavement,

she felt as if she were flying. She cut across the highway at an angle and into the jungle on the other side without a pause. She heard a car approach behind her and prayed it would distract Carlos long enough to keep him from noticing where she'd entered the jungle.

In another minute Lorraine knew she'd made a mistake. She hadn't gone more than twenty or thirty yards when she saw the cliff. Breathing painfully, her heart pounding, she stared down at the rocks jutting out of the river below. A jump or fall would kill her.

"No, no!" she wept frantically. She backed away from the ledge and started running parallel to the cliff, heading into the brilliant sunlight with the hope that if it blinded her, it would blind Carlos, too.

She raced ahead, squinting, breathless, fighting panic and fear. Her left eye had started to swell and she could barely see out of it.

Perhaps that explained why she didn't see Carlos until it was too late. He stood with the handgun pointed directly at her, his shoulders heaving with exertion.

Lorraine stopped abruptly. She couldn't breathe until she leaned forward, arms lifted awkwardly behind her, hauling in deep drafts of air. What surprised her was how calm she felt. Emotionless.

Maybe he'd already killed her and she just hadn't figured it out.

Then Carlos smiled, that smug smile she'd seen far too often, and Lorraine realized she was very much alive. But his look of triumph told her she wouldn't be for long.

Marjorie Ellis walked back into her kitchen and sank onto a chair. She'd been serious when she told Gary she intended to hand in her letter of resignation first thing Monday morning. She didn't want to leave her job, not when she was beginning to establish a new career, form new friendships, make more money. She was proud of her growing success in the corporate world.

But what else could she do?

She covered her face with her hands as she tried to analyze why everything had gone so very wrong.

This attraction to Gary Franklin had started early on, she admitted, almost from the day she'd been hired. After Mark's death, she'd continued working at the bank, but she related well to people, and several of her friends had suggested she try sales. It'd taken her a year to find the courage to give up the security of her nine-to-five job. Then she'd had a couple of negative interviews before landing the job with Med-X. She'd fit in right away; in fact, she'd succeeded beyond expectation. Everyone had been kind and helpful, offering helpful advice and frequent reassurance.

Especially Gary Franklin.

Yes, she'd liked him immediately. In those early weeks he'd been stiff and just a little pompous, but she'd soon discovered that was all a front. She'd worked hard to get him to smile that first time and felt like she'd made a million-dollar sale when he did. His smiles seemed to come more easily and more often after that.

Only recently had she found out he was engaged. It'd shocked her, and discouraged her, too. He'd never spoken of his fiancée. Not one word. She supposed he was the type of man who left his personal life outside the office.

Then she'd learned that his fiancée was vacationing out of the country. In Mexico, according to office rumors. It made no sense to Marjorie. The woman Gary had chosen to marry was taking an extended vacation only a few months before her wedding. An extended *solo* vacation.

Her mistake, Marjorie acknowledged, had been inviting Gary to dinner and introducing him to Brice. The two of them had hit it off instantly. And it wasn't just Brice who was crazy about Gary. She'd set herself up for heartache and had done it knowing there was no other possible outcome. Still, she couldn't seem to stop.

When she sent him away, Gary had looked lost

and at loose ends, a feeling she understood all too
well. She'd loved her husband, grieved for him—
and now she was so terribly lonely. Since Gary
was lonely, too, it'd seemed like a simple act of
kindness to ask him over for dinner. A way of
reciprocating after all his help. Deep inside, she'd
known her invitation was more than a courtesy,
more than a gesture of friendliness or compassion.
He was engaged; she should avoid any social involvement. But she craved his companionship, his
presence. She'd debated the wisdom of it all
morning, then thrown caution to the wind and put
the burden of refusal on his shoulders. The quick-
ness of his acceptance had calmed her worries. If
he didn't think there was anything wrong with
having dinner at her house, she didn't have to be
concerned, either.

She couldn't have been more surprised when
he kissed her that night. And in all honesty she
couldn't have been more pleased. She reminded
herself that it was wrong to feel like this. And
what about Brice? Had she set him up for heartache, too? He and Gary had talked baseball all
through dinner, and Brice had talked about Gary
constantly ever since. It was Gary this and Gary
that. Nor had it hurt any that Gary had spent an
hour playing catch with her son. It was almost as
if he'd come to her house to visit Brice—not that
Marjorie minded in the least.

"I think we should marry him," her son had announced when she tucked him into bed that night.

"Brice, I barely know the man."

"Then invite him back."

How easy this courtship and marriage business was to a nine-year-old boy. "He's already engaged."

Brice's eyes widened. "You mean he's going to marry someone else?"

"It looks that way."

"You gotta *do* something, Mom."

"Any suggestions?" she asked facetiously.

He frowned and shook his head. "Cook for him again. He really liked your lasagna."

Even now, Marjorie couldn't prevent a smile as she recalled his comment. It sounded like the corny old-fashioned advice her grandmother used to dispense.

"Mom! Mom!" Brice burst through the door from baseball practice. "Where are you?"

Marjorie glanced at the clock, surprised that practice was already over. No, it was eleven-thirty, later than she'd realized. "In here," she called.

"You'll never guess what!"

"Probably not," she agreed, forcing herself to smile.

"I saw Gary out front."

"Gary Franklin?"

"He was sitting in his car and he looked pretty miserable. Did the two of you have a fight or something?"

Marjorie wasn't sure how to answer that. "Um, not really."

"I asked him to come inside, but he said he couldn't. I was hoping he'd have time to play catch with me, but he said he had to get home. Then you know what he did? Can you guess?" Brice's eyes blazed with excitement. "He gave me his Ken Griffey, Jr., signed rookie card. *Gave* it to me, Mom." Her son held up the card as if he was holding a map for buried treasure. "Is that the coolest thing that's happened to me in my entire life or what?"

"He gave you the card?" Marjorie wanted to make certain she hadn't misunderstood him.

"For free," Brice assured her.

"Did...did he say why?"

"No, just that he wanted me to have it." Brice grew quiet then. After a moment he said, "I still think we should marry him. I loved Dad and everything, and I miss him a lot, but I think he'd like Gary, too."

Marjorie had felt the same thing herself.

"Will you?" Brice asked, looking up at her. "Marry him, I mean?"

Luckily the phone rang before she had a chance

to respond. Brice charged across the room as if answering the phone before it rang a second time was a matter of dire consequence.

He listened for a moment, then said, "It's for you." He handed her the portable receiver.

"Hello," she said, wishing she'd asked Brice to take a number so she could return the call. She wasn't in the mood for a chatty conversation with one of her friends from the bank or, worse, a spiel from a telephone solicitor.

Her disinterested greeting was met with a moment of silence. She was about to check the phone's batteries when she heard, "It's Gary."

Now it was her turn to lapse into silence.

"Listen," he said. She could hear traffic sounds; he was obviously calling from his car. "I don't want you to quit Med-X. If you refuse to work with me anymore, I'll understand. You can report to a different supervisor. I'll—"

"It isn't that."

"I'll request a transfer on Monday morning. You won't have to see me again."

Marjorie felt an immediate sense of loss. She *wanted* to see Gary, considered him her ally and friend. Her intense attraction to him had nothing to do with that. The thought of working at Med-X and not being able to go to him with her technical problems devastated her. No one else was as patient, as understanding. Not only that, she'd taken over the territory he'd covered before his promotion. She'd found his advice invaluable in dealing with his former clients. Half her success was actually due to him.

"Don't do that, Gary," she whispered.

Being a perceptive child, Brice left the room.

"Could we talk?" Gary asked.

"I...I don't think so." Marjorie couldn't see that it would do any good. She'd only want him to kiss her again and didn't know if she could disguise her feelings, especially outside the office.

"I'm an idiot," Gary said. "I can't tell you how sorry I am."

"It isn't you, it's me."

"I should never have kissed you."

Marjorie closed her eyes. "It was what I wanted." What she'd dreamed about for weeks.

"You did?"

"It isn't a good idea for us to talk except at work," she felt compelled to say. "It's better for us both if we nip this in the bud and not see each other again. I'll draft my letter of resignation over the weekend."

"You're serious about quitting Med-X?"

"Yes."

"Even if I request a transfer?"

"Yes." The temptation to stay was strong, but she couldn't let him uproot his life because of her. He'd been with the company far longer than she had. Her leaving was the fairer alternative. Briefly she considered asking for a transfer herself, but knew she'd still see him at the quarterly sales conferences and at other company events. Anyway, she couldn't tear her son away from his school, his friends, his familiar surroundings.

"Then I guess there's nothing I can do, is there? If you think of something, I'll do it. I'll do anything."

"Oh, Gary..." She felt like crying.

"*Is* there anything I can do?" he asked once more.

"No," she whispered. She turned off the phone.

Jack had witnessed terror in his life, seen it on the faces of others, even been the cause of it. But nothing from his past could have prepared him for what he felt when he saw Lorraine race across the highway with her hands bound.

As soon as he'd learned that Jason Applebee had tricked Thomas into giving him information about Lorraine, Jack had tried to reach her at the hotel. When there was no answer in her room, he hurried back. By pure luck he caught sight of her in the rear seat of a black car. Two men in front. Even a fleeting glance told him the driver was Carlos. The other had to be Jason. In a moment of craziness, Jack found a man with a vehicle and paid him an outrageous amount of money for the use of it.

Still, he was too far behind Carlos and Jason to catch more than a glimpse of the car as they sped through the streets and past the shantytowns that bordered the city. Somewhere along the way he lost sight of the car and drove around frantically, searching with no success. Then he'd taken the jungle road, and that was when he happened upon Lorraine. Carlos wasn't far behind. Jack saw him run into the trees at a different angle.

He slammed on the brakes and leaped out of the vehicle, racing after Carlos. He had no weapon. No gun. Not even a knife. But his intuition told him any delay would mean Lorraine's death. If his lack of weapons meant he died defending her, then so be it.

The jungle was impossibly thick, and Carlos was nowhere to be seen. Jack soon found what Lorraine must have discovered. A few yards into the dense vegetation, was the edge of a cliff. The river twisted around the jagged rocks below. Jack had never been fond of heights and stepped cautiously back.

Lorraine's scream propelled him into action and he fought his way toward her.

Carlos had her on the ground. Despite her struggles, he'd managed to rip off her blouse and in the process beaten her nearly senseless. Her face was bloody, her eyes swollen shut, and still she fought him, still she struggled.

Jack had never loved her more or admired her courage as much. With a cry that came from deep within his throat, he launched himself at Carlos.

Swinging around as he crouched over Lorraine, Carlos pointed a gun directly at him. To Jack's astonishment, Lorraine heaved herself up from the ground and slammed her head into Carlos's arm. The gun flew out of his hand and into the trees.

The reprieve was all Jack needed. He charged the other man, throwing him off Lorraine, but the force of the attack stole his breath. The wound in his shoulder had only partially healed, and his stamina and strength were much lower than normal.

What Jack lacked in brute strength, he compensated for with skill and finesse, punching Carlos repeatedly on his injured arm.

The man grunted with pain and returned the favor, barreling his ham-size fist into Jack's bandaged shoulder.

Pain spiraled down Jack's arm and he fell to his knees in agony. For an instant the world went black as he dealt with the crippling pain.

"You bastard!" Lorraine shouted at Jack's tormented cry. With a shout of outrage, she flung herself at Carlos, shoving him off balance.

Carlos staggered, then whirled around, ramming her into a tree. She slumped, unconscious, against its base. Her action—her courage—gave Jack time to let the stars dissolve from his eyes.

As soon as he could, he entered the fray again, going after Carlos with a vengeance. Carlos didn't wait for Jack, but raged after him, knocking him off his feet. He had the superior strength, but Jack was fighting for Lorraine's life as well as his own.

They broke apart and circled each other. Jack's eyes held the other man's, letting him know that this would be a fight to the end. Either he died or Carlos died. There could be no compromise.

In his weakened condition, Jack knew Carlos had the advantage. His strength would only hold out for so long. He'd lose, and when he did, the bastard would kill Lorraine.

Carlos lunged for him first, and they ventured dangerously close to the cliff's edge. Jack heard the rush of the water below. One wrong move and he'd fall to a certain death.

Out of the corner of his eye he saw that Lorraine had regained consciousness and had started to scrabble frantically, kicking through the underbrush for the gun.

With his back to the cliff, Jack had no way of gauging how close he was to the edge. It was then that he knew what he had to do. There was no other way to save Lorraine. No other way to stop Carlos.

Already he could feel his strength leaving him. Carlos had the momentum, the stamina…the hatred.

Jack acted quickly—out of need and determination. Out of love. He reached for Carlos and with his last reservoir of strength propelled them both toward the ledge.

Carlos threw out his arms in a desperate effort to save himself, but it was too late. Both men teetered there for a moment and then they went over.

The last thing Jack heard as he tumbled over the cliff's edge was Lorraine's horrified scream.

Sixteen

The Mexican Department of Rescue worked feverishly for the next few hours. Several emergency technicians had been lowered carefully down the side of the cliff and they were now examining the bodies.

No one could have survived a fall like that. Lorraine had known it the moment she saw the two men sprawled on the shore below. Carlos had struck the rocks and his body lay there, twisted and broken. Jack—her heart stopped beating every time she glanced over the edge—lay on the riverbank, face up. Lorraine fell to her knees, her pain too much to bear.

After she'd seen Jack and Carlos go over the cliff, she'd run into the middle of the highway, nearly getting hit by a fast-moving car. Thankfully, the young couple spoke enough English to understand that there'd been a terrible accident. They were the ones who'd contacted the authorities.

"Miss, miss, we need you to answer questions." The policeman, whose name tag identified him as Officer de Oro, hunkered down where she knelt. His voice was gentle, concerned. She didn't mean to ignore him, but his English was difficult to understand. "Can you talk now? Please," he continued. "There are many questions."

"I need to know if he's alive. I love him." Her voice cracked and she refused to move away from the cliff edge, refused to stop gazing down at Jack. Illogically she thought that her love would somehow help him if he'd managed to survive.

"No one could live after such a fall."

She knew it without his saying so and merely shook her head. Officer de Oro's words underscored her worst fears.

"What happened?"

Lorraine didn't know where she could possibly start. "I want my father," she whispered brokenly, and gave him Thomas's name. "I need my father. Could I call him, please?"

"Yes, we'll arrange that later," the policeman said. "Who is the dead man on the other side of the road?" he asked urgently. "Can you tell us that much?"

"Jason Applebee."

"American?"

She nodded. "He's the man who stole the Kukulcan Star." Her answer generated an immediate response. Officer de Oro leaped up and called over another policeman. They spoke in hushed tones before the second man hurried to the radio in the patrol car.

"He no longer has the Star," Lorraine said in a weak voice.

"Who does?"

"The Department of Antiquities."

"How can you be sure?" he asked.

"Because I gave it to them this morning." Was it only this morning?

"Do you have the name of the person you gave it to?"

"Dr. Marcus Molino."

He left her to speak to the second officer again. She noticed that the activity far below had increased, and now a member of the rescue squad raced over to speak to the policemen. He was in radio contact with the people working below. Lorraine desperately wanted to understand what was happening.

"Tell me," she said, turning to Officer de Oro when he hurried back to her side. "What did he say?"

"The man on the rocks is dead."

Carlos was dead, but she felt no sense of exhilaration. She barely even felt relief. Instead, she experienced a deep sadness—because she realized the next news she heard would be of Jack's death.

He'd died for her. He'd given up his life to save

her. He loved her. Neither of them had spoken the words; neither had found the courage to actually say them. But Jack had loved her. And she loved him, more than she'd ever known she was capable of loving.

What was she going to do? How could she continue the rest of her life without him? Right now, it didn't seem possible.

The man with the radio spoke to the other police officer again. A flurry of activity followed, with ropes and stretchers being assembled and instructions shouted.

"What's happening?" she asked, hope filling her heart. She struggled to her feet. "Tell me, tell me." She gripped the police officer by the arm and wouldn't let go until he told her.

"The second man is alive."

She nearly passed out with relief.

"But barely."

"Then we must get him to the hospital! As soon as possible. Please, please hurry."

Jack was alive. There was a chance. It bubbled up inside her, this surge of sudden unexpected promise. It was all she could do not to hug the man who'd delivered the news.

The ambulance was already there. The man from the rescue squad tried to steer her away from the cliff to have her injuries treated, but she wouldn't leave. Not until she heard the final word on Jack.

"He's alive!" She wept openly at the news. "Alive."

"Miss, miss, now you see the doctor?"

"Not until Jack is brought up from the cliff."

"But, miss—"

"I'll answer all your questions later," she assured him.

She kept her gaze trained on Jack, who was being brought up the face of the cliff by perhaps half a dozen men below, as many above, all working together. It astonished her that such a difficult rescue could even be accomplished. She was careful to stay out of everyone's way. The task seemed to take hours of coordinated effort; in actuality it was less than forty minutes.

As soon as the men carrying Jack reached the top, he was hurried into the waiting ambulance. The rescue team, their faces red with exertion, stepped back from the vehicle.

Before anyone could protest, Lorraine climbed into the back of the ambulance with the medical technician.

Once inside, Lorraine got her first look at Jack. As a nurse practitioner she'd worked with accident victims before, but this was the worst she'd ever seen. She was appalled by the extent of his injuries. It was a miracle he wasn't dead. She felt for the pulse in his neck, which was almost too faint to register. His internal injuries had to be massive, and he'd obviously broken a number of bones. Most likely he'd received a spinal injury.

The medical technician worked frantically, getting Jack hooked up to an IV and combating the effects of shock. Lorraine simply watched, holding Jack's limp hand. Watched and prayed.

The siren began to wail as they started down the highway.

The next two days were a blur in Lorraine's mind. Jack was taken almost immediately into surgery. His injuries proved as extensive as she'd feared, with plenty of room for complications and problems. She refused to leave his bedside, even when her father appeared.

As soon as Thomas Dancy took one look at her, she could see he was badly shaken. Both her eyes had been blackened, her nose broken, and the gash in the back of her head had needed fifteen stitches. Funny how she hadn't felt a thing, not one second of pain, from the moment Jack went over the cliff.

Every ounce of energy she had she gave to Jack. All her strength, her will, everything she had to give. He *had* to stay alive.

''Raine?'' Her father stood by the hospital bed

where Jack remained unconscious, attached to various monitors.

She fell into his arms, desperately needing his support. "I love him so much." She understood now that she'd never really been in love. What she and Gary had was more friendship than passion. They were friends and companions, fond of each other but not in love. In many ways Gary had been her mother's choice rather than her own.

"Can you tell me what happened?" Thomas asked gently.

"Not now." Others assumed she was fragile, that her state of mind had been compromised by her ordeal. Perhaps they were right; she was no longer a good judge of such things. Not that it mattered. What was important was being with Jack. She thought of nothing and no one else.

"Raine," her father urged. "Come to the hotel. Sleep."

"No." She shook her head. "I never told him," she said, glancing away from Jack to briefly meet her father's eyes. "I won't leave him."

"He loves you, too?" her father asked in a soft hesitant voice.

"Oh, yes," she whispered, knowing she could never explain in words the special relationship they'd shared. She never doubted or questioned Jack's love, just as he never doubted hers for him.

It was something neither of them could or would say. For Jack, love was an emotion he couldn't afford to express to a woman he assumed was married. As for herself, she'd gambled, certain she'd have time enough to tell him the truth.

If he died now, they both lost.

Her father sat with her. After the first barrage of concerned questions, he'd asked no more, and she appreciated that. It was as if he understood she had to see this to the end. Whatever that end might be.

The hospital was quiet. Night settled around her as she stayed at Jack's bedside, alone now. She held his hand in hers and pressed her lips to the inside of his wrist.

"Once you're out of here," she told him, "we'll—"

She wasn't allowed to finish. His heart monitor started to blare, a piercing alarm that shattered the night and brought hospital staff running. A glance at the electronic readout showed one long straight line. Cardiac arrest.

Gary Franklin had decided he would refuse Marjorie's letter of resignation. This wasn't a personal decision, he convinced himself, but one he'd made out of concern for the company. After months of training, Med-X had invested a lot of money in Marjorie Ellis, and it would be a detriment to the entire organization if she left now.

Just as he'd suspected, he found her brief letter on his desk Monday morning. Knowing exactly what he intended to do, Gary grabbed it and walked briskly to her office.

Marjorie looked up when he entered and closed the door. Surprise flared in her eyes. "I can't accept this," he announced.

"Can't or won't?" she challenged.

"Both." He gave her the company line, explaining that Med-X would lose a substantial sum of money if she walked out the door.

"Then I'll train my replacement before I go," she offered.

He hesitated.

"You can't force me to continue working here."

She had a point. "No, but I'd consider it a personal favor if you didn't leave the company in a bind. Also, you're working out beautifully here and we'd hate to lose you."

Marjorie sagged in her chair. He noted that she'd already loaded half the contents of her drawers into a cardboard box.

"I'm hoping you'll reconsider."

She wouldn't look at him. "I can't...I won't."

"If that's what you want, okay, but..." He couldn't find a diplomatic way of telling her how important it was to him that she remain at Med-X. The hell with the company. He wanted her on the job for purely selfish reasons.

"Why is it so critical for you to leave?" At first he'd assumed it was because of his... advances, he supposed the term was. But he'd analyzed each time they'd kissed, plus a few things she'd said, and realized she'd *wanted* him to kiss her. She'd enjoyed their kisses as much as he had.

"Why?" Her head came up and she stared at him. "You're engaged to marry another woman. I won't be your last fling. I'm not interested in an affair, Gary."

"An affair?" He nearly choked on the words. Not once had it entered his mind that she'd believe he was suggesting such a thing.

"Well, what else am I supposed to think?" she asked defensively. "That's where we were headed."

Gary couldn't deny the electricity between them or the truth of what she said. They *had* been headed directly for the bedroom. "You're right," he said, hardly aware he'd spoken aloud.

"I won't hurt this woman who's promised to be your wife..."

"Lorraine," he supplied.

"Furthermore, I won't be part of something illicit. Some furtive noon-hour affair."

That felt like a slap in the face. "I didn't, wouldn't..." He was too flustered to continue.

"Yes, you would. We both would."

"Okay," he said, thinking fast. "But now that we're aware of the pitfalls, we'll be careful. Before you walk away from a good job, I suggest you take a couple of days, give this some real thought."

She seemed to be considering his words.

"It's easy to let our emotions get carried away, but you're important to this company." *And to me.* But he didn't say it aloud.

Frowning, Marjorie bit her lower lip. "I'll give it a week."

"Good." A load had been lifted from his shoulders. He returned her letter of resignation and walked back to his office.

A number of business concerns demanded his attention, but he left them, his mind awhirl. Everything Marjorie had said was true. He was engaged. The thought of kissing another woman shouldn't have entered his mind. But he *had* kissed Marjorie, and he'd enjoyed it more than anything.

Sure, he missed Lorraine. Quite a bit in the beginning, but she'd been away for such a long time he didn't know what to think anymore. Even her father couldn't give him a definite answer about when she'd be back.

One thing was certain—he couldn't marry her. Not now.

It seemed like a simple decision, and he didn't understand why it'd taken him so long to reach it. If he truly loved Lorraine, he wouldn't be this attracted to Marjorie.

He jumped up from his chair and marched down the hallway to her office. When he saw she was talking on the phone, he felt intense disappointment. As soon as he could, he'd let her know.

Soon after that, he had a lunch meeting with a major distributor and then he spent the afternoon typing up a report for the company's CEO. Marjorie had gone out on some local calls. Before he knew it, the day was over.

Not until he was in his car did he think about stopping at her house. He probably shouldn't, but the thought of seeing her again was a temptation too great to resist.

Brice came running over the minute Gary parked in front of the house.

"How're you doin', kiddo?" Gary asked, and playfully jerked the bill of the boy's baseball cap down over his forehead.

"Great! Are you coming to see my mom?"

"Yeah. Is she around?"

"Yup."

Worried that she might not appreciate his walking into the house unannounced, Gary asked, "Would you mind telling her I'm here?"

"Sure. She'll be glad." The boy dashed up the steps and through the door; half a minute later Marjorie appeared. Gary could tell by the way she hesitated when she saw him that she felt flustered and uncertain.

"Hello, Gary."

"Marjorie." She remained on the top porch step, arms folded protectively.

"I won't take much of your time," he said, standing a safe distance away on the lawn. "I came to a decision today, and I want you to know what it is, since it definitely concerns you."

"Concerns me how? What kind of decision?"

"As you pointed out, I'm engaged. But I've learned something—I don't want to be engaged anymore. Lorraine and I... I don't know. She's terrific. Great. We dated for quite a while, and I more or less decided it was time to get married. She felt the same way. That's why it happened. But I'm breaking off the engagement."

"Is she back from Mexico or wherever she went?"

"No." He'd thought about that, too. If she was in Louisville, he'd talk to her that very day.

"So she doesn't know?" Marjorie pressed.

"Not yet, but I don't think she'll be too disappointed."

"How can you say that?" Marjorie demanded with such outrage, Gary retreated a step in surprise.

"There was no passion between us. No... sparks." He hadn't realized that until he'd kissed Marjorie. The sizzle between them was strong enough to shoot sparks into tomorrow.

"Sparks." She arched a brow.

"I'm not a fickle man, Marjorie. I want you to know that."

She didn't reveal any emotion. "Are you breaking the engagement because of me?"

Gary didn't know how to answer. The best policy was the truth, so he met her look squarely, unwilling to discount the intensity of what he felt for her. "Yes. I've been waiting my entire life for you. I refuse to let you slip through my fingers now."

"Oh, Gary." She was actually crying.

"Invite him to dinner, Mom." Brice stood at the screen door.

"Thanks, but I should be leaving." Gary headed back to his car.

"Gary."

He turned around.

She was wiping her eyes with one sleeve. "Would you like to stay for dinner?"

More than she'd ever know. "Would you like me to?"

She smiled and nodded, then held out her hand to him.

Gary didn't need a second invitation.

Jack didn't know where the hell he was. He opened his eyes and bright lights blinded him. He wondered if he was dead, then decided he was in too damn much pain for that. Pain was a good sign. It meant he was alive.

A nurse stood at his bedside, along with an elderly physician.

"Doctor?" Jack asked in Spanish.

The older man turned to him and smiled when he realized Jack was conscious. "So you've decided to return to the land of the living, have you?"

"How long have I been out?"

"A week."

The last thing Jack remembered was the convincing knowledge that he was about to die and take Carlos with him.

"How do you feel, Mr. Keller?"

"Like I fell off a cliff."

The physician grinned.

"How's the other guy?" He hoped to hell Carlos was dead.

"Mr. Applebee?"

"Him, too."

"Unfortunately, both Mr. Applebee and Mr. Caracol were pronounced dead at the scene."

"Carlos Caracol?" Jack wasn't taking any chances. Jason's death was news to him, but there hadn't exactly been time to ask Lorraine questions.

"You and your wife are the only two to survive."

Jack didn't correct the assumption, but turned his head away, not wanting to think about Lorraine.

"Your wife has been at your bedside from the moment you were brought into the hospital," the nurse told him. "She wouldn't leave you."

"How is she?" Jack's memory was foggy, but he knew Lorraine had taken one hell of a beating. "*Where* is she?"

"She's with her father having lunch," the doctor said. "Against her wishes, I might add. And as for her injuries, she's much better. Or she will be as soon as I tell her you're conscious."

Jack closed his eyes.

"You gave us quite a scare recently."

"I did?" Jack's eyes fluttered open again.

"You went into cardiac arrest a couple of days ago. It's been touch-and-go ever since. You have a strong will to live, Mr. Keller."

"It's his wife," the nurse corrected. "She said she refused to let you die."

He grinned. That certainly sounded like Lorraine.

"For days she's been sitting at your bedside, talking about your future together. She said she wants your child."

Jack's grin faded. Apparently Lorraine had decided to file for divorce. She was going to do it, going to ruin her life for him. He could see it happening already. She'd return to Louisville and rip apart two lives. Jack couldn't let her throw away her marriage because of him.

"Doctor," he said between gritted teeth. He barely had the strength to talk. He grabbed the man's coat sleeve in an effort to convey the urgency of his request.

"Do you need something more for the pain?"

"No."

"I'll get your wife," the nurse said.

"No!"

"Calm down, Mr. Keller. Whatever is wrong, we can take care of it."

Jack doubted that. "The woman out there isn't my wife."

He watched as they stared at him in stunned disbelief.

"She's wearing a wedding band," the nurse said, as if to disqualify his statement.

"She loves you," the physician said, frowning. "She's been unwilling to leave you this entire time. The only way we were able to get her out of the room now was because of her—"

"That ring was given to her by another man."

Both the nurse and the doctor continued to stare at him.

"If you go out there and tell Lorraine I'm alive, you'll be responsible for breaking up a marriage, for destroying a family." His hand tightened on the physician's sleeve. "Do you understand what I'm saying?"

The doctor's gaze connected with his.

"I love her, too," Jack whispered. He could feel the darkness closing in.

"What do you want me to do?"

"Tell her I died."

"No, Mr. Keller, that isn't possible."

"Tell her I died or...or I'll ruin her life." He had trouble saying the words. They stumbled off the end of his tongue.

"You love her that much?"

"Yes."

"Mr. Keller—"

"Do it...please." He wasn't a man who begged or pleaded, but he was reduced to it now. "She has a husband. A good man who loves her...who knows nothing about me."

The physician took a long time deciding, then, as if he found it acutely difficult, finally agreed with a nod.

"Thank you," Jack whispered. He could rest now. Could shut his eyes and sink into the beckoning oblivion.

He heard the soft crush of footsteps as the physician walked out of the room.

Jack lost track of time. It could have been five minutes, possibly ten; he didn't know. The next thing he heard was Lorraine's agonized scream.

"No, no! Please, no!"

Hearing her wrenched his heart. The sound of her sobs followed. Plaintive, pitiful, filled with an agony that touched all who heard them.

Jack closed his eyes and wished he could close off his hearing, as well.

From this point forward, he was dead to Lorraine and she was dead to him.

Seventeen

Six months passed before Lorraine was able to sleep through the night. Each time she awoke, an intense sadness settled over her—worse even than the harsh grief she'd experienced at the unexpectedness of her mother's death. Often she lay in bed, grateful for the darkness, for the silence, and clutched the memories of Jack to her heart.

Finally she understood the poet's claim that it was better to have loved and lost than never to have loved at all. In years past she'd scoffed at those very words, considered them foolish. No more. Even though she would have escaped this pain if she'd never met Jack, she knew she'd gladly go through it all again. Those weeks with him were the most precious of her life. She treasured each and every day.

It hurt, this pain that was sharper than anything she'd ever known, and still she was grateful.

"You've changed," Gary told her when they met for lunch early in the month of November.

She could only agree.

"You seem more...resilient."

"Talking about people who've changed," she said, turning the tables on him, "I hardly recognize the man you've become." They sat in a Thai restaurant, one they'd frequented while dating.

Gary had the good grace to blush. "I credit it all to love."

Had she never known Jack, Gary's words would have offended her, but oddly enough she understood. Jack's love had changed her, too.

Her former fiancé had married Marjorie Ellis within a month of Lorraine's return. At the time she'd been in too much pain to really care. Only later did she experience a bitterness mingled with regret and relief. She was happy for Gary and Marjorie, but it hurt that she'd tried to be thoughtful of him and he hadn't afforded her the same consideration.

In time she got over those feelings and found herself pleased that her friend had fallen in love. She'd always enjoyed Gary's company. But she knew she'd never truly loved him. Not the way she'd loved Jack. Her fondness for Gary couldn't compare to the intensity of what she felt for the man who'd given his life to save hers.

Gary set aside his menu. Lorraine wondered why he bothered to look. For as long as she could remember, he'd ordered the same dish every time they ate at the Thai Garden.

"Marjorie should be here any minute," he said. His eyes brightened as he said his wife's name.

Lorraine had met Marjorie on a number of occasions and liked her a great deal. She approved of the changes that loving Marjorie had brought about in Gary. He was more relaxed and spontaneous, more sensitive to others. It was obvious that they were meant to be a couple.

"Sorry I'm late," Marjorie said as she rushed toward the table. Slipping off her shoes, she stepped up to the padded cushions and lowered herself beside Gary in the private booth. "The doctor was behind schedule and—" She stopped abruptly as if she'd said something she shouldn't have.

It took Lorraine a moment to discern her meaning. "You're pregnant!" she said, eyeing the two of them.

Gary and Marjorie both seemed to freeze, awaiting her reaction.

"That's absolutely wonderful!" Lorraine was genuinely delighted. "I'm thrilled for you." She reached across the table and squeezed Marjorie's hand. "How far along?"

"Three months," Marjorie said. Gary, who'd never demonstrated a burning desire for parenthood, simply beamed.

"We didn't want to wait, seeing that Brice is already nine," he said.

"We didn't want to wait, period," Marjorie teased. She flattened her hand over her stomach. "The baby was a surprise, but not an unwelcome one."

Now Lorraine understood why Gary had invited her to lunch. "You're going to make a great father," she said, and meant it.

"I'm a little nervous about a baby, but Brice said if he could put up with dirty diapers and fussy infants, then so could I."

"Gary's great with Brice," Marjorie told her.

"I think that's because he finally has someone his own age to play with," Lorraine teased. The two women laughed, and so did Gary. Actually, Lorraine figured, it wasn't far from the truth. Gary was a baseball nut, and apparently so was Brice. Lorraine had recently stopped by the house on a Sunday afternoon and discovered Gary and Brice glued to the television, watching the World Series. They'd given each other high fives and hooted noisily until Marjorie and Lorraine were forced to adjourn to the kitchen.

"I prefer to think that Brice is mature for his age," Gary muttered.

The waitress came for their order. She glanced at Gary and Lorraine several times as if to say something wasn't right. It was a look they often received when Marjorie joined them. Since they'd dated for so long, people naturally seemed to consider them a couple.

"What are you doing for Thanksgiving?" Marjorie asked.

Was it that time of year already? Lorraine could hardly believe it. For months now she'd been dragging herself through each day, praying for the strength to endure, the courage to continue alone. That was the key word. *Alone.*

She was grateful now that her mother's house hadn't sold. Soon after her return from Mexico, she'd moved in, needing the comfort of familiar things around her.

"We'd like it if you could join us for dinner on Thanksgiving," Marjorie said.

Lorraine heard the invitation, but didn't respond until she noticed that Marjorie and Gary were waiting for her answer. Both regarded her with concern. Suddenly she realized the invitation had been prompted by guilt as much as by affection. It wasn't necessary; neither of them needed to feel guilty on her account. If Gary hadn't beaten her to it, she would have broken off the engagement herself.

"I...I'm not sure," Lorraine said.

"Will you be visiting your father?" Gary asked.

"No." Her quick response concealed neither her anger nor her pain. She didn't want to think about Thomas Dancy and in fact had refused to deal with the emotions that beset her every time his name was mentioned.

He should have told Lorraine the truth about Azucena, but instead, had left her to discover it on her own. That was, perhaps, what hurt the most. Thomas had failed her the same way he'd failed her mother. All those years, Virginia had loved him, idolized him, been faithful to him. Not once had she looked at another man. Not once had she been disloyal to his memory.

When Jack was first taken to the hospital, she'd turned to her father for emotional support, but she regretted that now. He'd tried to comfort her when the doctor came to tell her Jack had died, but she was beyond solace.

As soon as it could be arranged, she'd returned to Louisville, where she belonged. Her father had written her a number of times since, but she hadn't answered his letters. Wouldn't have known what to say if she had. Thomas Dancy had made a new life for himself, had another wife, other children. She was part of the painful past, tied to a dead marriage and a woman he'd betrayed. It would be better for everyone if she stayed out of his world—and kept him out of hers.

"Lorraine? We were talking about Thanksgiving?" Gary's voice cut into her musings.

"Oh, sorry," she whispered. "I'll let you know, okay?"

"Are you ready to talk about what happened in Mexico yet?" The question came from Marjorie, asked with kindness and compassion. Without Lorraine's ever having spoken about it, Marjorie knew she'd endured some horrible trauma.

"No," she whispered brokenly, "not yet." And perhaps not ever. Lorraine hadn't shared her memories of Jack. Not with Gary and Marjorie or her friends at work.

Gary was right. She *was* different, and always would be for having loved and lost Jack. Really, what could she tell them? How could she explain that she'd died that day in the jungle outside Mexico City? How could she explain that she only went through the motions of living now? That she struggled to make sense out of life and death, struggled to gain acceptance and peace in a world that seemed devoid of both?

Jack endured six hideous months. The pain was physical, the suffering emotional. Twice now he'd fallen in love, and both times it had been a disaster. Each day he lay in his hospital bed, the pain so bad it was impossible to sleep. But he welcomed the physical agony. It diverted his attention from thoughts of Lorraine.

His back, he learned, had been broken. That

came as no surprise. Nor did the five other broken bones, plus internal injuries. The doctors hadn't made any promises about walking again. Most seemed surprised he'd survived, but no one more so than Jack. He would have shaken hands with death any number of times. Been glad to give up the fight. Even now he cursed God for playing such a cruel trick. If he'd wanted a reward for the noble gesture of sending Lorraine back to her husband, this wasn't it.

The second week of November, Jack stood on his own for the first time since he'd entered the hospital. Stood, not walked. Sweat broke out across his brow at the amount of energy required to maintain an upright position.

Someone clapped loudly behind him.

Jack dared not glance over his shoulder for fear of losing his balance, precarious at best.

"Good going."

"Murphy?" Jack couldn't believe his ears. His knees gave out on him, and he fell back into his wheelchair. His strength deserted him; otherwise he would have whirled the chair around and cursed out his friend. He wasn't in the mood for company, and he didn't want anyone's sympathy.

Murphy's long strides devoured the distance between them. "You're a sight for sore eyes."

Jack turned purposefully away. "What the hell are you doing here?"

"What else? I came to see you."

Jack refused to meet Murphy's eyes. "Then you made a wasted trip."

His friend walked a circle around him, shaking his head. "A fine mess you've gotten yourself into this time."

Jack ignored the comment. He knew Letty and Murphy had been phoning weekly for updates on his condition, talking to Dr. Berilo and the hospital staff. Jack hadn't wanted to talk to them himself and hoped they'd get the message. Apparently they hadn't.

"Doc says you can leave the hospital soon," Murphy said, facing Jack.

"So I understand."

"Have you decided where you're going?"

"No." Jack preferred not to think about the future. His one and only decision had been to sell *Scotch on Water*. He couldn't go back to the cabin cruiser. Every night he'd be haunted by the memory of Lorraine and their time together.

"Are you returning to the boat?"

"Sold it," Jack muttered.

"You sold *Scotch on Water*?" Murphy didn't seem to believe it. "But you loved that boat."

"That time of my life has passed." It was all he intended to say on the subject. Murphy would never know the real reason.

"Don't you think it would've been better to wait and make such a drastic decision later?"

"Leave it!" he barked.

Murphy sat down in a nearby chair.

"Is that why you're here?" Jack asked sarcastically. "To check up on the boat?"

"No. Letty sent me. Said I was to bring you home."

Jack snorted. "Not on your life."

"Hey, good buddy, you don't know my wife the way I do. She's got a stubborn streak as wide as the Mississippi. So when she told me to bring you back, I knew I'd better do it."

Arguing was a waste of energy, but he wasn't going to involve Murphy and Letty in his troubles. "I'll take care of myself," he insisted.

Murphy gave no indication he'd heard. "Letty had me working on the old foreman's house. She's cleaned and repainted the place and ordered a hospital bed and whatever else Dr. Berilo suggested. Before I knew it, she had me widen the doorways to accommodate your wheelchair."

"I plan to walk again."

"You will," Murphy said swiftly. "This is just until you're able to get around on your own. I'm telling you, Jack, you don't know my wife. That woman's unstoppable once she sets her mind on something. I don't dare come back without you."

Well, Letty would just have to be disappointed, Jack thought.

"Another thing. Letty and Francine have been talking up a storm. Last I heard, Francine's hired a physical therapist who's flying out to work with you."

"Is that a fact?" Jack asked with a heavy dose of sarcasm. He appreciated all the trouble Letty and Francine, the wife of another ex-mercenary friend, had gone to, but he'd rather stay in Mexico.

"I tried to explain to Letty that I know you, and you prefer your own company. I tried, Jack, I really did, but she said you need family now and we're the only family you've got."

"I'm not a charity case."

"I should say not!" Murphy snapped. "You're paying for that physical therapist."

"Letty doesn't have time for this."

"I know that, too. With three children under the age of four, she's got plenty to do without worrying about you, but she's convinced you'll recuperate faster at the ranch with us than anywhere else."

Again Jack reserved his strength rather than argue. Murphy could say what he wanted, but Jack had no intention of allowing his longtime friends to play nursemaid to him.

Three days later, however, Jack was loaded

onto a medically equipped private plane and made the long trip from Mexico City to Boothill, Texas. He wasn't pleased to have Murphy step in and take charge of his life. But at this point Jack's options were few and far between.

He needed physical rehabilitation, plus people to assist him. And time. Lots of that. But it'd take more than time for him to heal. He'd never be the same again, emotionally or physically, and he knew it.

The flight to the ranch exhausted him, and staying awake long enough to get himself settled in the foreman's house was about all he could manage.

Just as Murphy had said, the structure, which was set apart from the main house, had been set up as a miniature hospital, complete with a bed, wheelchair, walker and more. He fell into a deep sleep the minute he pulled the covers over himself.

His dreams were full of Lorraine. Of her lying in his arms, talking about movies while he tried not to kiss her. Of the two of them sleeping, arms and legs entwined, on the deck, gazing up at the moon. He could hear the sound of her laughter. It rang in his ears like a forgotten melody. He felt the softness of her skin against his. It seemed so real.

His eyes fluttered open and he saw a figure sitting in the dark, rocking back and forth in a high-backed wooden chair.

"Lorraine?" he whispered. It had to be her. Must be her. Heaven help him, he didn't have the will to send her away a second time. How had she found him? Who'd told her?

"It's Letty," Murphy's wife whispered.

The disappointment was almost too painful to bear.

"Sleep," she whispered.

He yearned to tell her that he'd done enough of that in the past six months. If there was any justice in the world, he'd—

Jack's musings were interrupted by the sound of someone else coming into the room.

"How's he doing?" Murphy asked.

"He woke up briefly. He seemed to think I was someone named Lorraine, but he's asleep now."

Jack would have loved to shock them both by bolting upright, but he hadn't the strength. It demanded more than he could muster even to open his eyes.

"Did he tell you about her?" Letty asked.

"Not a word. He'll say something when he's ready."

Letty seemed to consider her husband's statement. "He'll recover."

"Dr. Berilo said as much."

"I mean emotionally," Letty explained. "He

loved Marcie and regrouped after they split up. He'll do it again.''

Little did she know, Jack thought. Technically Letty was right; he *had* loved Marcie. But what he felt for Lorraine was far stronger. He'd willingly surrendered a large part of himself, his heart, his very being—his life—when he'd asked Dr. Berilo to tell Lorraine he was dead.

It had been a noble thing to do, or so Jack had believed. What he hadn't realized at the time was how close to the truth it was. Without Lorraine, he found little purpose in life. Without her he was empty. He'd been willing to die so that she could live. Now he had a more difficult task to accomplish.

He had to learn to live without her.

"He must love her the way I love you," Murphy said.

In that moment Jack understood why he considered Murphy his family. Murphy knew him like no one else.

"Yes," Letty whispered.

They were right, both of them. Jack loved Lorraine with that same intensity. Enough to send her away. Enough to make his own life hell because she was no longer part of it and never would be again.

Thomas Dancy dismissed his last class, but remained in the classroom as he often did these days. He sat at his desk and studied his schedule, although his thoughts weren't on his work.

His American friend was dead, and Lorraine seemed to blame him. It was the only reason Thomas could conceive of for the fact that she completely ignored his letters.

Almost six months earlier he'd received a hysterical phone call from her about Jack. He'd immediately left the school and joined her at the hospital in Mexico City. Along with Raine, he'd kept vigil at Jack's bedside while his friend hovered near death. For countless hours, he'd talked to the hospital staff in an effort to glean what information he could. It was from the nurses that he came to understand the gravity of the situation. In his own way he'd attempted to prepare Raine for the worst.

When the inevitable happened, his daughter had wept as he'd never heard a woman weep. In her grief she'd collapsed against him. Her agony clawed at his heart, and Thomas recognized anew how much he loved his daughter. Her pain was even worse for him than the loss of his friend.

He was the one who led her out of the hospital, who spoke to the doctor and, with his help, made the burial arrangements. He'd had only a glimpse of the body through the door of Jack's room; it was all he could stand. Later that day, he'd tried to bring Lorraine home with him. She'd politely declined, which had confused him. Now, like her mother, she wouldn't answer his letters, and as each day passed without word, she broke his heart.

This was crueler than Ginny's abandonment. He'd accepted his wife's decision, but had pleaded with her when Raine turned twenty-one to tell their daughter the truth, allow her to make her own judgments.

Raine had done that, it seemed, and rejected him. Rejected his love.

This grief was the most painful yet.

"Thomas?"

Azucena stood at his classroom door. She was by herself, which was rare, and his fears were immediate.

"Is everything all right? The children?"

"They're fine," she assured him as she walked into the room. "They're with Consuela." Her cousin.

Azucena's beauty was unassuming, and at first glance few would find her pretty. He'd been guilty of that himself. For years he'd used her body as an escape from a hell of his own making. He'd loved Ginny, pretended in the dark of night that it was his wife's body he sank into, his wife who cried out in joy as she received him. But it had been Azucena who slept next to him, Azucena who comforted him when the dream came, who woke up with him in the morning. Azucena who gave him a second chance at life and bore him three wonderful sons.

Azucena who was his wife now.

She was by far the most beautiful woman he'd ever known, and his heart swelled with love at the sight of her. He started to get up, but she stopped him.

"Stay," she instructed.

"Stay?"

"I need you to write a letter for me."

"You don't need me to write your letters."

"In English."

His curiosity was keen now. "To whom?"

Azucena's gentle smile reached out to him. "Your daughter."

Little could have surprised him more. He wanted to tell her it would do no good. He'd poured out his heart to Raine, pleaded with her to respond—and she'd refused, with no explanation and apparently no regret. Her silence baffled him. Hurt him.

He took out a fresh sheet of paper and a pen while Azucena removed a folded paper from her pocket. "Please translate this into English for me," she said, and handed him the letter.

Thomas read it over and frowned. He read it a second time, then slowly set it aside. He loved

Azucena, but she was a simple woman with little education or knowledge of the world. "I don't think—"

"If you love me, you will do this."

It was unusual for her to ask anything of him. Thomas felt he had no choice. Besides, what did he have to lose? Lorraine hadn't responded to his letters, and he sincerely doubted she'd respond to Azucena's heartfelt message, either.

November 21

Dear Lorraine Dancy,

If I could put my arms around you and comfort you, I would. Your grief must be very great. You've lost your mother and Jack, and now choose not to answer your father's letters. I can only assume that you are disappointed in the man your father has become. As his wife, I feel I must come to his defense.

Your father is a good man. He loves you and he deeply loved your mother. Many times it was her name he whispered in our bed. I pretended not to notice. Only when he learned that I carried his child did he tell me about his daughter. He spoke of you with such tenderness that my fears vanished. You see, until then I didn't know how your father would react to my pregnancy. At that moment I realized he would love our child, too, even though he didn't love the mother. At least not then. He does now, very much, and we have three sons. Your brothers.

Thomas is afraid that you blame him for Jack's death, and that is the reason you haven't answered his letters. I think there is another reason. I think you have ignored his pleas because of me. In many ways I understand. My skin is darker than yours, and I don't speak your language. Nor am I beautiful like your mother was. Perhaps my greatest fault is that I love your father.

But, Lorraine Dancy, you love him, too. I know this. You would not have traveled to another country to see him again if not for love. At the death of your mother, you sought out your father. You needed him then, but I wonder if you realize how much you need him now. When Jack was in the hospital, it was your father you asked to see. Your father who rushed to your side, who held you as you wept, who cried with you. You need your father, and he needs you.

You love Thomas. I love Thomas, and in return he loves us both.

We are your family and you are ours. Please. I beg you not to shut him out of your life. For your sake and for his.

Azucena Dancy

Thomas read the letter twice to make the translation as accurate as possible. When he finished, he took Azucena's hand and kissed her palm.

"I thank God for you," he whispered.

She wrapped her arm around his shoulders and pressed his face against her soft belly.

"You'll come home now?" she asked.

Thomas nodded. Many afternoons he lingered at the school, not wishing to darken the home with his bleak mood or trouble his family with his sense of failure and loss.

"Good," she whispered.

Together they walked past the tiny post office and mailed the letter. But after all these months of silence from Raine, Thomas didn't hold out much hope she'd answer.

He turned to Azucena that night and made love to her for the first time in weeks. Afterward he held her close, grateful for her presence in his life. Mentally he released his daughter, set her free. He couldn't use her rejection as an excuse to punish himself any longer. He had a new family now, and Raine was welcome to join him and Azucena or make her own life without them. The choice was hers.

To his surprise, a letter arrived from Raine a week before Christmas.

Eighteen

It was Azucena's letter that persuaded Lorraine to confront her feelings about her father. She suspected Christmas had something to do with it, too. All around her, people were celebrating the festive season with their families. Lorraine had no family. And the only man she'd ever truly loved was dead.

She hadn't stayed for the funeral and deeply regretted that now. But at the time it had been more than she could bear. Perhaps she'd feel a greater sense of closure—as everyone called it these days—if she'd stayed in Mexico City. She hadn't even wanted to see the body; that wasn't *Jack,* that lifeless shell, bandaged and hooked up to monitors and IVs.

And she hadn't been able to tolerate the thought of being with her father, knowing how he'd misled her. She'd only wanted to leave Mexico.

Never had she felt more like an orphan. She missed her mother dreadfully, and the small traditions they'd observed over the years didn't feel right when she performed them by herself.

She did manage to dredge up the enthusiasm to buy a Christmas tree. But it sat undecorated for nearly a week before she started to trim it.

Halfway through the project, she realized her heart wasn't in it. She paused, sat down at her computer and without forethought, started writing to her father and Azucena.

December 14

Dear Dad and Azucena,
Standing alone in front of the Christmas tree convinced me to write. That and Azucena's letter.

She's right, I do need you. I wish I didn't. I lived without you nearly all my life, so it shouldn't be difficult to go on pretending you really are dead, the way Mom told me. But I find that impossible.

You made a new life for yourself, started another family. After being alone for more than six months now, I'm beginning to appreciate what it must have been like for you without Mom and me. At one time, I believed that you'd betrayed your marriage vows to Mother, but I don't feel that way anymore.

Azucena, thank you for opening my eyes.

Thank you for having the courage to write me and defend my father. He *is* a good man.

Dad. I don't blame you for Jack's death. How could I? If anything I'm thankful, so very thankful, that you brought me to him that fateful evening. In fact, loving Jack has helped me understand why Mom did the things she did.

From the day I found your letter and realized you were alive, I've been agonizing over one question. What made Mom lie to me? Why did she tell me you were dead? Especially since her love for you was so unmistakable. I saw it in her eyes any time she mentioned your name. Your wedding photo was on her bedside table, so it was the last thing she saw at night and the first thing every morning.

Now I think I understand a little better. Mom was the kind of woman who only loved once. She never divorced you or remarried because she gave her heart completely and totally to you. Why she chose to do what she did in lying to me, I can't say, but I have no doubt of her absolute devotion to you. I understand because it was that way with Jack and me. Now, here's the shocking part of our relationship. I disliked him on sight and he felt much the same about me.

Because I wore Mom's wedding band, he assumed I was married, and I let him think it. Many times since, I've regretted not telling him the truth. There just didn't seem an easy way to do it and when I tried he wouldn't listen. I thought there'd be plenty of time to explain after I'd squared matters with Gary.

You see, Dad, Jack and I weren't lovers, and yet we shared an intimacy I could never hope to find with anyone else. He is the only man I've ever truly loved. Mom and I are alike in that way. So, Dad, I don't blame you for what happened with Jack. Like I said, I'm grateful to you for bringing him into my life.

Again, Azucena, thank you for your letter.

Merry Christmas and much love to you all.

Raine

January 2

Dear Raine,

I can't tell you how happy Azucena and I were to get your letter. It was the best Christmas present I've ever received. Our time together last spring was far too short, and there was much to tell you, much to explain.

Perhaps I can answer some of your questions now and help you understand what happened between your mother and me. I loved Ginny, still do, and know deep in my heart that she continued to love me. Our love for each other was never in doubt. But as I mentioned the night I saw you, she remained in the States because she wanted what was best for you. So did I. You were always our first consideration. Your mother wanted a high quality of education and health care for you. Nor did she want to take you away from your grandparents who adored you. I was the one foolish enough to ruin my life, and I didn't want you or your mother to pay the penalty for my sins.

As I also explained, from the midseventies until you were about nine, your mother visited me on several occasions while you stayed with the woman you called Aunt Elaine. Ginny's visits were short and it was agony for her to leave. Many times I pleaded with her to agree that I should return to the States and accept my due. No prison sentence could be worse than the hell of being away from the two of you. Each time she persuaded me to remain in my adopted country. I wasn't strong enough to do what I knew was right. Now it's too late. Azucena and our three sons need me.

When you were five, your mother and I decided to tell you I was dead. It was a decision we made together. You were at the age when you started asking probing questions about your father. The circumstances of my leaving were too complex and difficult for a child to understand. Nonetheless, I always worried that someone might make the connection between the two of you and me, a man considered a traitor and worse. I worried that if people did know you were my wife and daughter, they would scorn you—and I couldn't stand the thought of that. It seems I worried for nothing, for which I am profoundly thankful.

What I didn't realize at the time we told you about my "death" was that your mother would come to believe the lie herself. I can't explain it in any other way. I think it was easier for her to let me go if she could convince herself I really was dead. As the next few years passed, her visits stopped and she only rarely answered my letters. For a period of time I drifted from town to town, more a prisoner than if I'd been locked behind bars. Only when I accepted a teaching position here in El Mirador and met Azucena did I have a chance to start a second life. Don't blame me for this weakness, Raine.

About your loving Jack. I will always be grateful for his friendship and I miss him dearly. He was an honorable man and a true hero. He gave his life for you and without knowing it, he saved me, too. Often it was his visits that kept me sane at a time when the world seemed beyond my control. He was a true friend. It makes me proud that my only daughter would give her heart to such a man.

You will heal, Raine. The terrible pain you suffer now will ease. This doesn't mean you'll forget Jack, or love him less. With effort you can learn to love again. I know.

Your loving father

For four months Lorraine and her father exchanged letters. Every night she eagerly checked her mail and sent off lengthy letters of her own. For the first time in her life, she came to know her father and to appreciate his wit and intelligence. He wrote often of his sons, Antonio, Hector and baby Alberto. The two oldest boys sometimes enclosed pictures they'd created for their big sister. Lorraine posted them on her refrigerator and smiled whenever they caught her eye.

Thomas encouraged her to visit again, to give Mexico another chance. Someday she would, she promised. As the weeks and months passed, she found herself thinking about the possibility. Then, on the anniversary of her mother's death, Alberto became seriously ill. Lorraine knew what she had to do—but she needed to talk it over with her mother first.

Taking a large bouquet of spring flowers, Lorraine visited the cemetery in early May. She arranged the tulips and daffodils about the gravesite, then stood next to Virginia Dancy's engraved marble marker.

"Hi, Mom," she whispered, staring down at the perfectly manicured lawn. This was her first visit since shortly before Christmas. Her throat felt thick, and tears gathered in the corners of her eyes.

"I was angry with you for a while," she said, her voice hoarse. "But I understand now why you did the things you did." She was silent as she thought about that for a moment.

"I'm not the same person I was a year ago." Lorraine knew she was wiser now. More mature. More tolerant, braver, a better person. Thanks to her love for Jack, of course, but also her growing relationship with Thomas and Azucena. She'd changed in other ways, too. Outer ways. For one thing, the style of her hair. She'd had it cut to a more practical length. She felt Jack would have approved of that. Bit by bit her casual wardrobe changed from tailored slacks and silk blouses to cotton shorts and T-shirts. Already she'd reaped a small harvest from the garden she'd planted and that winter had taken up knitting. Gary and Marjorie's newborn daughter was the recipient of her first project, a beautiful—even if she did say so herself—yellow baby blanket.

"I've grown up," she added softly. "Dad and I write now—a couple of letters a week. His wife is a lovely, gentle woman, and his three sons are beautiful. I know you'd want him to be happy— that's why I'm telling you this. He is, you know. Happy for the first time in ages. He's got a wonderful family and he's made peace with his past. He still believes the war was wrong, but he deeply regrets his involvement with the bombing."

She waited a few minutes and then brought up the subject she'd come here to talk to her mother about. "I've decided to put the house on the market," she said. "I waited because...well, because it helped me deal with losing you and Jack. I might have continued to live here if Alberto hadn't come down with strep throat last month. El Mirador doesn't have a medical clinic, and Dad ended up taking Azucena and the baby into Mérida to see a doctor. By the time they got there, Alberto's temperature was 106 and he had scarlet fever. He nearly died. The town needs a medical clinic and a trained medical professional. Do you realize what I'm saying, Mom? What I want to do?

"Alberto should have been on antibiotics much earlier, and he would have been if El Mirador had a clinic. Dad and I've written to each other about this several times now. I'm going to take the money from my inheritance and the sale of the house and use it to build a clinic in El Mirador. So many people want to help. Gary got Med-X to donate supplies, and even Group Wellness wants to contribute. If you don't mind, I'm going to name the clinic after someone you never met, someone I've told you about. His name was Jack Keller.

"You probably wouldn't have liked him," she said, and smiled sadly. "In the beginning I didn't, either, but I came to love him and in time you would have, too."

Peace settled over her. An inner peace that told her she'd made the right decision. There was nothing more for her in Louisville. Her father, his wife and her three half brothers, all the family she had in the world, waited for her in a Mexican village on the Yucatán Peninsula. There she would build a lasting memorial to Jack. There she would make a new life for herself the way her father had all those years ago.

"Jack, Jack." The six-year-old boy raced across the yard, rimed with autumn frost, to join Jack at the fence. They stood together watching a number of llamas graze contentedly in the pasture.

"How's it going, Andy?"

"Good." The boy was the spitting image of Jack's friend and fellow mercenary, Tim Mallory. He leaped onto the bottom rung of the fence and folded his arms over the post. "Hey, you're walking without your cane!"

"Yup." His offhand response showed no hint of the massive effort and patience this accomplishment had required. Jack had lived in Texas with Murphy and Letty for nearly a year, using the time to recover his strength and learn to walk all over again. He'd never intended to stay that long, but his physical therapy had been extensive.

Recently Cain and his wife, Linette, had visited him from their cattle ranch in Montana and brought their two daughters with them. Cain's girls were relatively close in age to Murphy's boys, and the kids had gotten along famously. Cain had hoped for a Deliverance Company reunion, but Tim and Francine couldn't get away. Their llama ranch on Vashon Island up in Washington State was thriving, and Tim Mallory had a small but growing herd.

When he could travel comfortably, Jack went to visit Tim and Francine himself. He'd originally planned to stay a couple of days, but found he enjoyed the view off Puget Sound. It reminded him of Mexico and the years he'd spent aboard *Scotch on Water* and those all-too-brief weeks with Lorraine.

"Mom says one day no one'll know you used to walk with a cane," Andy said. He rested his chin on the top of his hands and heaved a deep sigh.

"Hey, there's Bubba!" the boy said next, pointing toward a llama at the far end of the pasture.

"Bubba?" Jack asked, grinning.

"Dad and him don't get along very well, but I know he gives Bubba some extra feed every day."

"Did you ask him why?"

"Yeah."

"And what did he say?"

Andy shrugged. "That Bubba did him a favor once and he hasn't forgotten it."

Jack knew all about that favor. Six years ago, the very night Andrew Mallory was born, two hired assassins had paid a visit to Vashon Island. Their job had been to eliminate Tim and Francine. Unbelievably enough, the timely appearance of the big llama had been a lifesaving intervention.

"What else did your mother say?" Jack asked. "About my walking, I mean." At one time Francine had been the best physical therapist on the West Coast. She'd been in charge of his rehabilitation from the beginning.

"She said—" Andy paused and let out a slow breath "—it would take longer for your heart to get better. Did your heart get hurt when you fell off the cliff, Uncle Jack?'' He turned and regarded Jack quizzically.

"In a manner of speaking.''

"What's that mean?''

"It's difficult to explain.'' Jack didn't want to talk about Lorraine and, in fact, hadn't. Not to Murphy or Tim or their wives. But that didn't mean she was ever far from his thoughts. Although it'd been a year and a half, not a day passed that he didn't think of her.

Bits of memory came to him at the oddest times, often when he was least prepared to deal with them. He couldn't help wondering what had happened to her once she'd returned to the States. Was she happy? Had she told her husband about him? How had Gary Franklin reacted? Had she forgotten him and gone on to have the baby she'd wanted so badly, badly enough to mention to Dr. Berilo's nurse? The thought of Lorraine with a child wrenched his heart. Only recently had he come to realize how much he wanted children himself. It was seeing his friends with their sons and daughters....

"Is Andy talking your ear off?'' Tim joined him at the fence.

"Hardly.'' Jack enjoyed the boy's company and his energetic bursts of conversation.

"Some pretty freakish weather going on around

the country," Tim said, glancing up at the sky, which was a clear bright blue with clusters of high clouds.

"Looks downright perfect to me," Jack murmured. In fact, he liked Washington and had given some thought to purchasing a few acres here himself. Somewhere near the water. Early on, in a moment of pain, he'd sold *Scotch on Water*. He'd done it knowing he'd never be able to sleep on the boat again and not think of Lorraine. Little did he realize then that he wouldn't be able to sleep *anywhere* and not think of her.

"The weather here seems fine," Jack said.

"I'm talking about what happened in Louisville, Kentucky."

"Louisville?" Lorraine and Gary lived in Louisville.

"You didn't hear?"

"No." It required an effort to conceal his interest.

"Tornadoes in the area. They've done a lot of damage to the city. The news is full of pictures." He shook his head. "Hard to believe a storm could cause so much destruction."

"How many people were killed?"

"Five so far, but they're sure to discover more bodies in the next day or two."

"That's a lot," Andy inserted.

"It wasn't just one part of the city, either,"

Tim continued. "From what the newscaster said, quite a few neighborhoods were affected. Crazy how one house'll be leveled to the ground, while the house across the street is untouched."

That night, Jack stayed up late and watched the news reports for himself. Afterward he couldn't sleep. Whenever he closed his eyes, Lorraine was there, and when he did manage to drop off, his dreams were filled with her. In one, he was searching but couldn't find her. Her voice grew weaker, more plaintive and urgent. Then he saw her, buried under a huge pile of rubble. No matter how hard he dug, how frantic his efforts, he couldn't reach her. He awoke in a cold sweat.

By the time dawn swept over the pasture and the nearby water, bringing the bright crisp sunshine of November, Jack had packed his bags and booked a flight out of Sea-Tac for Louisville.

"You're leaving?" Francine said as she poured him a cup of coffee.

Jack took his first restorative sip and nodded.

"Any particular reason?" Tim asked. He secured the straps of his coveralls and reached for a mug from the kitchen shelf.

"Yes," Jack said. He didn't elaborate. He caught husband and wife exchanging a look.

"Is it important?" Francine asked. She buttered toast and piled it on a platter.

"Yes." Her questions were a subtle way of

telling him it might not be a good idea to take on too much just yet. After all this time, he was still as weak as one of Tim's newborn llamas. He was sick and tired of being sick and tired.

"Where are you headed?" Tim pried. "Kentucky?"

Jack was surprised he'd been that readable. "What if I am?"

Tim and Francine sat next to each other, across the table from him. "Is she there?" Francine asked.

No one outside of Mexico knew about Lorraine—and yet they all seemed to know. The hell if Jack could figure it out.

Both husband and wife waited for his response. "I don't know where she is now, but I suspect it's Louisville," he said grudgingly.

"And you're going to find out," Tim announced with finality, as if this would be the romantic conclusion they'd all been expecting.

While Jack hated to shatter their illusions, he thought he'd better do so. "I just want to make sure she's okay. That she doesn't need anything."

"You'll talk to her, won't you?"

"No," he insisted.

"Why not?" Tim asked.

"Because then I'd probably have to talk to her husband."

That shut the two of them up quick enough,

Jack noticed. He should have set the record straight a lot sooner.

Jack flew out of Sea-Tac that morning and landed in Louisville four hours later. Luckily the airport hadn't sustained any damage. It took him forty-five minutes to secure a rental car and locate his hotel. Once he'd checked into his room, he pulled open the nightstand drawer and found a Louisville telephone directory.

"Gary Franklin," he muttered as he opened the white pages to the *F*s and ran his finger down the columns until he came to the listing. Only one G. Franklin. Lorraine had mentioned her husband's name just once, but it had stayed in Jack's mind. He'd repeated it often, reminding himself that this was the man who loved her and waited for her at home.

Reaching for a pad and paper, Jack wrote down the address. He'd been serious when he told Tim and Francine that he had no intention of speaking to Lorraine. None. But for his own peace of mind, he needed to know she was unhurt.

Exhausted from the long flight, Jack knew he would have been well advised to wait until the following day before venturing into the city's neighborhoods. But he'd never been a patient man, and the storm had heightened his anxiety.

He grabbed the car keys and headed out. With a map of the city and the concierge's directions, he drove until he found the part of town where Lorraine lived. When he saw a street sign that said Dogwood Lane, he knew he was close.

Jack followed the house numbers until he came to the one he was looking for: 323. It appeared that the house, the entire neighborhood, had escaped the worst of the storm. He felt immediate relief. This was what he'd come for; now he should drive directly past and be done with it.

Instead, he pulled over on the opposite side of the road and sat there with the engine idling.

The house was ordinary enough. One story, painted a pale shade of yellow. The structure itself was like thousands of others built shortly after the Second World War. The type that often sported a white picket fence...and a couple of kids playing out front.

There was a convertible parked in the driveway, top down. He saw something yellow in the backseat. He strained to see what it was and remembered that yellow was Lorraine's favorite color.

A yellow baby blanket, tucked into an infant carrier.

Lorraine must have recently had a baby. A baby. Lorraine and Gary's. He closed his eyes and waited for the pain to subside into numbness. It was what he'd wanted for her, what he'd hoped would happen.

Swallowing tightly, Jack turned the key in the ignition. He had his answers, he told himself again. He'd found out everything he needed to know. More than he'd wanted, actually. Now he could go back to his life without her ever realizing he'd been there.

He'd just eased the rental car back into the street when out of nowhere a baseball slammed into his windshield. The force of the impact shattered the glass.

Nineteen

"**Y**ou okay, mister?" Two boys raced to the passenger window and peered inside at Jack.

"I was until about two seconds ago," Jack muttered, somewhat dazed.

"Brice?"

The boy whirled around and looked over his shoulder. "It's my dad!"

"You were the one who threw the ball," the second kid said. "I'm outta here." With that, Brice's pal took off running.

Jack put the car in Park and climbed out to study the damage. A man approached from the same side of the street as Lorraine's house—a businessman, if the dark suit he wore was any indication.

"What happened?" he asked, directing the question to Brice.

The boy had obvious difficulty meeting his father's eyes. "Todd and I were just practicing and I decided to see how far I could throw with my left hand and..." He paused, staring at the ground.

"The baseball collided with my windshield," Jack completed for him. "Other than the window, no harm's been done." He downplayed the damage. "Accidents happen."

"Must have been one helluva pitch," Brice's father said, examining the broken windshield on Jack's rental car.

"I'm really sorry," Brice said, his voice quavering.

The man placed his hands on Brice's shoulders and looked at Jack. "Naturally we'll pay for all damages."

Jack nodded, thinking it would probably be best to exchange information quickly, then leave. He didn't want to stick around in case Lorraine happened to come outside.

"Were you injured?" the kid's dad asked.

"No. If you'll give me your insurance information, I'll take care of everything myself."

The man released his son's shoulders and gave him a reassuring pat on the back. "Great. And thanks for not yelling at the boy. It was an accident, but one that won't be repeated—right, Brice?"

"Right!"

Jack smiled at the obvious respect between father and son.

The father took out his wallet and removed his insurance card. "Gary Franklin," he said, and extended his hand.

Jack's head jerked up. Then, seeing the man's hand, he thrust his out and they shook hands. "You're Gary Franklin?" he asked before he could stop himself. He wondered if he had the wrong man.

"Do you know me?"

Jack shook his head.

Jack was spared any further need to explain when a woman approached with an infant held securely against her shoulder. "What happened?" she asked, looking sternly at her son. Her frown said she had a fair idea but wanted Brice to tell her himself.

"My baseball hit Mr.—" He paused, waiting for Jack to supply the name.

"Jack Keller," he said. He hoped it wasn't obvious, but he couldn't stop staring at the woman. The baby, too.

Judging by the intent expression on Gary's face, he must have noticed. "This is my wife, Marjorie," he said, and wrapped an arm lovingly around her shoulders. "And our daughter, Alana."

Jack's instantaneous surge of relief was difficult to explain. Even more difficult to understand. Clearly this wasn't the Gary Franklin who was married to Lorraine. The fact that this baby wasn't hers shouldn't be cause for a lighter heart. Jack had cut Lorraine free, sent her on her way to live a good life with the man she'd loved enough to marry long before she'd met him.

"You have a beautiful little girl," Jack said. "How old is she?"

"Eight months," Marjorie answered. "Listen, there's no need to do all this in the middle of the street. Won't you come inside, Mr. Keller?"

"Jack Keller," Gary repeated his name slowly. "I knew a man by that name. Unfortunately I never met him, but I heard enough about him to know I would've liked him."

"It's a common enough name," Jack said as they walked toward the house.

"You might say Jack Keller is a friend of a friend." Gary opened the screen door that led to the living room. The house was cluttered without looking messy. Evidence of the baby was everywhere. A rocking chair with a flannel sheet draped over the back. An infant swing situated next to the sofa. Toys scattered about. An empty baby bottle on the coffee table.

Jack hadn't intended to accept the family's invitation to come into their home. All he needed was the Franklins' insurance information. And yet... He felt oddly drawn to the young couple.

Even though this Gary Franklin wasn't Lorraine's. Or maybe because of that.

"Do you want to see your name?" Brice asked. At Jack's puzzled look, he moved toward the television set and lifted a photo from the cluster assembled there.

"Brice," his mother said, stopping him, "I don't know if that's such a good idea."

"Why not?" Brice asked.

"Because that Jack Keller's...gone."

"Oh." Brice set the framed snapshot back on the television.

"I don't mind," Jack said, his curiosity aroused.

The boy reached for the photo and brought it over to him. But the picture wasn't what he expected. Far from it. It was so much of a shock, in fact, that he knew it would forever change the course of his life. The photograph wasn't of a man, as he'd expected, but of a woman. Lorraine. Her beautiful face smiled back at him.

The sight was enough to wildly affect his heart rate. She stood in front of an adobe structure, a new building, between Antonio and Hector Dancy, her tanned arms around each boy. All three of them were grinning.

For an instant he almost didn't recognize her as the woman he'd once known. She wore khaki shorts and a sleeveless blouse. Her hair was short.

And her eyes...they reflected happiness and—he could sense it—pain. He wondered if she'd walked through the same valley he had these past eighteen months. Had she found a shaky sense of peace, as he had? If so, he suspected it hadn't come easy.

Neither had his own.

All he'd had to sustain him these long months had been his memories. He didn't have her picture, nor did he have the luxury of some memento from their time together. But none was necessary, or so he'd believed. Then again...

Apparently he didn't know as much about her as he'd thought.

When he managed to drag his eyes away from Lorraine and the boys, he received yet another shock. A wooden sign hung over the doorway. He had to squint to read it: The Jack Keller Memorial Health Clinic, in English and in Spanish.

"Is something wrong?" Gary asked.

Jack lifted his gaze from the photo and shook his head.

"You look like you've seen a ghost."

"That's the way I feel," Jack didn't mind telling him. "It appears we have more to discuss than I first realized."

Lorraine had lived in El Mirador six months now, and it felt as though she'd been part of the community all her life. Her Spanish was still rudimentary, but she was working on it. Antonio and Hector took great pride in teaching her new words, and she, in turn, practiced English with them.

As soon as she'd announced her intention of building a medical clinic in Jack's memory, she had more offers of help from the people of El Mirador than she knew what to do with. The clinic, with living quarters for her, was constructed in record time.

The building itself was only the start. Her friends at Group Wellness back in Louisville had raised more than $25,000 for medicine, and Med-X had donated medical supplies, with a commitment for the following year, as well.

Lorraine's last hurdle before moving into Jack's clinic was her certification to practice medicine in Mexico. With her father's help—he filled out the forms—and assistance from a government grateful for her efforts in returning the Kukuloan Star, Lorraine was ready to open her doors to the public in less than two months.

The first day she'd been shocked by the number of patients waiting outside the clinic. The line had stretched out the door and down the narrow walkway.

At the end of her first week Lorraine knew this was exactly the right thing to do. Before, everything in her life had felt pointless. Unnecessary. In El Mirador her medical skills were badly needed. Knowing she was helping others also helped her; she had learned to accept both her past and her future. Teaching here had done the same thing for her father.

For the first time since losing Jack, Lorraine slept through an entire night. A whole day sometimes passed without her thinking of him. And when he did drift into her mind, she wasn't overwhelmed by blinding grief. She sensed with certainty that he would have approved of her returning to El Mirador and doing this work.

Sometimes, especially at the end of a long day, she'd sit back, put up her feet and wish he could somehow see her. How different she was from that self-righteous, prudish woman he'd first met. She'd changed so much since then, but she hadn't understood the full extent of her transformation until recently.

All her life, her mother had insisted that life was full of compensations. When one door shuts, another opens was how she put it. Lorraine hadn't given the matter much thought until she realized how much she'd come to love her three half brothers.

Jack was lost, but her heart was full again. Antonio, Hector and Alberto returned her love in full measure. The older two usually stopped by to spend time with her late in the afternoons. More often than not, they dragged her home with them for dinner. Two or three nights a week, she joined her father and Azucena for meals. The more she came to know Thomas, the more she loved and respected him. Again and again she wished she'd known him sooner, and she still struggled not to blame her mother for the long years of separation.

Her relationship with Azucena, too, had grown into one of affection and mutual assistance.

Alberto, her youngest half brother, had made a full recovery. The chubby toddler was her greatest joy. His round happy face lit up with delight when he saw her. He would race cheerfully to her side, knowing she'd lift him high in the air, and his infectious laughter would echo through the house.

In some ways it was as if these cherished little ones were Lorraine's own children. The family she would never have with Jack. He'd shown her how much love her heart could hold, and now that love spilled over, embracing her young brothers.

In the stillness of late afternoon Lorraine sat at her desk and finished up the last of her paperwork. The door opened, and half expecting Antonio and Hector, she set her pen aside.

"I'm in the office," she called out in Spanish.

When no one answered, Lorraine got up and walked to the door. She kept regular hours, but didn't hesitate to see a patient after closing time.

She stepped into the waiting area and saw a man framed in sunlight, standing just inside the clinic door. But this wasn't a man—it was a ghost.

The ghost of Jack Keller.

One so real, so lifelike, it was all she could do to keep from running into his arms. Reaching for a chair, she clenched her fingers over the top to anchor herself. All the while she greedily drank in the sight of him.

Dear heaven, he seemed so real!

Her heart pounded wildly. Fear coursed through her, although she believed this particular ghost would never hurt her. Her concern was for her sanity. She was afraid that somehow, some way, her mind had slipped. That loving Jack with such intensity had pushed her beyond reason.

Or perhaps she'd been working too hard, she thought in those first shock-filled seconds. Spending too many hours at the clinic. Not taking enough time for herself.

Sweet Jesus, could Jack actually be real? Could he possibly be alive? Had God and the universe made some horrible mistake? Had Jack been sent back to her to make it right?

She yearned to say his name, to call out to him. To bring this dream to life. And yet she feared that if she spoke he might disappear.

Not yet. Please not yet. Let me have him for a

few minutes more. But finally she couldn't bear not knowing any longer.

"Jack?" His name trembled on her lips.

His features relaxed and his eyes softened as he walked toward her. With exquisite tenderness he pressed his palm to her cheek. His hand felt warm and solid, and for an instant Lorraine thought she might faint.

Needing to hold on to him, she covered his hand with her own and urged his palm toward her lips, where she planted a single soft kiss.

"Oh, Raine." He caught her by the shoulders and his mouth swept down on hers as though waiting another moment was more than could be asked of him.

She'd dreamed of this so often, it was difficult to know if it could actually be happening. If this *was* a dream, she didn't intend on waking anytime soon.

She wound her arms around his neck and, leaning into him, kissed him back. Hunger and urgency, love and need. They blended until coherent thought escaped her. She and Jack strained against each other, mouths seeking, their passion fierce. She buried her fingers deep in his hair and held tight, almost as if that might prevent him from leaving her again.

"Am I dreaming?" she whispered, desperate

for answers. "Tell me, please. Is this really happening?"

He eased his face from hers and closed his eyes. "It's real, Raine, it's real. I'm here. I'm alive."

Sobbing, choking, hardly able to breathe, she clung to him, her hands digging into his shoulders. It wasn't possible. Dr. Berilo had told her Jack was dead. He'd sat with her, comforted her. Jack's presence here, now, was beyond comprehension.

"I'm sorry," Jack repeated between kisses. "I'm sorry, so sorry," he whispered again and again.

"What happened?" she pleaded, needing answers and yet fearing them, too. Still, her desire for the truth overcame her fears. "Tell me," she demanded. "I need to know."

He found a chair, then sat her down and kneeled in front of her. He looked into her eyes for a long moment before cradling her face with his hands.

"Jack, please. Tell me!"

An eternity came and went before he spoke. "I thought you were married."

That didn't explain why Dr. Berilo had told her Jack was dead.

"You loved me," he whispered. "Did you think I didn't know?"

She felt lost in a fog, not understanding where she'd taken the wrong turn, how this could have happened. Love should have brought them together, not driven them apart. Love was meant to be a bond.

"And I loved you enough to convince Dr. Berilo to tell you I'd died."

"Oh, God." She closed her eyes to keep the room from spinning out of control.

"I loved you enough to keep from ruining your life."

"Loved," she said. "Past tense?" She didn't know who to blame—herself for the initial lie or Jack for being so damn noble.

His answer was to draw her toward him for another kiss. "Past, present, future and every tense in between. I had to prevent you from making the biggest mistake of your life."

"But I'm *not* married!" she protested.

"I didn't know that at the time."

And it was her fault for not telling him.

"I didn't know," he said again. "You wore a wedding band, so I assumed, reasonably enough, that you were married."

And when he'd asked her for the name of her husband, she'd given him Gary's. It hit her then, the gravity of what she'd done. Because of her one small lie, they'd wasted eighteen months of their lives. His own lie had robbed them, too, but

Lorraine accepted full responsibility. The blame was hers.

The sobs began, welling up from deep within her. She wept as if she would never stop, as if regret and sorrow had overwhelmed her.

"I know, I know," he murmured, pulling her close.

She came into his arms and he wiped away her tears. She grew quiet, exhausted from crying, and then passion flared between them again, the way it had that day in Mexico City. By the time the kissing ended, neither could speak.

They held on to each other for a long time, until Jack finally said, "About this business of your having a husband?"

"Yes?"

"As soon as we can arrange it, that part will be true."

Twenty

Lorraine read the text a second time, trying to clear her thoughts. Concentrating on her studies was difficult because she was so anxious for Jack's return. The wonderful news about the baby bubbled up inside her and spilled out in small giggles every few minutes. She couldn't help it—but she really did need to study for an important chemistry exam the following day.

True to his word, Jack had her at the altar less than a week after his arrival in El Mirador. Father García had performed the ceremony. Thomas and Azucena stood up for them and the entire town of El Mirador had celebrated. Even now, nearly two years later, Lorraine had trouble taking it all in. Most of the people in the small waterfront village were very poor, but they had an abundance of love and generosity. Lorraine's wedding to Jack was the perfect opportunity for them to show her how much they appreciated the clinic.

Table upon table of food had been set up in the town square, and small homemade gifts were lovingly offered to her and Jack. The wedding celebration had gone late into the evening and Jack had been forced to steal her away, to the cheers and laughter of the entire town.

Their honeymoon was incredible. Lorraine's heart smiled each time she remembered what had proved to be the most marvelous week of her life. Jack had docked a newly purchased cabin cruiser near a small uninhabited island off the Yucatán Peninsula, not far from El Mirador. They'd spent their days swimming and snorkeling, exploring the colorful coral reef, and their nights...their nights had been spent exploring each other.

That she could actually be in Jack's arms and love him this completely—it was a gift she'd never expected to receive. In those early days their lovemaking had been frantic, as if they feared their being together couldn't last. He held her close afterward and they clung to each other. Almost always she'd weep in his arms in sheer wonder and joy. Jack seemed to understand her need to cry following their lovemaking. She cried for all the long lonely months they'd wasted. For the miracle of being together now.

In the weeks following their honeymoon they had long talks about the future. Increasingly Lorraine had become aware that what El Mirador and the surrounding villages needed was a fully qualified physician. Jack had encouraged her to reapply for medical school, to finish the education she'd cut short.

It was Gary Franklin who'd told her about a retiring general practitioner who was looking for volunteer work. He'd been considering the Peace Corps. Lorraine wrote him and told him about the clinic—now renamed The Virginia Dancy Medical Center—and he'd come down with his wife for a two-week visit. Lorraine knew the moment she met Dr. Samuel Wetmore that he'd be a perfect choice to replace her while she earned her credentials. After taking a crash course in Spanish, he'd journeyed to El Mirador and worked with her until Lorraine received word that she'd been accepted into her third year of medical school at the University of Kentucky.

Now her schooling was almost over—and she was pregnant. The baby shouldn't have been a surprise to either of them, but Lorraine had been stunned at the news. Her shock had soon turned into the purest joy.

She didn't know how she could possibly concentrate when all she wanted to do was dance around the apartment.

Lorraine heard the door open and knew Jack was home at last.

He'd barely made it over the threshold when she flew out of the study and hurled herself into his arms. Before he could ask, she had him pinned against the door and involved in a series of deep hungry kisses.

They were both breathing hard by the time she finished.

"To what do I owe this greeting?" he asked, cocking one eyebrow. "Not that I'm complaining, mind you."

Lorraine kissed the underside of his jaw. "Because you're wonderful."

"That's true," he murmured.

"And virile," she added, and started to unbutton his shirt.

"That, too."

"And potent."

"So it's been said." He paused suddenly in the task of unbuttoning her blouse. His gaze met hers, and he frowned. "Exactly what do you mean by potent?"

Lorraine led him into the bedroom. "You don't know?" She didn't give him a chance to respond. Instead, she kissed him and undressed him at the same time. His own hands were busy removing her clothes.

Soon they were on the bed, their mouths greedily seeking and finding each other, their bodies on fire with need. He moved over her and she opened to him—her heart, her future, all her being—and sighed with immense satisfaction as he slowly linked their bodies. As he moved, she relished the feel of him against her bare breasts and stomach. Although he'd been brutally injured in the fall from the cliff, the muscles of his back and shoulders remained firm and hard. Her fingertips roamed his skin, and she traced his scars, each one a badge of courage.

Afterward Jack held her close and whispered into her ear, "You'd better explain what you said earlier."

"You mean you *still* can't figure it out?" She smiled at him mysteriously.

"Lorraine?" He paused and swallowed hard before continuing. "Could you be...is there any possibility you're pregnant?"

"Yes! Oh, Jack, isn't it wonderful?"

He went very still. Lifting her head, she smiled up at him again, this time with unconcealed delight. "Don't tell me you hadn't guessed."

"I hadn't guessed." His voice sounded odd, raspy and shaken.

"Oh, Jack, I'm so happy about it."

He buried his face in the curve of her neck. "I can't believe it." His kiss was filled with tenderness. "What about finishing school, working at the clinic? We hadn't planned on a baby this soon."

"Some of the best things in life are unplanned."

He laughed outright. "Isn't that the truth!"

"I've got it all figured out," she told him, snuggling close to his side.

"I want you to finish school." He pressed his hand against her flat stomach as if to welcome the child growing inside her.

"I will, I promise. And I'm looking forward to my residency—and then working at the clinic."

"I'll help with the baby."

"I'm counting on that. When we move back to El Mirador, Azucena will watch the baby during the day. I know Dr. Wetmore will stay on another couple of years to run the clinic—and you can start that boat-building company you've been talking about."

Jack chuckled. "You do have this all figured out, don't you?"

"I have a few other plans, but we don't need to discuss them now."

"You mean to say there's more?" He laughed and kissed the top of her head. "I swear, marriage to you is about as much adventure as a man can take."

Coming from an ex-mercenary, that was quite a compliment.

A trilogy of warm, wonderful
stories by bestselling author

DEBBIE MACOMBER

Orchard Valley, Oregon

It's where the Bloomfield sisters—Valerie,
Stephanie and Norah—grew up, and it will
always be home to them.

When their father suffers a heart attack, they gather at his
side—the first time in years they've all been together. Coming
home, they rediscover the bonds of family, of sisterhood.
And, without expecting it, they also find love.

ORCHARD VALLEY

MIRA

On sale mid-June 1999 wherever paperbacks are sold!

Look us up on-line at: http://www.mirabooks.com   MDM308

Let **DEBBIE MACOMBER** take you into the **HEART OF TEXAS.**

Let her take you back to...

PROMISE,
TEXAS

Dear Reader,

In promise, Texas, people know that family, home, community are the things that really count. They know that love gives meaning to every single day of their lives.

Some of the people in promise are from old ranching families—like the westons and the pattersons, who first came to the hill country more than a century ago. and there are newcomers like Annie Applegate, who agrees to marry a widowed veterinarian for the sake of his children...and discovers that this marriage can lead to a great deal more.

MDM502A

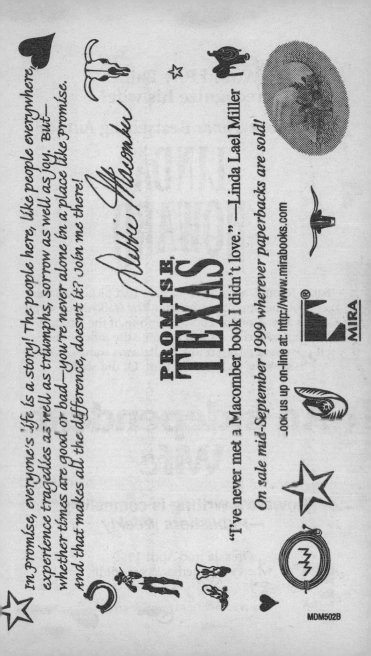

If you loved this romantic tale by

DEBBIE MACOMBER

Don't miss the opportunity to receive this author's
other titles also available from MIRA® Books:

MIRA

Look us up on-line at: http://www.mirabooks.com   MDMBL0599